Baby City

a novel by
Freida McFadden
& Kelley Stoddard

Baby City

"Somewhere on this globe, every ten seconds, there is a woman giving birth to a child. She must be found and stopped."

– Sam Levenson

Foreword

Labor and Delivery. Sunshine and Roses. The Babies! The JOY!

The nurses and physicians that work on the labor floor must hear it a thousand times, if not more, in their lifetime, "Oh, what a wonderful job you must have, bringing life into this world!"

Yes, yes we do.

On the good days, we have an amazing and awe-inspiring job. In our over-scheduled, planned-to-the-minute society, labor is one of the last forces we can more guide than truly control. We have a great privilege and honor to help mothers and babies arrive through Labor and Delivery safely.

"Safely" being the key word, because we also bear the burden of seeing the dark side of Labor and Delivery. The sadness. The heartbreak. The heart-pounding, muscle-clenching fear. The fact that things can go wrong in a blink of an eye. All of these extremes combine together to make Labor and Delivery one of the most intriguing, exhilarating, fascinating, and exhausting professions to choose.

The stories in Baby City are representative of some of the more common scenarios that can be encountered on any Labor and Delivery floor, in any city, on any given day. If the stories feel familiar, it is because they happen in many different ways, over and over again, with slightly different variations, throughout the nation, and throughout the world. This novel, while a work of fiction, provides a very real glimpse behind the curtain of the perception of the orderly labor floor, into the true whirlwind of perpetual motion that lies beneath the well-known façade, and gets to the heart of what makes Labor and Delivery so very special… the people who work there.

Kelley Stoddard, MD

Chapter 1

I am going to make this medical student cry.

I don't know how I know it, but somehow I can sense it. I know it the second she walks into the resident room on Labor and Delivery at Cadence Hospital, her perfect blond ponytail swinging behind her. And I'm certain of it when she holds her slim hand out to me and says, "Hi! I'm Caroline! I'm the new medical student!"

No, I am not exaggerating those exclamation points.

"I'm Emily," I say. (Note the lack of exclamation points.) I stay in my seat, but I reach out to take her hand, which is as smooth as a baby's bottom. And I've touched a lot of babies' bottoms lately, considering I'm working on Labor and Delivery right now. "I'm a third year resident."

My co-resident and sometimes friend, Jill, who also happens to be the chief resident for OB/GYN, looks down at Caroline's outstretched hand and shakes her head. She leaves Caroline hanging as she says, "I'm Dr. Brandt."

Actually, maybe Jill will make her cry.

"I'm so excited to be here!" Caroline says, practically bouncing on the heels of her practical shoes. She's wearing the requisite blue scrubs—if she weren't, Jill would be chewing her out as we speak. "I'm really interested in women's health."

"Do you want to do OB/GYN?" I ask her.

Caroline shakes her head, trying not to look too horrified at my question. Most people are freaked out by the very idea of doing what we do every day. I have Caroline pegged as more of a family medicine or pediatrics type.

"I want to go into family medicine," Caroline says. Bingo. Then she adds, "But I'm considering a fellowship in women's health."

Jill snorts. She doesn't think much of family medicine residents who want to horn in on our territory.

This is our second day on Labor and Delivery, which somebody years ago nicknamed Baby City, like one of those discount places that sells TVs or computers. Baby City, as in *bring home the baby of your choice in any shape or size at low, low, low prices*! Of course, it isn't really an accurate comparison. You don't get to choose the shape or size of your baby. And I definitely would not describe the prices as "low, low, low." If this were a real store, we'd definitely go out of business.

We were sort of hoping that we wouldn't get a medical student this month. I do believe in teaching and all that crap, and I was excited about having medical student when I first started out in residency. But since then, I've learned a very important lesson: most medical students are very annoying. Occasionally, we'll get some rare gem who is just wonderful and who makes our lives easier. But the vast majority seem to be lazy, whiny, and disinterested.

Or in Caroline's case, overenthusiastic. Which is very possibly the worst of all.

Caroline hovers in the center of the room, as if afraid to sit in our presence. Jill looks up in disgust, and rubs her temple with one skeletal hand. In residency, many people tend to get either really fat or really skinny based on what they do with food when they're stressed out. Jill obviously starves herself when she's under stress, as evidenced by the fact that I can make out every single bone in her hand. I bet I could count her ribs.

I wouldn't say this to her face, but if Jill gained about 15 pounds, styled her hair, and put on some makeup, I think she would be gorgeous. She has wispy white blonde hair that is clearly natural based on the roots and the fact that there's no way she has enough time to dye it. Her crystal blue eyes are always slightly bloodshot with purple circles underneath, and her high cheekbones only make the hollowness of her cheeks more exaggerated. I don't think I've ever seen Jill looking any less than gaunt and completely exhausted.

But she's only got one year of residency left. Maybe after that, she'll start taking care of herself again.

"Emily," she says. "They just put The Princess in a room. Why don't you take Caroline here to go see her?"

"The Princess is here?" I ask. "Why?"

"Elective C-section," Jill says.

I sigh. Figures.

I turn to Caroline. "Do you want to come see a patient with me in triage?"

Caroline's eyes light up like she's a puppy who just found out she's being taken for a walk so she could go pee.

"Oh, yes!" she gushes. If she had a tail, she'd be wagging it.

Baby City consists of three parts. The first part is what you traditionally think of as Labor and Delivery: a bunch of rooms where women's cervixes are busy dilating or else they're busy trying to push out their babies. The second part consists of an operating room for C-sections, D & C's, or whenever other procedures may be required over the course of bringing babies into the world.

And the last part is Triage. That's where the women go when they think they're in labor, are waiting for a C-section, or have some other pregnancy-related problem that is yet to be diagnosed. That's where our patient, The Princess, is waiting.

The Princess is well-known to pretty much every resident in OB/GYN. We take turns doing outpatient clinic throughout residency, and The Princess seems to show up there almost daily. If this woman breaks a nail, she needs her OB/GYN to check it out and make sure it's not early labor. She's been asking for a C-section since she was 32 weeks pregnant. The part that surprises me is that we're actually doing it. When did we start letting the patients run the asylum?

Caroline follows me down the long hallway to Triage. I'd prefer if she walked next to me, but instead she walks directly behind me. I feel like I have a stalker. I keep turning my head, to see if she's still behind me, and being slightly disappointed to find her there.

The Princess is in Room 2 in Triage. I pick her chart off the door, and quickly ascertain that she is only 37 weeks pregnant. Pregnancy is supposed to last 40 weeks, so I can't imagine why she would be getting an elective C-section three weeks before her baby is done cooking. Presumably, there's a good reason. None of the attendings that I work with would deliver a baby early just because the patient asks him to.

Well, none except one.

I knock twice on the door to the room where The Princess is waiting. She's lying on the table, her long dark hair impractically loose. And she has on way, way too much makeup for a woman about to have major abdominal surgery. (Although I think any amount of makeup is probably too much for that.) The first thing I notice is that she's on her cell phone, and when she sees me enter, she holds up a manicured finger to indicate she will just be a minute.

So I wait.

I recognize in this day and age, everyone has a cell phone. So it's not completely crazy to expect that occasionally you will walk into an exam room and find the patient using one. I don't like it, but I accept it. But most of the time, the patient will quickly say something into the phone along the lines of, "The doctor's here. I need to go." I wait for The Princess to say something like that, but she doesn't. She seems to just be continuing her conversation as if I'm not even standing there. Moreover, the conversation seems to involve some juicy gossip from work. Seriously, you would not *believe* what Dave said to Angie.

I clear my throat twice, and am this close to throwing her chart on the floor and storming out of there, when The Princess finally says, "Okay, I've got to go have this baby now." And then she hangs up the phone.

"Well?" she says to me impatiently. "Are they ready for me yet?"

"Not yet," I say through my teeth. I can tell she has no idea who I am even though we've met several times, so I say, "I'm Dr. McCoy."

The Princess nods, and then her eyes rest on Caroline.

"Why did you bring your daughter with you?"

Okay, I realize that I am very tired and probably look it, but I really don't think I look old enough to be the mother of a 24-year-old. I mean I'm only 30 years old. Not even 30 and a half.

"This is Caroline," I say. "She's our medical student."

The Princess shakes her manicured finger at me. "No medical students."

"Mrs. Woodhouse," I say. "This is a teaching hospital."

"I told Dr. Brandt *no medical students*," she says firmly.

So Jill knew about this when she sent me in here with Caroline. That bitch. I'm going to get back at her for this.

"That's all right," Caroline says quickly. She smiles brightly at The Princess, who looks like she wants to make Caroline cry just as much as I do. "I can get you something while you're talking to Dr. McCoy. Is there anything you would like?"

The Princess nods. "Yes, I would like a vanilla Coke Zero."

The Princess is not allowed to have anything to drink, because she's about to go into surgery. She knows it, I know it, and Caroline ought to know it, but clearly does not.

"I'll be back in a jiffy!" Caroline says.

I probably ought to stop her. But I don't. It will give her something to do. I'm pretty sure there's no vanilla Coke Zero anywhere in the hospital.

"Mrs. Woodhouse," I say. "I'm looking through your chart, and somehow they haven't recorded the reason for scheduling your C-section so early. Is your baby measuring large?"

"Oh no," she says. Then she adds proudly, "I only gained 15 pounds in my entire pregnancy."

Actually, The Princess looks pretty fabulous for being 37 weeks pregnant. A lot of women are gigantic by this point and also very swollen. But she looks like a model of pregnancy. If I ever get pregnant, I want to look like her at 37 weeks.

"So here's what happened," she says. "A few nights ago, my belly got itchy. I mean, really itchy."

I wait for her to tell me more. Were her liver tests elevated? Was she cholestatic? Did her blood pressure go up? What was the indication for this early delivery?

But it turns out the story is over. That's it. She's having her baby because she's itchy.

"Dr. Buckman said I was full-term," she explains. "I mean, there's no reason for me to continue being pregnant and keep getting fatter. He said the itchiness might mean I'm getting a new stretch mark. Ew, can you imagine?"

I grip The Princess's chart hard enough that the papers start to crinkle. Dr. Buckman, the doctor with 50% C-section rate. That explains everything.

The Princess sighs and adjusts her body on the table. She hasn't gained much weight, and most of it is in her belly. She looks the way I used to look when I was a skinny little kid and I put a soccer ball under my shirt and pretended to be pregnant.

Every resident, myself included, wants The Princess to deliver her baby, because that means she'll be out of our lives. But we can't be selfish right now. I look down at her belly and think about that tiny little baby inside. That baby deserves another three weeks to grow in the best possible environment. It doesn't deserve to come out gasping for air, because its mother was *itchy* one night. I have to advocate for this baby. God knows, somebody has to.

It's up to me to convince The Princess not to have this baby today.

Chapter 2

I can see The Princess reaching for her phone, so I know I've pretty much reached the limits of her attention span. If I don't convince her quickly, she'll go back to texting her friends or playing Minecraft or whatever.

"Listen," I say, trying to use my most friendly voice, like we're two old buddies chatting over cosmopolitans, "I've got this amazing cream that really helps with itchiness. The patients I've given it to say it works miracles."

The Princess just stares at me.

"Also," I add. "It's supposed to prevent stretch marks."

The Princess's painted lips form a straight line.

"Interesting," she says in a tone that makes it clear that she does not find anything I'm saying in the least bit interesting.

I force myself to smile. "If you use the cream, then you won't have to have the baby early. You can wait until the baby is full-term, and you won't even get any stretch marks. Won't that be great? I know the itchiness is bothering you a lot, but like I said, the cream will really help you with that."

And now I'm just babbling.

The Princess's lower lip juts out in a pout.

"I'm not going to get bumped, am I?" she whines. "I've got to have this baby today, you know. I already filed the disability paperwork. I really can't wait any longer."

I'm wasting my breath—I may as well be talking to the wallpaper. This baby is going to be born today, like it or not.

"By the way," The Princess says. She lifts up her shirt and I see that below her belly, she has drawn a line in black permanent marker. "I was looking at my friend Cindy's C-section scar, and this is how big it is. I don't want my scar to be any bigger than this line."

I examine the black marker smeared across her pelvis. It looks like her belly has grown a Charlie Chaplin mustache. I can't imagine any baby being small enough to fit through that incision. Maybe if she was giving birth to a baby kitten. But there isn't any full-term human being that would fit through that narrow black line. Unless Harry Houdini delivered her friend's baby, her scar was undoubtedly larger than that.

"You know," I say. "If you deliver the baby vaginally, you won't have any scar at all."

"Oh no," The Princess says, horrified. "I don't want to get all torn up down there. That's disgusting. Anyway,

Dr. Buckman said that my cervix wasn't, like, *in favor* of having the baby right now."

Okay, I'm done arguing with The Princess.

"So you won't make the incision any bigger than that, right?" she presses me.

"Sure," I say.

She won't be able to see what we're doing during the surgery anyway, thank God. We'll deal with the consequences later.

I leave The Princess's room, longing for a stiff shot of whiskey. Luckily, Caroline shows up at that moment with the next best thing: a can of vanilla Coke Zero. I don't know where she got it and I don't care. I grab the can from her hand, pop the tab, and take a long swig. Ah, that hits the spot. It's too early for whiskey anyway.

The smile fades from Caroline's face.

"I thought Mrs. Woodhouse wanted that," she says carefully, afraid to offend me.

"Mrs. Woodhouse is NPO for her surgery," I remind her.

NPO means you can't eat.

"Oh," she says meekly. She wrings her fingers together. "Um, I was just wondering…"

Those are my least favorite words to hear out of the medical student. I brace myself and say, "Yes?"

"What are the indications for primary C-section?" Caroline asks.

All 37 weeks of my irritation with the Princess comes rushing to the surface. I couldn't take any of it out on her, but I can damn well let Caroline have it.

"Next time you have a question," I say in a low voice that isn't yelling but may as well be, "make sure it's not something you should've read about the night before." I shake my head, to indicate that Caroline has really disappointed me. "The answer to your question is available in *any* OB/GYN review book."

Caroline's eyes widen. "Oh, I..." she stammers.

Hey, maybe I could make her cry on her very first day.

"A word of advice," I say. "It's a good idea to show up on your first day *prepared*."

"Sorry," Caroline says. Her jaw trembles, but I don't see any tears yet. Well, there's always tomorrow.

As I brush past her to return to the labor unit, I see Caroline fumbling with her phone, probably to look up the indications for C-section. I can guarantee she won't find itchiness among them.

————

A large part of rotating on Baby City is sitting around and waiting. After all, babies come out when they're good and ready. But things can get incredibly exciting and you don't have a moment to sit down, eat, pee, or sometimes even breathe. On the other hand, then there are large chunks of time where you're just staring at the wall, watching the paint dry.

This is one of those times.

When Caroline and I return from Triage, we head over to The Pit to wait. Years ago, the resident room on Labor and Delivery was nicknamed The Pit. The room is in the dead center of Baby City, so there's no window. Jill says back in the day there was no ventilation in the room and it would be freezing cold in the winter, and sweltering in the summer. Since then, a single vent has been installed to make the room marginally tolerable. But the nickname stuck.

The Pit is about the size of a jail cell. (I'm not sure why that's the first comparison that comes to mind.) There's a computer in one corner of the room, more plastic chairs than the room can comfortably accommodate to the point that we're always tripping over them, and a giant whiteboard on the wall. If this really were a jail cell, there would probably be a bed, as well as a toilet in the corner of the room, and I can't say that either of those additions would be unwelcome.

There isn't a whole lot to do right now. Jill is fumbling with her phone—she recently got one of those new huge smartphones and she hasn't quite figured out how to use it yet. She keeps shoving it in my face and saying things like, "Emily, how do I add this phone number to my list of contacts?" How should I know? I have an iPhone. Those things are idiot proof. And I need it, because my brain is so exhausted and filled with information about my patients that I don't think there's any room left to store knowledge about other types of smartphones.

I settle into one of the uncomfortable plastic chairs, and pick up the lukewarm coffee I abandoned to go see The Princess. It tastes terrible but I drink it anyway. I've been awake since 5 a.m. this morning, and I'll be asleep on my feet by noon if I don't have my coffee.

Caroline doesn't sit down though. She hovers over me, swaying slightly in my direction. She's making me really claustrophobic, which isn't that big a challenge in this tiny room. "Is there anyone I should see?" she asks me.

"No, not right now," I say. And then I add, because it obviously needs to be said: "Sit down."

Thank God, Caroline settles into one of the many plastic chairs (good doggie), and digs through the bookbag she brought with her this morning. She pulls out a copy of an OB/GYN review book and makes a big show out of opening it up. I yawn and take another sip of my coffee.

And then I shut my eyes. Just for a second.

"Um, Emily?" I hear Caroline's voice saying.

Go away, medical student. "Yes?"

"What does the chart on the board mean?"

I crack open my eyes. She's referring to the table we keep on the giant whiteboard, which keeps track of women in labor. I probably should've explained it to her when she arrived. That's what a good resident, one who isn't completely exhausted, would have done. I glance over at Jill, who is fully absorbed with her phone. I guess it's up to me.

I struggle to my feet, and make my way somewhat unsteadily to the whiteboard hanging from the wall. There's only one name up there right now.

"This is a list of the women having babies," I explain. "The first column is their name. The second is their age. The third is how many weeks pregnant they are. The fourth is how dilated their cervix is, then how effaced the cervix is, then how high up the baby is."

"Oh." Caroline bites her lip. I can tell she's struggling to balance her desire to ask me a question over her fear of me. Desire to ask the question apparently wins out. "When is the woman fully dilated?"

Jill, who had been previously fiddling with her phone, slams it down on a table with a loud snap. She rests her icy blue eyes on Caroline's face.

"What rotation is this?" she asks in a sharp voice.

Caroline eyes dart around like a trapped animal. "What?"

"I'm just wondering what rotation you think this is," Jill says. "I mean, I know you don't think it's Labor and

Delivery, because if you did, you'd be able to answer the most basic question about labor."

Caroline bites her lip.

"Really, tell me, I'm curious." Jill folds her arms across her chest, waiting for a response. "Do you think it's... Psychiatry? Anesthesiology? Radiology?"

I can't help but stifle a laugh. Ever since we were newbie residents, Jill has always been known for her quick wit. She's actually bitingly funny, although recently her snarkiness has been leaning more in the direction of mean than hilarious. But she's still often hilarious, especially when someone else is the object of her mockery.

"It's OB/GYN," Caroline finally says, her voice cracking slightly on the words.

Jill raises her eyebrows at me. "Look at that, Emily. She knows what rotation this is. Go figure." She glares at Caroline one last time before getting up out of her seat to leave the room. "Maybe tomorrow she'll actually come prepared."

Caroline hardly breathes until Jill has disappeared from the vicinity. When the sound of Jill's footsteps has faded, Caroline bites her lip again and says to me, "Is it five centimeters?"

I sigh.

I could be nice and tell Caroline that ten centimeters represents a fully dilated cervix. It's not like it would be hard to do. But truth is, I'm just as irritated by her stupid question at Jill is. "Look it up," is all I say.

I used to be a nice person, I swear.

I had hoped that both Jill and I yelling at her would be enough to deter any further questions, but that doesn't appear to be the case.

"I was wondering," she begins, "when I will get to have some outpatient clinic time? Since I'm doing Family Medicine, it would really benefit me to see some pregnant women in an outpatient setting. Or maybe learn how to do Pap smears."

"Yeah," I say. "If things are slow, we can send you over to clinic in the afternoon. Maybe sometime next week we can do that. There's plenty of time for it on this rotation."

Caroline nods happily. See? I can be nice sometimes.

———

After we've been sitting in The Pit for about half an hour, one of the Triage nurses, Pam, peeks her head in to our room. Pam is one of those incredibly efficient nurses who has been a nurse since before we were born, and always seems a little bit amused by the fact that *we're* the ones giving *her* orders when she probably knows about five times as much as anyone here, possibly including the attendings. She crosses her arms and raises her eyebrows at us.

"Are you ladies planning to see the new woman who came in to Triage?"

Jill sits up straight. "There's a patient in Triage?"

Pam nods. "She's 38 weeks and says she's in labor."

Jill looks over at Caroline accusingly.

"One of your jobs is to keep track of who comes into Triage," she says. "You should *own* Triage. Make sure the patients are seen before we even know they're there."

"Oh," Caroline says. She looks at us questioningly. "So... should I go see this patient?"

Jill looks at her like she's just asked a question too stupid for words. "What do *you* think?"

Caroline scrunches a fistful of her blue scrubs in her hands. "Um, yes? I should?"

Pam decides to take pity on her, and taps her on the shoulder. "Come with me, sweetie," she says.

"I think medical students are getting stupider," Jill announces when Caroline is gone.

"She's not so bad," I say, even though Caroline has been annoying me more than anyone. I'm not sure why I feel a need to defend her.

"You're right," Jill says. "They've been this dumb all along." She smiles wistfully. "Do you remember when I got that medical student to do my laundry?"

I do. It was during my intern year. Jill told the med student on OB/GYN that he was completely incompetent at medicine, so he may as well make himself useful by doing her laundry. Then she handed him a bag of laundry, which he proceeded to bring to the laundromat across the street and wash for her. He even separated her white and colors.

Jill swore up-and-down that it was all a joke and she never actually intended for him to do her laundry. Especially when the program director yelled at all of us for abusing medical students. But honestly, I wonder. I know for a fact that Jill really hates doing her laundry.

"Don't make Caroline do your laundry," I say.

"That was a *joke*," Jill says, but she winks.

I'm debating whether I need to further convince Jill that it would be a mistake to foist any more personal chores on Caroline, but then Jill becomes completely absorbed by her phone, so I figure that whim has passed.

"Emily," she says. "How do you switch windows on the internet browser?"

I roll my eyes. "How should I know?"

Jill grins at me. "Aren't you some kind of techie nerd?"

"No way," I say. "That's definitely not true."

"Then how come you're named after the doctor in 'Star Trek?'" she challenges me.

I glare at her. She knows I hate it when people make "Star Trek" jokes about my name. Yes, the doctor in the original "Star Trek" is named Dr. McCoy, and yes, that is also my name. And that stopped being funny about five minutes after I graduated from medical school.

Jill laces her fingers together to plead with me. "Come on, please help me. I'm ready to chuck this phone at the medical student."

I think that there's probably at least a 50% chance of that happening either way, but I decide to take pity on Jill and attempt to help her. It's always a good idea to be nice to the chief resident.

It's a lost cause though. I'm even more clueless than Jill is. Jill and I are huddled over her phone, hopelessly trying to figure out how to open up a new browser window, when we hear a male voice from above us.

"What you *doing*?"

Male voices are pretty rare in The Pit. With only one exception, all of the residents are female. All the nurses are female. We have two male attendings, and all the rest are female. So any voices deeper than an alto are pretty unexpected in here.

I look up and see (surprise, surprise) a guy standing in the center of the room. He's wearing green scrubs, which means he's not a regular in OB/GYN, since we always wear blue as a rule. By his age and the mildly exhausted expression on his face, I suspect him to be a resident, but he doesn't look familiar to me.

And believe me, I would recognize this guy. He's extremely adorable. After I do a once over of his lanky-but-firm body, tousled light brown hair, and green, green eyes, I've already fallen half in love. He honestly has the greenest eyes I've ever seen. Usually when you say somebody has green eyes, there's generally some blue or brown mixed in. But this guy's eyes are the color of fresh grass. I don't generally make a point of ogling men's eyes, but it's hard not to find those green eyes incredibly sexy.

Then I look at his left ring finger and see the wedding band in place, and I quickly fall out of love. Dammit.

Jill lifts her eyes, regards the intruder briefly, then says, "I can't get my phone to open up a new browser window."

The guy holds out his hand, extending his long fingers towards Jill's phone. "Give it here."

I know this probably confirms some kind of awful stereotype about men and women, but damned if this guy doesn't teach Jill just about everything she needs to know about her phone in the next 15 minutes. She's been struggling with that phone for a month now, nagging every single one of us residents to try to figure out how to use it. Finally she hit paydirt.

"Thanks!" Jill says to the guy as she pockets her phone. Now that she's no longer distracted, she finally takes in the green scrubs and realizes that this is not a person she knows. He's an intruder in Baby City. She narrows her blue eyes at him.

"Who are you?"

The guy laughs. He has an adorable laugh. Damn that wedding band.

"I was wondering when you were going to ask me that," he says. "My name is Eric Kessler. I'm an emergency medicine resident and I'm rotating here this month."

Jill's eyes widen and her lips curl in disgust, like she woke up and just realized she had been making out with her dog or something.

"Oh *God*," she says, and storms out of the room.

The resident, whose name is apparently Eric, seems completely befuddled for a moment because he doesn't realize that this is completely typical behavior for Jill. Finally he turns to me and frowns.

"Is she always so pleasant?" he asks.

I shrug. "It's nothing personal," I say. "It's just that when you guys rotate here, it ends up being a lot more work for us. You have no clue what you're doing, and we basically have to treat you like a medical student. Worse, because at least the medical students have to do what we say. So it's really just a big pain in the ass."

Eric nods thoughtfully. "Are *you* always so pleasant?" he asks, a smile playing on his lips.

I smile sheepishly. "Sorry, it's been a long day."

"It's only eight in the morning," he points out.

"Exactly."

Eric grins at me. Damn, even his *teeth* are adorable.

"Well," he says. "If I'm such a pain in the ass, maybe I'll just sit down in the corner and try not to touch anything."

Eric sits himself down in one of the plastic chairs. He folds his arms across his chest, and very blatantly tucks his hands away under his armpits. This guy really has the look of an ER resident. He sort of... scrappy. Muscular, but in a wiry sort of way. He looks like the kind of guy you'd like to have with you if you got stranded on a desert island. He could probably build a defibrillator out of a coconut.

"Okay, how about this?" I say. I've got The Princess's C-section starting any minute now and it does look like things are picking up a bit. It would be good to have Eric manning Triage. "Our medical student is seeing a patient in Triage, a woman who thinks she's in labor. Why don't you have her present the patient to you?"

He nods. "Yeah, I think even a dumb emergency medicine resident can handle that."

"Do you want me to show you where Triage is?" I ask.

He shakes his head. "Nah, I think I can find it."

"Okay," I say. "Good luck." As an afterthought, I add, "I'm Emily, by the way."

"I've already surmised that from your badge," Eric says, gesturing at the ID badge hanging from the pocket of my scrub top. He reaches out like he's about to touch it, but then thinks better of it and pulls his hand away. "Dr. Emily McCoy, I presume."

"You better wear your badge while you're working here," I say. "If you don't, your new friend Jill will go ballistic."

Eric smiles wryly. "Is there anything I can do that *won't* make Jill go ballistic?"

"She's very protective of her patients."

"Like a mama hen."

"Sort of." I hesitate. "Don't ever say that mama hen thing to Jill. It will make her go… well, you know."

"Yeah, I'm a fast learner," Eric says.

With those words, Eric turns and jogs in the direction of Triage. If he has any other questions for me, I don't hear them. Because at that moment, a nurse grabs me and tells me it's time for The Princess's C-section.

Chapter 3

While The Princess is getting her spinal anesthesia, I stand outside the OR, waiting for Dr. Buckman to arrive. Unlike the general surgical operating rooms, we only have one operating room in Baby City. It's fully equipped though with everything that an obstetrician might theoretically need (surgical instruments for everything from tubal ligations to cesarean sections to hysterectomies, esoteric forceps, a variety of sutures, a suction D&C machine, and our very own dedicated surgical scrub team), and there's a nice big sink right outside the door, with three spouts to accommodate multiple people scrubbing at once.

Dr. Buckman is running very late, as usual, and there's no point in scrubbing in until he gets here. Dr. Buckman has a habit of showing up 30 minutes to an hour after whenever you tell him he supposed to be somewhere. Whenever he's the attending in clinic, we always spend a large chunk of time just waiting for him to show up.

The scrub nurse peeks her head out of the OR.

"Dr. Buckman here yet?" she asks. "The spinal has taken effect and Mrs. Woodhouse is getting antsy."

I glance off in the distance, then at the clock on the wall. "Tell her he'll be here any minute."

The scrub nurse looks like she doesn't believe it any more than I do, but she disappears back behind the swinging doors. Thank God the nurses are around to deal with The Princess. If they make me go in there, I'm going to be really pissed off.

And then, miracle above miracles, Dr. Buckman materializes in front of me. It would be nice, since he's nearly an hour late, if he at least pretended to appear out of breath. But instead, he looks like he just sauntered out of a spa. And it shouldn't come as any surprise to me that he isn't wearing scrubs—that would be far too much to hope for—instead, he's dressed in a tennis shirt and shorts.

"My game ran a little bit late," Dr. Buckman says to me.

It's now 9 a.m. on a Monday morning and he's on call for Baby City. Why exactly was he playing tennis? Okay, no judgment. I hope that when I'm his age, I have a life too.

"Let me just go change," he says.

"You do that," I mumble under my breath.

I twiddle my thumbs for a bit, because I know The Princess won't let me touch her until Dr. Buckman arrives. The scrub nurse sticks her head out again and asks where the hell he is, and I inform her that Dr. Buckman at least is in the building, albeit dressed for tennis right now. It will just be a little bit longer.

It takes him a baffling 15 minutes to change from his tennis clothing into scrubs. I'm not particularly fast at changing clothes, but I think I could've changed into scrubs about 20 times during that period of time. What took so long?

No judgment, no judgment.

Dr. Buckman and I scrub in together, but I let him enter the OR first so his will be the first face that the patient sees. The Princess is lying supine on a stretcher, anesthetized from the waist down, but she still manages to prop herself up on her elbows when she sees him. She offers him the largest smile I've ever seen come out of that woman.

"Dr. Buckman!" she exclaims. Her eyes light up like she's starstruck. I almost expect her to start fanning herself. "I'm so glad you're here!"

It shouldn't surprise me that The Princess has this kind of reaction to Dr. Buckman. It's actually pretty common. The first time I heard a patient refer to Dr. Buckman as "that handsome doctor," I didn't know who they were talking about. I don't find Dr. Buckman particularly attractive. At all. He's 40-something and chubby, with a receding hairline and eyes that are so close together, it makes me think he's always scheming something, which may very well be the case.

But the patients *love* him. The Princess is practically slobbering over herself for him. She doesn't even care that her husband is right next to her, although to be fair, he seems to be doing something pretty involved with his phone right now. (He's not supposed to have his phone out in here right now, but I suspect that if I say something, I'll be the one who gets in trouble.)

"Mrs. Woodhouse," Dr. Buckman says in his silky smooth voice. "Do you know how privileged I feel to be delivering your baby?"

This is worse than any line I've heard delivered in a bar, but The Princess is lapping it all up. She beams at him. "Did the resident tell you about the incision?"

Dr. Buckman frowns. "No. She didn't."

They both glare at me accusingly. Crap, I forgot about The Princess's teeny tiny incision. Oh well.

The Princess lifts up her gown, and sure enough, her little Hitler belly mustache is still there. I listen as she explains to him about her friend Cindy, and how a human being was somehow lifted out of an opening the size of a walnut. Dr. Buckman nods with his brows scrunched together, making a concerned face. Jill calls it his "constipated face."

"It's not a problem, is it?" The Princess asks.

"Of course not," Dr. Buckman says. (Clearly lying through his teeth.)

Next comes my favorite part, which is when we get to put up the drape so that The Princess can no longer see what we're going to do. The drapes are used during a C-section because it's obviously very weird to see your belly being cut open and also we don't want to have any fainting husbands. But in The Princess's case, I'm pretty sure the drape it is to keep her from rattling off instructions to us through the entire surgery.

As I adjust the drape, I keep getting distracted by what sounds like a loud humming sound. It sounds like a bee is loose in the OR.

"What's that noise?" I swat at some imaginary insect above my head and nearly break sterile.

"That's the CD I brought with me," The Princess says from behind the drape.

"Is it broken?" I ask.

"No," The Princess snips at me. "This is a meditation that is used as an adjunct to anesthesia for soothing pain relief."

I should probably just shut up now, but I can't help myself. "You shouldn't feel any pain from the surgery," I say.

"It's not for me," The Princess clarifies. "It's for the baby. Don't you think birth is painful? I want my baby's first moments to be perfect. It will lay the groundwork for his entire life."

I'm itching to tell her that if she really wanted her baby to be perfect, she wouldn't be having an elective C-section three weeks before the baby is ready to be born. But I keep my mouth shut. I don't want to be the first resident to get into a fight with the patient during her C-section.

Dr. Buckman is looking down at the black pen mark on her belly. After a moment of thought, he picks up the marker from the instrument tray, and extends the line that the Princess made about an inch in either direction. The line is now about the size of a normal incision or even a bit on the large side.

"Scalpel," Dr. Buckman says to the scrub nurse.

She hands him the scalpel, and then Dr. Buckman holds it out to me. He raises his eyebrows at me and nods at the incision line.

"Go ahead, Doctor," he says quietly but firmly.

The Princess is not going to like this at all.

Chapter 4

We deliver The Princess's six pound three ounce baby boy without further complication. He appears healthy, despite having been deprived of three weeks of gestation time. And we put a dressing on The Princess's incision, so she had yet to discover how long it is. That will be a fun conversation, I'm sure.

I go straight to Triage after the section. It seems like things have picked up a bit. Aside from the patient Caroline saw, two other patients have just arrived. Hopefully, Eric took care of most of the work and it will be quick for me to see this patient.

Caroline and Eric are sitting together at the desk outside the patient area. Their heads are leaning towards each other, and Eric is talking softly to her. He's probably giving her advice, maybe telling us what bitches all of the OB/GYN residents are. Well, screw him.

"Did you see that patient?" I ask them.

Caroline nods and eagerly stands up. She holds up a tiny white notebook in front of her face and starts to recite: "Mrs. Anderson is a 27-year-old woman who is 38 weeks and one day gestation with her first—"

"Is she in labor or not?" I interrupt. I don't have time for this crap.

Caroline looks at Eric for help. "I… I don't think so," she says.

"You don't *think* so?" I repeat.

"She's not," Eric says firmly. "Her contractions aren't regular and her cervix is closed."

"How do you know?" I challenge him. "You feel a lot of cervixes in the ER?"

"Yeah," he says. "I do. You think I can't do a pelvic exam? Her cervix is closed. Like a safe."

I yank Mrs. Anderson's chart from off the desk in front of them and flip through the pages. Caroline got the gist of it right—the patient is having her first baby and is 38 weeks and one day gestation. She had an appointment with us two days ago and her cervix was closed at that time. So Eric may very well be right, although there's a part of me that really wants to prove him wrong.

I put down the chart and march into Mrs. Anderson's room. Caroline scurries behind me, but Eric hangs back, not even curious as to what I'll find. That confident bastard.

Inside the room, I find a young woman dressed in a hospital gown, with her husband sitting next to her, holding her hand. The woman has frizzy hair pulled into a frizzy ponytail, and has what I believe are the largest, thickest glasses I have ever seen, until I look to her left and see her husband's glasses. I recall the detail from the chart that the two of them are both engineers. Maybe they could help Jill with her phone.

"Hello," I say. "I'm Dr. McCoy. I'm the OB/GYN resident here today. I hear you've been having a lot of contractions."

Mr. Anderson looks incredibly excited when he hears my name. "Dr. McCoy? Like on 'Star Trek?'"

Mr. Anderson looks like the kind of guy who has watched a lot of "Star Trek" episodes. He looks like he probably has a real opinion about who's better, Captain Kirk or Captain Picard.

I wince. "Yes, like on 'Star Trek.'"

Honestly, if I had ever watched "Star Trek" before going to medical school, I might've seriously reconsidered my decision to become a doctor, and subject myself to a lifetime of hearing that joke.

Mrs. Anderson has a monitor attached to her belly, which is recording both her contractions and the baby's heart rate. From the chart, I noted that the contractions were indeed not regular although some of them were close together. The heart rate is a nice healthy 130s.

"Dr. Kessler says I'm not in labor," she says, frowning as she touches her belly protectively. "But I really feel like I am. I know the contractions haven't been regular here, but they were at home. I'm *certain* that I must be in labor."

"Sometimes contractions can slow down when you're resting," I explain. "I'd really like to take another feel of your cervix to see if you're dilated at all."

"Dr. Kessler said it was closed," Mrs. Anderson says.

I smile at them. "He may be right," I say. I wiggle my fingers at them. "But I have magic fingers. Let's see what I find."

Mrs. Anderson manages a small smile.

I get her up in the stirrups while I put on sterile gloves. I want more than anything for this woman to be dilated, so I could tell "Dr. Kessler" that he's wrong. But even as my hands are sliding inside her, I know what I'm going to find. Mrs. Anderson's cervix is so closed and so thick and high that my finger can barely reach it.

Meaning that there's no way her baby is coming out of her today, at least not in that direction.

"Sorry," I say. "The cervix is closed. The contractions were probably Braxton-Hicks."

Mrs. Anderson's face falls. She looks like she's going to cry. If she does, I'll let Caroline comfort her.

"Couldn't you just induce her?" Mr. Anderson speaks up. He pushes his glasses up the bridge of his nose.

Induce her? Who does he think he's talking to? Dr. Buckman?

"I'm afraid not," I say. "The way her cervix feels, an induction would most likely fail. Then she'd end up with a C-section."

"We *really* wanted to have the baby today," Mrs. Anderson says hopefully.

Mr. Anderson nods. "If she's born today, her birthday will be a perfect square. She'll never have another opportunity like that again."

I wish there were a trophy that I could hand to them for having the stupidest reason I've ever heard for wanting to have their baby early.

"Well, do you know when I'll likely go into labor?" Mrs. Anderson asks.

"I'm sorry," I say. "I just don't know right now."

"Dammit, Jen," Mr. Anderson says. "She's a doctor, not a *psychic*."

That's a "Star Trek" joke. On "Star Trek," Dr. McCoy was always saying things like, "Dammit, I'm a doctor, not a torpedo technician," or something like that. I swear, I've never watched the show.

"I'm sorry," I say again.

"It's okay," Mrs. Anderson says. She brightens. "Maybe I'll deliver on *Labor Day*. Wouldn't that be funny?"

Possibly the worst thing about doing Baby City in August is that I'm going to get a whole month of people making that joke. I'm definitely not surprised to hear it coming out of the Andersons.

Mr. Anderson manages to squeeze in one more "Star Trek" joke before I escape from their room. Outside, Eric is sitting at the desk, looking through the chart of the new Triage patient. He lifts his eyes to look at us.

"Well?" he asks.

"Not in labor," I admit.

"Look at that, the dumb ER resident was right," he says with a grin. He needs to stop being so damn cute. "Who would have thunk it?"

"You got lucky," I retort.

Except I don't really think he got lucky. I think, for once, the ER resident they sent us actually knows what he's doing. But I'm sure Jill will manage to find some other reason to yell at him.

————

I told Caroline to write up a note on Mrs. Anderson, and it's beginning to seem like she's making it her life's work. Granted, her handwriting is immaculate, but who really cares? A woman came in *not* in labor, with no complications. That should be the whole note: "Not in labor, no complications." There, done.

The note should have taken her all of 60 seconds to write. But in the time it takes me to see a second patient on my own and write up that patient, she's still working on it.

"Are you done yet?" I say to Caroline. I already admitted my patient to Baby City, as she was actually in labor. Eric saw a second patient too, who was also in labor, and he made himself useful by drawing up her admission orders. Caroline is still writing up her physical exam.

Caroline purses her little pink lips together. "Almost."

"Okay," I say. "You have exactly one minute to finish your note. Starting... now!"

Caroline's eyes go wide and she starts scribbling manically. I know I shouldn't be too hard on her, since this is her only her second rotation of the year. She isn't used to writing notes. Still, this is getting ridiculous.

At the end of the 60 seconds, I practically have to pry the note out of Caroline's hands. I honestly think she'd like to take it home and keep working on it tonight.

"Can I say goodbye to Mrs. Anderson?" she asks me.

Is she kidding me?

"Fine," I grumble. God, I'm a softy.

I start to head back in the direction of Baby City, where Jill is presumably holding down the fort. We now have three women in labor, which is slightly respectable. There's actually a chance we might get to see a baby emerge from a woman's vagina today.

I've made it halfway down the hallway when I hear Caroline yelling out my name.

"Emily!" she screams. "Mrs. Anderson's water just broke!"

No way.

I do an about-face and head back to Triage. This makes no sense. Mrs. Anderson's cervix was locked up tighter than a bank vault. How could her water have broken? If it's true, she's almost certainly headed for a C-section today.

No, more likely Mrs. Anderson just peed on herself.

"We need to find out if this is actually amniotic fluid," I explain to Caroline. I rifle through a drawer, shoving aside a bottle of urine dipsticks, and come up with a blank slide. "Go get a sample of the fluid and look at it under the microscope."

"Cool," Caroline breathes and I roll my eyes.

Okay, it *is* a little cool.

Caroline practically skips off to Mrs. Anderson's room, gripping the slide in her hand. I wonder if I should remind her to wear gloves when she gets the sample. Oh well.

Eric, who is sitting at the desk finalizing his orders on his admission, looks up at me.

"Mrs. Anderson's water really broke?" he says.

He seems as skeptical as I feel.

"We'll see."

It takes far too long for Caroline to get the sample from Mr. Anderson. What is she *doing* in there? Delivering the baby herself? I'm just about to march into the room and ask her what's been taking so goddamn long, when she bursts out holding the slide triumphantly in her right hand.

"Got it!" she cries.

With Caroline, everything she does seems like a bit of a miracle.

I roll my eyes again and take the slide from her. We have a microscope in the back of Triage for this very purpose—it's ancient, but it does the trick. I slip the slide under the lens of our rusty microscope and peer down at the sample. Under the microscope at low power, amniotic fluid has the very characteristic appearance of a fern leaf. I've seen that pattern a million times and I could recognize it in my sleep. And I know immediately that this is not amniotic fluid. It's something else, something that I don't see nearly as often, but is extremely recognizable.

"Oh God," I say, backing away from the microscope. "Oh *God!*"

I think I'm going to be sick.

Chapter 5

"Oh God," I say again, covering my mouth this time.

Eric has been looking over our shoulders, and my exclamations have apparently piqued his interest. He nudges me aside and peers through the lens of the microscope himself. Apparently, he recognizes the image as well, because he bursts out laughing.

Caroline is staring at us.

"What?" she asks. She moves over to the lens of the microscope and looks at the slide herself. Her light brown eyebrows furrow together. "I don't get it. What is it?"

"It's sperm!" I nearly scream at her. A few people turn to look at me, but I don't care. I am just that disgusted. "Those two... they were having *sex* in there. And they told you it was... Christ, can't you tell the difference between ejaculate and amniotic fluid?"

Caroline's face goes bright red.

"I thought it looked like amniotic fluid," she mumbles.

"Ejaculate is white," Eric volunteers, still snickering.

I grab the slide off the microscope tray and toss it in the hazardous waste bin. Then I wash my hands for like five straight minutes, because seriously, ew.

The nurses are watching me to see what I do. I'm so angry that my hands are shaking. I know Eric and pretty much all the nurses think the whole thing is funny, and I guess it's a little funny, but I feel like that nerdy couple played us for fools. I mean, they made us look at *ejaculate* under a microscope. And they had sex in our freaking examining room. The whole room is going to need to be sterilized now.

I give myself a minute to try to calm down then I burst into the Andersons' room without bothering to knock first. (Considering everything, it probably would have been wise to knock.) They stare up at me, shocked by my intrusion on them.

"You had sex in here?" I snap at them.

I see them exchange looks, obviously debating if they should deny it or not. Mr. Anderson fixes an innocent look on his face, and says, "What do you mean?"

I'm a doctor, dammit, not an *idiot*.

"I just looked at a slide of fresh sperm," I inform him. I fold my arms across my chest. "Do you want to discuss this or should I have security escort you out?"

Mrs. Anderson has two little pink spots on her cheeks.

"No," she murmurs. "Please don't. I'm really sorry, Dr. McCoy."

"Did you think we wouldn't notice?" I ask her angrily. I'm definitely not ready to accept any sort of apology.

"It's not what you think," she says softly. Her eyes are welling up with tears, and I almost feel a tiny bit sorry for her. Then I remember she just had sex in this room and I feel a lot less sorry for her. "We really wanted to have the baby today, and you know how they say that sex can sometimes precipitate labor. So we figured we'd give it a try. I really did think my water had broken, but I guess…"

I sigh, deflated by her tears.

"Go home," I say. "You can come back when the contractions are regular and less than five minutes apart or if your water really does break."

Mrs. Anderson nods. I trust that she isn't going to try another stunt like this again. But even so, I don't take my eyes off her or her husband until they are out the door.

———

During the rest of our shift, a few women come in and are admitted, but nobody gets dilated worth a damn. We get a few other people in Triage whom I end up sending home. Some of them were outright ridiculous. For example, one lady came in who was two months pregnant and asked to be put on early maternity leave because she was just so damn tired. Caroline actually attempted to plead her case.

Signout to the evening shift takes place at 6 p.m. in The Pit. Basically, that consists of Jill and I handing off our patient load to the two residents who will be manning Baby City tonight. The night shift will be handled by Holly Park and Ted Patterson, who both show up at six o'clock on the dot.

Holly is in the same year as me, and she's my best friend in this place. Ever since the first day of residency, the two of us just hit it off. We like the same kind of movies (action, no chick flicks), the same kind of music (hard rock), and the same kind of clothes (scrubs, what else?). We've made it a point to go out for margaritas at least two or three times a month, no matter how busy we are.

Holly also happens to be 28 weeks pregnant right now.

Obvious question: Has Holly's pregnancy put a damper on our friendship? Honestly, maybe a little bit. We can't go out for margaritas like we used to… it's just not the same when Holly is getting Coca-Cola. And I worry that after the baby comes, Holly and I won't have much time to hang out, considering how little time we have right now. But I try not to think about that. Mostly I'm happy for my best friend. Really.

Holly lingers at the doorway to the Pit, her blue scrubs nearly concealing the bulge of third trimester. (Scrubs are great at hiding any sort of weight gain or loss.) Holly is Korean... I think. She told me once, but it slipped my mind, and I worried I might seem racist if I asked her a second time. She's one of those adorably chubby girls, and it took a long time before I got over the urge to want to pinch her cheeks. I mentioned this compulsion to her once, and she said that if I ever touched her cheeks, she would drop kick me.

I don't doubt that she would do it. Holly is short, but tough. She grew up in the city, in a rotten neighborhood, and to hear her tell it, she had to beat up at least one person every day on her way to high school.

Right now, Holly seems to be completely fascinated by something, which piques my interest. I stare where she's looking, but I can't figure it out. She nudges me, and nods in the direction of Eric, who is talking to one of the nurses.

"Who's that?" she asks.

"Eric Kessler. He's the ER resident. Jill already hates him."

Holly winks at me. "Yum."

"Easy there, pregnant lady." I grin at her. "I think those hormones are getting a little out of control. What would Mr. Park say?"

I always call Holly's husband Mr. Park. His name is James, but somehow it's funnier when I say Mr. Park.

Holly rolls her eyes. "No, I mean for *you*."

I shake my head. "Married."

Holly's face falls. Holly really wants me to meet a nice guy and get married. Her hopes for this have escalated since she got pregnant. She's got it all planned out to how I'd have a baby right away so we can have play dates together. Obviously, she's in fantasyland.

Although there is a romantic possibility lately that I haven't told her about. I don't like to keep secrets from Holly, but I can't bring myself to tell her this one. Not until I know it's for real.

Ted Patterson is standing in the center of The Pit, staring at the whiteboard, a perplexed look on his face. I've only had a few interactions with Ted, and he seems perpetually perplexed. He's tall and lanky to the point of being gawky, with more hair on his body than a human being should rightfully have. He's got thick black hair going almost 360° around his forearms, and the stubble of his facial hair goes all the way up to his cheekbones. It goes without saying that he's sporting a unibrow.

Holly and I have hypothesized that he was only accepted here because they didn't want the program to be 100% female. Ted is our token male resident, so they made sure he was extra burly. I don't mind so much the idea of all-female residents. Although I definitely think that our menstrual cycles are syncing up.

This is Ted's first year of OB/GYN residency and it's his first time on Baby City. Holly glances at Ted, a worried expression on her face.

"I can't believe I'm going to spend the next 12 hours babysitting this guy," she whispers.

"It won't be that bad," I try to reassure her.

"It will," Holly insists.

"Come on…"

"Emily," she says. "He couldn't even find Baby City."

I suppress a smile. "Stop exaggerating."

"I'm not exaggerating!" Holly's brown eyes are wide. "I found him in the elevator, going up and down, checking every floor, trying to find it."

I laugh. "Hey, at least you don't have to deal with a medical student who follows you into the bathroom."

It's the eternal dilemma. Which is worse? A co-resident who is an idiot or a medical student who follows you into the bathroom? Before we can debate the matter further, our attending, Dr. Ford, makes his entrance.

Dr. Ford is a big fat guy with sweaty dark hair who always walks around with a big goofy grin on his face. I've only had a handful of conversations with him, but that's been enough to know way, way too much about his personal life. Dr. Ford doesn't seem to have a clear sense of boundaries between what he can and can't talk about with his residents. That's why I know when his teenage daughter got her first period and that his wife has a third nipple. I guess having a sense of humor is his way of coping with being surrounded by women all the time.

Dr. Ford rubs his stubby hands together as he contemplates the whiteboard. "So what have you ladies got for me today?" he asks. Then he sees Ted and grins like it's Christmas. "Oh, excuse me, I didn't realize there was another *gentleman* in our midst."

Ted's face reddens and he raises his hand in an awkward hello. But Dr. Ford isn't ready to let him off the hook just yet.

"You must be Ted," Dr. Ford says.

"That's me," Ted says, squirming in his blue scrubs.

Dr. Ford grins. "It's always good to see another man entering the field."

"Thanks," Ted says.

Ted smiles, happy about the attention. Oh Ted. You have absolutely no idea what's coming.

"You know what they say about male OB/GYNs, don't you?" Dr. Ford says.

Ted's shakes his head. He's probably hoping it's something positive. Unlikely.

"All male OB/GYN are either queers or perverts," Dr. Ford recites. He cocks his head at Ted. "I'm a pervert. Which one are you?"

Ted's eyes go wide. He opens his mouth, but no sound comes out.

Dr. Ford's eyes fall on Ted's left hand, where he's wearing a wedding ring.

"Married," Dr. Ford observes. "A pervert then, I guess."

Ted wisely keeps his mouth shut. I'm just grateful that Dr. Ford does not elaborate further on exactly why he's a pervert. I suspect it has something to do with third nipples.

———

On days that I don't feel like the world has run me down with a Mack truck, I opt to walk home from Cadence Hospital rather than take the usual subway trip. Don't be too impressed. It's only two subway stops to my apartment, but sometimes that's more than I can manage.

You might be wondering how I can afford an apartment in Manhattan on a crappy resident salary. First off, it's a tiny studio apartment. It's horrible, honestly. I have just enough room for a single bed, one bookcase, and a small dresser of clothing. I have a kitchen, but it's only the bare minimum: a narrow refrigerator, an oven that only works about 50% of the time, and a sink that's coated in rust. I do have a closet, which doubles as the bathroom.

Still, I probably wouldn't be able to afford the place if it wasn't in a truly horrible neighborhood. My apartment has been broken into twice, probably courtesy of the methadone clinic across the street. Luckily, I have nothing worth stealing. Well, at least I don't anymore.

I survive on frozen dinners, ramen, and hot dogs. The first thing I do when I get home is grab one of the frozen mini pizzas from the freezer, and pop it in the microwave. It tastes better from the oven, but I don't feel like getting involved in an epic battle to get the heat to turn on right now. After two minutes, the cheese on the pizza is bubbling, and I bring the pizza with me to my tiny, creaky bed/dining table. This is where I eat dinner every night. Sadly, the only action that my bed ever sees is pizza action.

But I'm about to do something worse than eating pizza in bed. Much worse.

I pull my phone out of my purse, and I bring up my list of favorite numbers. Without hesitation, I select David's number.

David is my ex-husband.

Yes, I have an ex-husband.

How can I be divorced? I'm only 30 years old. If someone had told me when I was a kid that I'd be divorced by 30, I'd say that I would've made some pretty bad missteps in my life. Divorced people are older, with fake nails and dyed hair and possibly British accents. I'm too nice and normal to be divorced.

Except, as it turns out, even normal people make mistakes.

I met David Graham at an ice cream social during the second week of my freshman year of college. I was spooning strawberry ice cream into my mouth and trying not to fret about the dreaded freshman 15 when my roommate Natalie nudged my shoulder, and said, "Don't look now, but there's a cute guy checking you out."

I looked up in the direction that Natalie was pointing, and indeed noticed a pair of brown eyes looking me over, which immediately averted when their attention was noticed. The owner of the brown eyes was indeed cute, with dark brown hair that flopped over his forehead, and an adorably shy smile. He also had a cleft in his chin, which my friends in high school had always jokingly referred to as a "chin butt" (and not particularly kindly), but his chin butt was small and actually suited his face quite well.

Later that evening, the cute boy introduced himself at the ice cream table as David. We got to talking for several minutes before David accidentally squirted chocolate sauce on my shirt.

"I'm so sorry!" he cried.

"It's okay," I said quickly. I must have really liked him, because I wasn't even all that mad about the chocolate sauce. And *nothing* gets out chocolate.

David handed me a napkin. "Let me make it up to you. I'll take you out to dinner tomorrow night."

I'm still not entirely sure whether or not he spilled that chocolate sauce on me intentionally.

On our first date, David was more of a gentleman than I had ever experienced in my 18 years. As soon as he parked in front of the small off-campus Italian restaurant, he leaped out of his seat in order to be able to open the passenger side door. He even pulled out my chair for me at the restaurant. After a lovely dinner, the check arrived and I made an attempt to at least pay the tip, but David was adamant.

"I'm paying," he insisted. "Girls don't pay."

"Yes, we do," I said.

"Not with me, they don't."

If a man said that to me nowadays, I would probably think he was a chauvinist pig, but after years of dating high school boys who usually made me pay my own way on dates, I found his chivalry refreshing and endearing. On that first date, I fell a little bit in love with David Graham.

During spring break of our senior year of college, David and I took a trip to New York City. He led me up to the top of the Empire State building, and as we held hands and looked down at the stretch of glowing city below us, I thought to myself that I couldn't have imagined a more romantic moment.

Until David got down on one knee.

"I can't live without you, Em," he said as he presented me with a tiny diamond. "Will you marry me?"

I said yes, of course. If I hadn't, he might've thrown himself off the Empire State building, but that wasn't why I said yes. I was in love with him. What I didn't realize at the time is that I had fallen slightly more in love with New York City than with my future husband.

We spent the year after college backpacking through Europe, making out in such romantic locations as the Eiffel Tower or while trekking through an alp in Switzerland. When we got back, we got married. It felt like the best day of my life.

I'm not really sure how everything fell apart.

After our exciting year in Europe, we returned to our home state of Ohio, I started medical school, and David started working in a 9-to-5 job as a payroll officer for a clothing store. Since David had more free time than I did, he took over most of the chores around the house, such as cooking or vacuuming. But instead of being grateful to him, somehow I started to lose respect for him. David may have been sweet and romantic, but he wasn't ambitious like me and my new friends. He used to talk about getting a Master's degree in math or a degree in accounting, and even thought about law school. But now he seemed perfectly happy to be a payroll officer for the rest of his life and have a couple of kids. To me, that just seemed pathetic.

One evening, I was sitting at a diner with David and a few of my new medical school buddies. We were talking about mnemonics that people were using to memorize anatomy, and each one of us were reciting our favorites.

"To Zanzibar by motor car," my friend Mark said. "That's for the branches of the facial nerve."

"That's terrible," said Joe, another of my classmates, known for a particularly raunchy sense of humor, often featuring midget jokes.

"You got a better one?"

Joe grinned. "Ten zebras bit my cock."

Mark winced. "That's at least nine more zebras than I'd like biting my cock."

Everyone at the table laughed, including David, but I could tell his laugh was somewhat forced. He didn't get it. The medical jokes just aren't funny if you're an outsider. Even if they involve zebras biting penises.

It seemed like every time David came out with me and my new friends, it was awkward. David didn't know any of the same people we were talking about and he had no interest in our newly learned medical jargon. Usually he'd spend most of the evening smiling politely. I became jealous of my friends who were dating other guys in the class, who knew what they were going through and had similar goals in life.

When I started to get interested in OB/GYN as a specialty, David didn't hide his disapproval. When we first got married, we had tentatively agreed to start trying for kids during residency. But I made it clear to him that OB/GYN residency was not a great time to start having a baby. There's no time for motherhood during an OB/GYN residency, I told him. "I'm beginning to wonder if there's going to be time for *me*," David had grumbled.

Honestly, I had started to wonder the same thing.

When I started talking about residencies in New York City, and how fun it would be to spend my training there, David put his foot down. He had grown up in Toledo and he had no intention of leaving the Midwest. He wanted to buy a house, not have a couple of kids tucked away in a tiny one-bedroom apartment. He was not going to leave Ohio, and if I loved him, I would stay too.

I decided to let the fates decide. I applied to residency programs in Toledo, Detroit (less than an hour from Toledo), and New York. I told David that I ranked the Ohio and Michigan programs first, but that was a lie, and I think deep down he knew it. My first five choices were all programs in New York. When I told David that I matched at my third choice, Cadence Hospital in New York City, he just shook his head at me.

"Well," he said. "I guess that's that."

We were divorced before I left the state.

I don't know when exactly I realized that I'd made a terrible mistake. I'd like to say it was the second I boarded the plane for New York, but more likely it was during one of the disastrous dates I've been on in the 2+ years I've lived here. One guy actually picked his nose in front of me. I'm not even kidding. It's lucky that I'm so busy at work, because my love life is a big fat zero.

David is so much more wonderful than I gave him credit for. He's good-looking (chin butt aside), he sweet, he's romantic, and he's intelligent if not incredibly ambitious. And most of all, he wanted a family. Back when I was 25, having a baby was the last thing I wanted. But now, more and more, it's all I can think about. It's hard not to when you spend your life delivering other people's babies.

About six months ago, I gave David a call, knowing I'd be fighting an uphill battle to get him back. At first he was reluctant to talk to me, but then he remembered how we used to be best friends. Slowly but surely, we're falling back into our old rhythms. I miss him. And I'm pretty sure he misses me back. I told Holly a while back that I was thinking of calling David and she warned me against doing it, but I think she was wrong, which is why I've kept it from her. She was definitely wrong.

David's phone rings only twice before he picks up. I take it as a positive sign that he's so eager to talk to me.

"Hey, Em," he says.

"Hey yourself," I say. "Did I catch you at a bad time?"

"No, it's actually a good time," he says. "You saved me from having to watch 'Family Guy' while I eat dinner."

That was something that always used to bug me about David. At the end of a long day, I'd want to just veg out and watch TV during dinner. He always wanted to have a *conversation*. About our *days*. It felt like torture at the time.

And now, look how things have changed. David is watching stupid cartoon sitcoms during dinner and I'm the one calling him.

"How is work?" I ask.

"Fine," David says, without elaborating. "And what are you up to? Delivering babies?"

"You got it," I say. "And I have the most annoying medical student ever working with me."

David laughs. "I'm surprised," he says. "I would've thought you'd love having a minion to do your bidding."

"I would," I agree. "I mean, if she'd come home with me and do my laundry and wash my dishes, that would be great."

"Oh, you mean that's frowned upon?"

"Mostly," I say. "But I did manage to trick her into getting me a vanilla Coke Zero."

"Coke Zero," David scoffs. "Em, you can't afford to be drinking Coke Zero. I saw those pictures you posted last week on Facebook. If you lose any more weight, you're going to get knocked down by a burst of amniotic fluid."

Like Jill, when I'm stressed out, I tend to forget meals. I was a perfectly normal weight in medical school, but now that number has been dwindling down. I'm not sure how much I've lost because I haven't gotten around to purchasing a scale. Anyway, that's why scrubs have drawstrings.

But who cares about my weight? The main point here is that David is looking at photos of me on Facebook. I'm no love expert (that's an understatement), but I think that's a good sign.

Maybe David is over being pissed off at me. Maybe he's willing to give us another chance.

Step Two: Post sexy photos of myself on Facebook.

(Step One being to obtain sexy photos of myself.)

Chapter 6

Oh my God, 5:15 a.m. is way too early this morning.

In general, waking up at five in the morning is not a big deal to me. Actually, it's a little bit on the late side. On GYN rotations where we're doing surgery, I usually have to be at the hospital by now. Waking up when the sun is already peeking through the horizon seems like such a luxury.

Except today.

The conversation last night with David went exceptionally well, and we ended up staying on the phone past midnight. It didn't get sexual or anything, but definitely very flirtatious. I couldn't bring myself to hang up when things were going so well, so I sacrificed the sleep instead. (Life lesson: There's always tomorrow night to sleep.) Anyway, I think I'm immune to sleep deprivation. I function better on two or three hours of sleep than most people can function on seven or eight hours. I thrive on it.

Although I have to admit, I am really, really tired right now.

I would love to blast myself with steaming hot water right now. Unfortunately, my shower doesn't do "blast" and it doesn't do "steaming hot" either. So basically, I end up stepping through a lukewarm drizzle, then find my way into a (relatively) clean pair of scrubs. I sort of float my way to the hospital in that fog where everything you're doing just feels sort of surreal.

I grab a coffee on the way to the hospital. Coffee saves my life. Show me a doctor who doesn't drink coffee, and I'll show you… a sleeping doctor.

As I walk into the building, I'm mostly awake, and the familiar smells of the hospital give me that extra bit of adrenaline to make it through the morning. The hospital has that anti-septic smell, a combination of Clorox, Lysol, alcohol foam, Hibiclens, mixed with the heavier, musky odor of illness and bodily fluids. And every floor has its own unique smell tossed into the mix. The internal medicine floor smells of fecal matter, the surgery floor stinks of necrosis, and Baby City, located on the second floor, smells like baby powder.

By the time I arrive on the second floor, I am not only awake but slightly buzzed. In contrast to Holly and Ted, who look half-dead.

"You will not have any deliveries today," Holly informs me. She's sitting in the corner of the room, her limbs strewn about her, her straight black hair half unraveled from her ponytail and falling in disheveled clumps around her face. "We have officially delivered every baby in the city who will be born for the next two months. There are simply no more babies to be born. Maybe ever."

"It couldn't have been that bad," I say.

Holly just looks at me. I guess it was that bad.

Jill arrives a few minutes after I do, and Caroline walks in a few minutes after that. It's somewhat gratifying that Caroline looks slightly less bright-eyed than she did yesterday. Maybe she won't have quite as many annoying questions today. Jill's eyes snap up when Caroline enters the room.

"Why are you so late?" Jill demands to know.

Caroline looks down at her watch, then helplessly back at Jill. "I thought we started at six. I'm five minutes early."

"The job of the medical student is to arrive 30 minutes before her residents," Jill recites. She narrows her eyes at Caroline. "So you, my dear, are 25 minutes late."

Caroline glances around the room, maybe looking for someone rising to her defense. Good luck with that, Caroline. Finally, she sinks into a chair and mumbles, "Sorry."

Jill enjoys a moment of satisfaction for having broken the medical student's spirit before she nudges me. "Hey, where's that ER resident? Is it Edgar?"

"It's Eric," I correct her. "I haven't seen him."

Jill looks at her watch. "He better get here soon. He's late."

"I thought you hated him."

"Yeah," she says, "and this is why."

I'm not even going to try to argue with that logic.

The final arrival is Dr. Ford, appearing rumpled but still with that goofy grin on his face. He's dressed in blue scrubs like the rest of us, the top stretching over the large bulge of his belly, and there's little smear of blood on his collar. It looks like he had a rough night too.

"This is a sorry group of residents," Dr. Ford comments.

Everyone mumbles a greeting.

Dr. Ford rubs his hands together. "Okay, let's liven things up a bit," he says. "I'm going to tell you guys a joke."

There are times when it really sucks to be at the mercy of the crazy attending. Jill looks up at Dr. Ford like she wants to reach out and strangle him. Holly may very well go into labor if Dr. Ford doesn't stop talking soon.

"So a couple weeks ago," Dr. Ford begins, "Bill Buckman tells me he's got this terrible headache. I say to him, 'Bill, I get headaches all the time. And you know what always works like a charm? I go home to my wife, nuzzle my head between her breasts for an hour, and then my headache is gone.'" Dr. Ford pauses, to make sure we're all listening to this story about his wife's breasts. We are. Unfortunately. "So the next day, Bill comes into work, and I ask him about his headache. He says to me, 'Doug, you were right. I tried what you said and now my headache's all gone.'" He pauses again for drama. "Then Bill says, 'By the way, Doug, you got a really nice house.'"

I look at Ted, and see the corners of his lips twitching slightly in a smile. Caroline's brows furrow together. I don't think she gets it, but she's afraid to say so.

"It's just a joke," Dr. Ford reassures Caroline. "I wouldn't really let Dr. Buckman nuzzle with my wife's breasts."

Good to know, Dr. Ford.

"Okay," Dr. Ford says, looking at Caroline. "Your turn to tell a joke."

Caroline's eyes widen in panic. "I don't know any jokes."

"Good," Jill says. "Let's go over the patients then."

"No, wait," Dr. Ford says. He looks back at Caroline with a very serious expression on his face. "How can you not know a joke? Everyone knows at least one joke."

She hangs her head in shame. "I don't." She sounds like she's confessing she doesn't know how to read.

"I know a joke," Ted volunteers.

"Let's hear," Dr. Ford says, rubbing his hands together.

"*No*," Jill says, but she's too late and seems like she's outnumbered.

"So there's this doctor delivering a baby," Ted begins. "As soon as the baby comes out, he holds the baby by the ankle, swings it around his head, and throws it at a wall. The baby hits the wall, slides down and lands in a garbage can. Everyone in the room is looking at him like he's crazy." Much like the way we're all looking at Ted right now. "But then he says, 'It's okay, the baby was already dead.'"

Ted is grinning proudly, but his smile slips slightly when he realizes that we are all staring at him in shock. Maybe there's a time and a place for dead baby jokes, but that place is not a Labor and Delivery unit.

Dr. Ford finally breaks the awkward silence by clearing his throat. "Okay, why don't we go over the patients now?"

Signout goes fast. Holly was right—half the city had their babies last night and now they are no more babies left to be born. Good thing, because that jolt of caffeine from my coffee is beginning to wear off already. I need a refill.

When we finish, Ted and Holly stand up to leave. And that's when I see a familiar, evil glint in Jill's eyes. Poor Ted. He actually thinks he has a chance of going home after that nightmare shift.

"Ted," she says sharply. "Did you do the circumcisions from last night?"

Ted lifts his bloodshot eyes. I doubt he got even a minute of sleep last night, but I don't have much sympathy. We've all had crappy calls. "Huh?"

"The circumcisions," Jill repeats. "I assume a bunch of male babies were born last night. Did you circumcise the ones who wanted it?"

I bite my tongue to keep from making a joke about how I'd hazard a guess that none of the babies would've wanted it.

"No," Ted says. He's looking at her warily.

"So whose responsibility is that exactly?" Jill asks him. "Do you think it's *my* responsibility?"

I can see the wheels turning in Ted's brain as he tries to figure out if there's any possible way to get out of this. There isn't. Give up, Ted, before you make things worse for yourself.

Ted finally comes up with the utterly uncreative, "I'm really tired."

Rule Number One of OB/GYN residency: Never *ever* complain that you are too tired to do your work.

Jill's lips curl into a sardonic smile.

"You poor thing," she says sweetly. "I had no idea you were *too tired*." She pokes Holly in the arm. "Holly, did you hear this? Ted is too tired to do his circumcisions."

Holly looks like she's about to punch him in the nose. "Oh, you're *tired*, are you?"

Ted's face turns bright red. "I didn't mean…"

"Maybe you should sit down," Jill suggests. "Put your feet up. Maybe Holly here can fetch you a pillow."

"I was just saying, I'm just a little bit tired…" Ted stammers.

Holly gets up in Ted's face, practically standing on her toes. "You don't know what tired is, Buster."

Ted hangs his head in resignation. "Okay, I'll go do it now."

A few minutes later, I'm about to go check on one of the few remaining laboring patients when I happen to notice Ted standing at the nursing station, furiously looking through one of his handbooks. His unibrow is furrowed, and there's a slightly worried expression on his face. I've got a bad feeling about this.

"Ted," I say.

He doesn't look up so I tap him on the shoulder, which causes him to startle. For a moment, he reminds me of a very hairy newborn.

"Hey," he mumbles.

"Ted," I say again. "You've done a circumcision before, right?"

Ted hesitates. "Yes," he says in a way that makes me think that he probably has never done a circumcision before.

I sigh. "Do you need me to help you?"

Ted shakes his head. "I'll be fine."

I raise my eyebrows at him. "Are you sure?"

Ted nods. "Yeah, no problem."

That's weird. I can't figure out why he doesn't want my help, except maybe he thinks it will be faster to do them without me. The wrong way is often faster.

That or it's some guy thing, where he doesn't want to admit he needs help from a woman. But if that's his attitude, he's going to sink fast in this residency.

I'm debating if I should insist on going with him when I hear a nurse calling out my name. I decide to let Ted have a go at it on his own. After all, what's the worst that could happen?

———

The clock in The Pit reads 6:45 a.m. when Eric finally shows up. Which makes him incredibly, unacceptably late.

He's not wearing scrubs either, which is another cardinal sin. He's dressed in a worn, gray T-shirt, and jogging shorts. The fact that he's also wearing sneakers and has a V-line of sweat on the front of his shirt makes me think that he actually was jogging just now. I hate to admit it, but my jaw drops a little bit at the sight of him wearing those skimpy clothes. The boy may be lanky, but he's got muscles. Damn.

Jill has a sixth sense of when somebody has broken the rules. It's actually a little bit spooky. The second Eric walks in, Jill materializes next to him. Her hands are already folded across her chest and there's a deep crease between her eyebrows.

"You're late!" she barks at him.

Eric raises his eyebrows. "What are you talking about?" he asks. "Don't you guys start at seven?"

"Six," Jill practically spits at him.

"Wow, that's inhuman," he says. "You know we start our day shift at eight in the ER?"

Jill just shakes her head at him.

"Okay, okay," Eric says, holding up his hands in surrender. "I'll be here at six from now on. Sheesh." He wipes his brow and I notice his hair is slightly damp with sweat. "Hey, you ladies got a shower here?"

"There's a shower for residents," Jill snips at him.

He offers her a half smile. "I'm a resident."

"*OB/GYN* residents."

Eric shrugs. "Fine. I'll just sit here and stink."

He strides across the room, and plops himself down in a chair. He makes a big show out of putting his hands behind his head. He does really smell sweaty. I sort of hate myself for thinking it's sexy.

However, Eric's manly odor is obviously not having the same effect on Jill. She crinkles up her nose.

"Go use our shower. It's next to our call room. The nurses will tell you where it is." She adds, "But don't think this means you can ever use our call room."

Eric salutes at her, then gets up out of his seat, and heads down the hallway. Jill yells after him: "And put on blue scrubs!"

"I hate blue!" I hear him yell back.

When Eric is out of sight, Jill turns to me and shakes her head.

"And as for you, young lady," she says, planting her fists on her hips. "Will you please stop drooling over him? It's kind of pathetic. He's not that cute, seriously."

"I'm not drooling," I say. I wipe my mouth self-consciously, just to make sure. I'm really not!

Jill snorts at me.

"I'm not," I insist. "Anyway, he's married."

"And don't forget it," Jill says, shaking her finger at me. "You know, if you're interested in a nice guy, my husband's brother—"

"No," I cut her off. "I have dated everyone's husband's brother and I don't like any of them."

"He's pretty hot," Jill says. "Besides," she adds, "if my husband can put up with me, you know he must come from a family of saints."

"What are you talking about?" My face twitches into a smile. "You're completely delightful."

"Hey, I'm comfortable with my bitchiness," Jill says with a shrug. "Come on, at least meet the guy. What have you got to lose?"

"My dignity."

Jill rolls her eyes. "Says the woman who sticks her fingers up about two dozen vaginas each day."

"Right. I've got almost none left. I've got to preserve it."

I'm pretty sure I haven't heard the last about Jill's brother-in-law, but fortunately, I get a stay of execution when a nurse shows up and tells us that a patient is waiting in Triage. And I recognize this one's name.

Chapter 7

I see a lot of patients in the course of any given day, and certainly hundreds over the course of a year. The truth is, most are pretty forgettable.

The opposite is not true. Random patients will show up in clinic and remember every detail of the last time I did their Pap smear, because apparently my Pap smears are quite memorable. I usually have no clue who they are. I got really good at pretending though. The trick is to find some small detail in the chart I can cling on to that would make them think the experience was as memorable to me as it was to them. *Yes, that was the greatest Pap smear I've ever performed.*

Then there are the patients that I hate. Luckily, that's the minority. Each resident has a short list of patients that we hate, and we make deals to get out of seeing them when their name shows up on the clinic list. The Princess is one of the lucky ones that we all seem to hate.

And finally, there are the patients that I love. Patients who somehow manage to make my day better just in the course of their visit. The ones who I see on the schedule and give a little fist pump.

Marissa Block is one of those patients.

I pull her chart off the doorway in Triage, trying to remember how far along in her pregnancy she is. I'm dismayed to see that she's only 24 weeks. Marissa is not a complainer. If she's here, there's something seriously wrong. I doubt she'd show up because her back hurt or she's just kind of tired.

Sure enough, it turns out she's having contractions. Scary contractions.

Inside the examining room, Marissa is dressed in a blue hospital gown. She's hugging her arms to her chest, and she looks terrified as she lies propped up on the examining table. There's a monitor stuck to her belly, which has already revealed that her contractions are regular.

You wouldn't know it to look at her now, but Marissa is a junior partner at one of the biggest law firms in the city. She's both the first female partner and the first African-American partner the firm has ever had. At her best, Marissa is incredibly intimidating. She's tall with a broad frame, and is built sort of like a female linebacker. Her artificially straightened black hair is always pulled back into a severe bun, but now that bun has mostly come unraveled.

"How are you doing, Marissa?" I ask her. I call most patients by their last name, but Marissa instructed me in no uncertain terms that I need to call her by her first name.

She always calls me Dr. McCoy. I'm in greater need of respect than she is.

Marissa manages a weak smile. "I'm okay, Dr. McCoy. I don't know what all the fuss is about."

Marissa is 42 years old and on pregnancy number five, but is still childless. She told me she made partner in her firm at age 36, and soon after, started trying to have a baby. After a year and one miscarriage, she was diagnosed with polycystic ovarian syndrome (PCOS). She decided to try IVF, meaning in vitro fertilization. Her own fertilized egg was implanted in her uterus, a procedure that isn't covered by many insurance companies and costs a bundle. Luckily, money wasn't an issue for Marissa. In vitro fertilization got her three more pregnancies over the next three years, and three more miscarriages. The twin pregnancy was especially devastating.

A few weeks ago, Marissa and I were celebrating that she finally made it past the treacherous first trimester, when all her prior miscarriages occurred. We knew that she was high-risk, being advanced maternal age (over age 35), but her amniocentesis was completely normal and the pregnancy had been going well so far. There was no particular reason to think anything would go wrong.

Except here we are.

"Okay," I say, in my best voice that exudes the confidence of somebody who believes Marissa will be just fine. "Let me take a look at your belly."

Marissa pulls up the drape covering her lower legs and allows me to lift her gown. The first thing I notice is how hairy Marissa has gotten. In the past, she's always been impeccably groomed. However, pregnancy tends to make you a little bit furry and so does her PCOS, and I guess she's been so busy, she let it get away from her. There is a *lot* of hair there. If someone told me I was looking at a man's abdomen… well, it would be surprising because men don't usually get pregnant, but the hair pattern is consistent with that.

I'm trying really hard not to react to Marissa's bushiness, but I guess my face gives me away. I have an awful poker face.

"I was going to get waxed this weekend," she says defensively.

I shrug like she isn't the hairiest patient I've ever examined since I stopped seeing the male half of the population. Part of being a doctor is pretending that everything is totally commonplace, no matter how weird it is. That third eye on your butt? Yeah, we see that all the time.

"Don't even worry about it," I tell her.

I can tell right away that Marissa is measuring small. By 20 weeks, her uterus should be at her belly button (our fancy name for belly button is *umbilicus*). Even though Marissa is four weeks past that point, her uterus is only slightly higher than the umbilicus. She's measuring small *and* she's having contractions. I'm seriously worried right now.

And then her pelvic exam confirms my fears. Marissa is two centimeters dilated and her cervix is thinning out. This baby is trying to be born. Like, now.

I allow Marissa to sit up from the table before I give her the bad news. She struggles a bit on the way up, trying to find her balance. "Marissa," I say. "We're going to need to admit you to the hospital. Now."

The protocol at this point is to put Marissa on complete bed rest. We'll give her dose of steroids to help her baby's lungs mature and then start tocolytics. The word tocolytic is Greek: *tokos* is the word for childbirth and *lytic* means to dissolve. Basically, these agents prevent women from giving birth. I'm hoping that all of these interventions together will at least buy her a few more weeks.

Marissa's face falls. "Today?"

No, after you're crowning in the shower tomorrow.

"Yes, today."

Marissa toys with the hem of her hospital gown. She won't meet my eyes.

"Dr. McCoy," she says. "I have this incredibly important meeting this afternoon at work. It's for this case I've been working on for months. We're about to settle and I don't know what's going to happen if I'm not there. I *have to* be there."

If Marissa were anyone else, I would be livid by now. But I respect her and I know how hard she's worked to get to where she is in her career. I get it. It's a little hard to throw stones, considering I threw away my entire marriage for my career.

"Marissa," I say patiently. "It is imperative that you stay at the hospital. The life of your baby is at stake. Maybe you can Skype into the meeting or something…"

Marissa is shaking her head. "I can't. You don't understand. I just can't…"

"You're in labor, Marissa," I say. I'm trying to use my scary voice.

She bites her lip thoughtfully. "What if…" I don't know what she's going to say, but I can already tell it will be completely unacceptable. "I can go to the meeting, and come right back here afterwards? The meeting will be over at five. Six, at the latest."

"You'd be taking a very big risk," I warn her.

Marissa smiles confidently. "Taking risks is what got me where I am today."

I just shake my head at her. "This is a mistake, Marissa."

"Dr. McCoy," she says. "Your career is very important to you too. I'd think of all people you'd understand. I can't just walk out on my job right in the middle of the most important deal of the year. Can't you understand that?"

I'm trying to muster up the words to contradict what is actually a very good point when my pager goes off. The number comes from the newborn nursery, and the attached message is 911. That means whatever the page is, it's urgent. I can't imagine why on earth I would be getting an urgent page from the newborn nursery unless…

Oh crap. Ted is down there.

Even though I'm worried that Marissa is a flight risk, I have to return this page right now. I make Marissa swear on her baby's life that she won't leave then I run to the nearest phone.

Unsurprisingly, the other line picks up after about half a ring.

"Emily?" It's Ted's breathless voice.

"What's wrong?" I ask him.

"I was doing a circ on this baby," he begins, the anguish mounting in his voice. "And… and…"

"*What?*"

"I cut it off."

I frown at the phone. "You're *supposed* to cut it off."

"No," Ted says. "You don't understand. I cut off... the whole thing. His penis."

My heart sinks. Oh my God, this is really bad. Really, really bad. Why did I trust Ted to do this on his own? Why didn't I go down with him? Now some poor little baby is missing a penis, and it's all my fault.

"Ted, what the hell?" I scream at him.

"It was just so *small*," he moans. "It's just this tiny little minuscule nub... I mean, you need a *microscope* to really see..."

Okay, damage control time. Ted cut off of a baby's penis. There's nothing we can do about that. But maybe we can preserve the penis and get it reattached. They can do that, right? They reattached Lorena Bobbitt's husband's penis, and that was years ago. Penis reattachment surgery must be much better by now.

"How are you controlling the bleeding?" I ask him. "Has the nurse started an IV?"

There's a long pause on the other line. "Bleeding?"

Holly was right about Ted being an idiot.

"You cut off his penis." You genius. "I assume he's bleeding pretty substantially?"

Another long pause. "Not... really. Maybe a few drops."

A few *drops*?

"Ted," I say impatiently. "Did you cut off his penis or not?"

"Hang on," Ted says, and before I can squeeze in another question, I hear him drop the phone. I really think I should probably get over to the newborn nursery, but at the same time, I still think I need to guard the door to Marissa's room. The second she gets a call from work saying she needs to leave, she'll take off.

Ted is gone long enough that I'm about ready to give up on him and dash down to the newborn nursery. But about five seconds before I give up hope, his voice comes on the other line.

"Never mind," he says, and hangs up the phone.

What the hell???

Remind me not to let Ted circumcise any sons that I might have.

As much as I don't want to, I'm pretty sure I have to go down to the newborn nursery and make sure Ted did not just neuter a baby boy. But Marissa is definitely a flight risk. I can't leave without making sure she's staying.

The problem with Marissa is that she smart. She knows the risks of preterm delivery, and as much as she wants this baby, she has worked incredibly hard to build her career. She's not just going to blow off an important case, not without a damn good reason. Which means I have to give her a speech worthy of a presidential candidate to convince her to stay.

I'm steeling myself to go back into Marissa's room when a tap on my shoulder startles me. It's Jill.

"Emily," she says. "Can you do rounds on the postpartum patients today?"

My shoulders sag in relief. I know that if anyone is capable of convincing Marissa to stay, it's Jill. Jill cares about the babies more than anyone else. I mean, we all care about the babies a lot. But Jill cares about them at the expense of everything else.

For example, if Jill sees a pregnant patient who reeks of cigarette smoke, she literally will not let the woman leave without extracting a promise to never smoke again and handing over all the cigarettes in her purse. Most women are quickly shamed into doing the right thing, but there have been a few cases where Jill has resorted to scare tactics that got her reported to her attending physician.

That's the thing about Jill though. She doesn't care if she's putting her entire career in jeopardy. She just cares that the babies are safe.

So I know she'll make sure that Marissa's baby is safe.

"Hey Jill," I say. "I'll go do postpartum rounds, but do you think you can help me convince a patient to let herself be admitted?"

Jill raises her eyebrows. "Who is it?"

"Marissa Block. Have you seen her before?"

"The lawyer, right? What she's here for?"

"Twenty-four weeks gestation, regular contractions six minutes apart, and two centimeters dilated." I shake my head. "I wanted to admit her, but she says she has some important meeting she has to go to."

A knowing smile spreads across Jill's face. She's dealt with women like Marissa before many times, and they never ever get the best of her. I think she derives some sort of enjoyment out of scaring the shit out of people. Anyway, she's really good at it.

Jill rubs her hands together. "Give me two minutes with her."

Jill is fumbling with her phone as she marches into Marissa's room. Marissa is talking into her own phone, and it sounds like she's barking orders at some lackey. If some file isn't on her desk by noon, somebody is going to be looking at the want ads for a new job. In another life, I really think Marissa could have made it as an OB/GYN. She'd have been great at it. Maybe that's why I like her so much.

Marissa clicks off her phone when she sees us. She hastily pulls up the sheet covering her legs and tucks a strand of hair behind her ear.

"Mrs. Block?" Jill asks crisply, lowering her phone but not putting it away.

Marissa nods, narrowing her eyes. "Yes?"

"My name is Dr. Brandt," Jill says. "Dr. McCoy here says that you're reluctant to let us admit you today."

"Right." Marissa seems more convinced than ever that she is on her way out. Yelling at her lackey seems to have reasserted her confidence. "I'd be happy to come in this evening or tomorrow, Dr. Brandt, but I'm just too busy today. I don't think my baby is going to be born today. I *know* it."

Jill studies Marissa thoughtfully for a moment. "You're 24 weeks pregnant, aren't you?"

Marissa nods again.

Jill holds up her phone. I don't need to look because I already know what's on it, but I look anyway. It's a photo of a 24 week old preemie. Even on the small screen, the photo is horrifying. The baby is lying in an incubator, looking half dead, intubated, IVs coming out of both arms, a feeding tube stuffed into his tiny nose, cardiac monitors taped into place. Although I think the most heartbreaking part is a tiny little pink hat on the baby's head with a little pom-pom on the top. It's just a reminder that there is somebody who gave that tiny baby that hat, someone who loves her.

"This is what your baby will look like if you go to work today," Jill says. "With such an early preemie, the risk is considerable for respiratory failure and being hooked up on a ventilator indefinitely, bleeding into the retinas with blindness, bleeding into the brain. If you go to this meeting today, your baby might never walk, might never talk, might not even have the cognition to ever know who you are. All because you couldn't miss one meeting." Jill lowers her hand and stuffs her phone back in her pocket. "But of course, it's your decision, Mrs. Block."

I look up at Marissa's face. She has gone very pale. She doesn't look like a linebacker anymore. She looks more like a scared mother who is worried her baby is going to die.

"Okay," she says in a small voice. "I'll stay."

"Good," Jill says, then turned on her heels as she leaves the room.

Chapter 8

One of the incredibly exciting duties of the Baby City residents is to follow postpartum patients until their discharge home. Usually it's a pretty simple task. Most are fairly healthy and complications are not common. I worry most about the C-section patients, who are at risk for wound infections, but even that is fairly rare.

Probably the hardest part about seeing these patients is the barrage of questions I get from the new mothers, most of which involve their breasts. When is my milk coming in? Why do my nipples hurt so much? Why are my breasts so big and will they stay this way? (That last bit is usually asked somewhat hopefully.)

After I check on the baby that Ted circumcised (totally fine, by the way), Caroline tails me to the postpartum unit. I didn't ask her to come but somehow she feels that it's her task to follow me everywhere I go. Sometimes I make a quick turn or walk in zig-zag, hoping to lose her. It never works. She is always. Freaking. There.

The first two patients we see are quickies. Both are vaginal delivery patient who are doing well. The third is the C-section, and she needs to have her staples out. Finally, I've discovered a use for Caroline!

"Caroline," I say. "Would you take Mrs. Bennett's staples out?"

Caroline gives me that deer in headlights look that she has managed to perfect recently. "How?"

I look at her incredulously. "You've never taken staples out before?"

Caroline squirms in her short white coat. "This is only my second rotation."

"What was your first rotation?"

"Psych."

Well, that explains a lot.

"Okay," I sigh. "Let me show you how to do it."

An attending once said to me that there is nothing like teaching a student who is eager to learn. Well, I can honestly say that there is *nothing* like teaching Caroline. I am sort of starting to understand now why some parents smack their children. She asks me question after question after question, and keeps leaning into my field of vision so that I can't see what I'm doing. I mean, it's not like removing staples is rocket science or anything but you at least need to be able to see the staples. I can't do it blindfolded. (Or in this case, with Caroline's big blonde head obscuring my field of vision.) Caroline's face is so close to Mrs. Bennett's surgical incision that she's practically licking it.

At least Mrs. Bennett is nice about the whole thing. She then lets Caroline take out a couple of staples to practice. She doesn't even get upset when Caroline exclaims, "Oh my God, it's just like removing staples from a piece of paper!"

"So Mrs. Bennett is going home today," I tell her as we finally leave their room. "I have a list of the medications she's on. Do you think you could write her prescriptions for me?"

Caroline's eyes widen. "You mean, like on a *real* prescription pad?"

"Um, yes," I say.

Caroline clasps her hands together excitedly. I can't believe she is so worked up over writing a few prescriptions. I'm worried that if I ever ask her to do something that's *actually* exciting, she might keel over. In any case, when we return to the nurses' station, I hand over my prescription pad and a typed list of Mrs. Bennett's medications, then leave Caroline to have a blast.

The next patient on my list to see is The Princess.

I've been dreading her postpartum visit ever since the surgery. Her incision is huge. I can only imagine how furious she's going to be when I peel back that bandage. She'll probably scratch out my eyes with her long, manicured fingernails.

But what choice do I have? Somebody has to see The Princess.

I postpone it as long as I can by peeking in on two repeat C-section patients, but it has to be done. I'll just blame everything on Dr. Buckman. Maybe I'll get lucky and she'll only scratch out one of my eyes.

When I get into The Princess's room, I have to admit, she looks fantastic for being one day postpartum. Her belly is substantially smaller—it's actually hard to believe that she just gave birth. And she's managed to comb her hair and apply a fresh layer of makeup. She looks far better than I do right now.

"Dr. McCoy," The Princess says, when I walk into the room. Her baby is nowhere to be seen. I suppose he's in the newborn nursery. I wonder if he's the one who had the tiny penis that Ted almost cut off.

"Hello, Mrs. Woodhouse," I say, swallowing down a lump in my throat. "I'm here to check your incision."

"I already looked at it this morning," The Princess says.

Oh crap.

"Did you?" I say, as casually as I can muster.

A lot of women don't want to look at their incision, because it freaks them out. Too bad The Princess isn't one of them. Not that I'm surprised.

"Of course," The Princess says. "And I have to say…"

I hold my breath.

"You guys did an amazing job," The Princess finishes, a smile touching her fire engine red lips.

I can only stare at her in disbelief. "We did?"

"Absolutely," she says. "The incision is even smaller than the line I drew. It's just what I wanted! Dr. Buckman is amazing. What a great surgeon."

"Yeah," I breathe.

I can't believe we got away with it.

My interaction with The Princess has improved my mood considerably. So much so that there's little bounce to my step as I walk back to the nurses' station to locate Caroline. I'm further cheered by the fact that Caroline has little stack of prescriptions next to the pad I gave her. She actually helped me by doing some of my work. Go, Caroline!

Caroline looks alarmed when she sees me approaching, which is my first inkling that something is wrong. She has a little pink spot on each cheek and her eyes are blue orbs of guilt. That's when I look down at the pile of prescriptions and realize that the top prescription has several words crossed out on it.

A sinking feeling in my chest, I grab for the rest of the pile and sift through it. I let out a low groan. There's not one usable prescription in the bunch.

Is she kidding me with this?

"What the hell, Caroline?" I say, slamming the pile down on the table in front of her.

"Um," she says. "How do you write a prescription?"

This shift will never end.

———

I guide Caroline through the tedious process of writing prescriptions for the patients. I really didn't realize how hard it was to write a prescription, or how many inane questions could be asked about it. I understand that her only previous rotation was psychiatry, which does not prepare you for anything, but I would think at least you would learn how to write prescriptions on psychiatry. I mean, what else do psychiatrists do aside from prescribe drugs for crazy people?

If I spend any more time teaching Caroline, I think I'm going to need a psychiatrist.

I finally have to go back to Baby City to catch the baby of a multip (woman who has had several babies in the past) who came in only two hours earlier. The nurse told me that the baby is pretty much crowning—after the third baby, they just pretty much fall out of you. I look over at Caroline, who is writing her final prescription. She's yet to witness a delivery, which is what this rotation is sort of all about.

"Hey," I say to her. "Want to deliver a baby?"

Caroline's eyes widen. "Whose?"

"This woman, Mrs. Kilpatrick, who's having her fourth baby," I say. "It should be fast and easy."

Caroline actually starts jumping up and down in the air. I didn't think anyone over the age of five could do that.

"Oh my God, that would be great!" she squeals. "Let me just go to the bathroom and I'll meet you down there."

"Okay," I say. "Don't take too long. This should be a quick delivery."

Caroline nods and skips away. Why do I get this feeling she's going to screw something up?

Chapter 9

I race down to Baby City, where the nurse and Dr. Ford are waiting outside the patient's room. This is definitely an urgent situation. I quickly gown up and burst into the room, where Mrs. Kilpatrick's legs are spread apart. Mr. Kilpatrick applauds when I enter. "There she is," he says. This guy knows the drill.

"Thank God," Mrs. Kilpatrick laughs. "Doc, if you didn't get here in the next five minutes, this baby was just going to squirt right out of me."

The lady didn't even get an epidural. She's a rock star. When and if I ever have children, I want to skip right to the fourth delivery.

As I was told, the baby is already crowning. I instruct Mrs. Kilpatrick to push, and the baby pops out with one solid push for the head, then one push for the body. Mr. Kilpatrick cuts the cord, and a mucus covered baby is plopped down on Mrs. Kilpatrick's chest while I deliver the placenta. No vaginal tears as far as I can see. Dr. Ford stays in the back corner and doesn't have to lift a finger to help me. He doesn't even have time to tell a dirty joke.

If only every birth could be as simple.

I'm leaving the room when I see Caroline outside the door, donning a pair of gloves. She beams at me.

"I'm ready!" she says, still bouncing slightly on the heels of her shoes.

"You missed it," I say.

Caroline's face falls.

I don't have much sympathy. "I told you to get here fast," I say with a shrug.

"I had to go to the bathroom," Caroline says in a small voice.

"Next time," I say, "hold it."

————

I wish there were a pill I could take to keep my stomach from growling when I'm hungry. It's not like I desperately need food, but that churning in my belly is an annoying reminder that will not shut up. If not for my stupid stomach, I think I could go several days without eating with no problem.

When I get back to The Pit, my stomach is growling furiously. I look at my watch—the cafeteria closed five minutes ago and it's unlikely they'll take pity on me and let me have some leftover chicken salad. It looks like I'm going to have another savory meal from the vending machine. That or I can raid the patient kitchen, but that's mostly crackers and stale muffins.

The thought of yet another lunch of bacon-flavored potato chips does not seem appealing. Worse, somebody is eating a cheesesteak nearby and the smell is tantalizing. I wonder if they'd let me buy it off them. Hell, I'd pay ten bucks for even a bite. Thirty bucks for two bites.

The smell grows stronger and is actually making me feel almost lightheaded with hunger. I am slightly considering going hunting with a scalpel, when Eric peeks his head into the Pit. He's holding a plate in his hand, which contains the offending cheesesteak.

Good. Maybe I can bully him into giving me some.

But before I can think of an adequate threat, Eric places the plate down majestically in front of me.

"For you," he says.

I look up at his green eyes, so overcome with gratitude that I nearly burst into tears. Man, I am tired.

"You looked like you needed to eat," he says. "I didn't want you passing out and falling face-first into some patient's vagina."

The guy is a poet.

"I love cheesesteak," I sigh. I pick up that cheesesteak and take a big bite. It's still warm. The steak is so juicy that a little bit dribbles down the corner of my mouth. I quickly wipe it away. Eric might be married, but I still don't want him seeing me with food all over my face.

"It's the one thing that the cafeteria doesn't mess up," he says. "And I'm pretty picky about cheesesteaks, considering I'm from Philly."

"You're from Philly?" I ask, around a mouthful of cheese and steak. There really isn't time to pause for conversation.

"Not exactly," he amends. "I'm from a suburb about 20 miles away." He adds, "I'm still tough though."

"Yeah," I say. "I've heard that about kids from the suburbs."

"Hey, be nice." Eric winks at me. "I just bought you a cheesesteak, lady."

That wink makes my stomach churn in a way that has nothing to do with hunger. I'm pretty sure that when a guy winks at a girl, it means he's flirting. And if a guy buys a girl food, that is definitely flirting. I'm not imagining it.

And this doesn't strike me as the kind of harmless flirting between two friends. This is real, honest to God, "I like you *like you*" kind of flirting.

Let's face it, Eric is incredibly, devastatingly cute. Under ordinary circumstances, I'd be quite happy that he's flirting with me. Except for the fact that he's married. *Married.* I am not about to get involved with a guy who's married. That is bad news. And I'm not going to believe any story about how he and his wife don't get along, and they're going to get separated any day now. I don't have time to waste on bullshit stories like that.

Plus, even if he were interested, I feel confident that things are going to work out with David. David and I have this huge history together. We're meant to be together. I just have to make him forgive me.

Eric sits down next to me and my breath catches in my throat. I inch away from him slightly, hoping to stave off any advances from the married guy.

"Feel better?" he asks.

I eye him warily. "Yes…"

He grins at me. "Good. So here's the thing…"

Okay, I feel dumb. He was never flirting with me. This whole cheesesteak thing was just an excuse to ask me for a favor. I'm simultaneously disappointed and relieved. "Yes?"

"I've got this patient who is ten centimeters dilated right now," he says. "She's almost ready to start pushing, just waiting for the baby to descend a little bit. It's a really uncomplicated pregnancy and labor, and the nurses say they'll take me through it. And I know Dr. Ford will come in at the end. But I just thought maybe you could…"

I raise my eyebrows at him. "You want me to sit with you while you're helping her push? I'm a doctor, dammit, not a babysitter."

Crap, now even *I'm* making the stupid "Star Trek" jokes. Eric is too cute. It's scrambling my brain. Luckily, he doesn't seem to judge me for it.

"Look," Eric says defensively. "It's just… I haven't delivered a baby since my internship and I'm worried that…"

"You'll drop it?"

"Among other things," he says, smiling sheepishly. "Please, Emily? I know you're very busy but I'd just feel better if you were there."

"What about Jill?" I'm half kidding.

Eric just gives me a look.

"Fine," I grumble. Actually it's a very reasonable request. If I'd realized that Eric hadn't delivered a baby since his internship, I probably would've offered to come in with him anyway. I can already tell that Eric isn't the kind of person who asks for help unless he really feels that he needs it.

Caroline, who has not given up hope of delivering a baby in the next few hours, pops in to The Pit to report on the patient, Mrs. White, who she is following from this morning. It's a primip (woman having her first baby) who came in after her water broke. She was only dilated to two centimeters so we started Pitocin to get things moving along.

"I checked Mrs. White and she's four centimeters now!" Caroline reports excitedly.

"Great," I say.

Maybe Caroline will actually get to deliver a baby today. Provided she doesn't get any further calls from nature.

"Also," Caroline says, looking down at her clogs, "Dr. Ford told me this morning that there's a GYN clinic tomorrow. Would it be all right if I went?"

"Caroline," I say tightly. "This is your second day on Labor and Delivery. There will be plenty of time for you to do clinic, but you're still learning the ropes here. Just be patient."

Caroline's face falls but she nods in understanding. Then she skips away to write her a note on Mrs. White. Why is she always skipping and jumping? I can't help but roll my eyes. It's like a reflex.

Eric sees the look on my face and snickers. "You hate her, don't you?"

"It's more like mild distaste." I sigh. "Why can't she bug Jill for change?"

"Because Jill is terrifying?"

"I need to be more terrifying," I resolve.

"You're close," Eric says. "I mean, you're a *little* terrifying. But you're not quite up to Jill's standards." He squints at me thoughtfully. "Maybe you should wear an eye patch?"

"Shut up," I say. "You're too scared to deliver a newborn."

"Ouch," Eric says, but he's grinning at me. (I still sort of think he's flirting.)

At that moment, a young nurse named Trish comes to find us.

"Dr. Kessler," she says. "Mrs. Tanner is ready to push."

I look over at Eric and see a slight twinge of fear on his face. It's sort of gratifying, because he seems so damn sure of himself most of the time. He stands up, brushes off his hands on his blue scrubs (he gave in to Jill!), and turns to me.

"Ready, Dr. McCoy?"

The delivery room for the Tanners is incredibly serene. This is exactly the sort of place where I'd like to be born, if I hadn't already been born. The lighting is dim, and there is soft music playing that reminds me of a river flowing. Mrs. Tanner has an epidural going and is calmly waiting to start pushing. Her husband is standing by her side, holding her hand, and smiling benevolently.

Unfortunately, the serene atmosphere doesn't last very long. Like most primips, Mrs. Tanner does not immediately get the hang of how to push. Eric is positioned to catch the baby, but Mrs. Tanner is giving these weak little girl pushes that are doing nothing to bring the baby through the birth canal. I consider calling Dr. Ford and asking him if we should get the vacuum, but then I decide to give her a little time. The vacuum isn't enough to get the baby out all by itself anyway. She's going to need to learn to push.

"Is it almost out?" Mrs. Tanner asks hopefully.

Ha. That's what we call "wishful thinking."

"No," I say. I'm trying to think of a nice way to tell her that she sucks at pushing. "Can you feel the contractions? Do you want us to turn down the epidural?"

"I feel it," Mrs. Tanner insists.

"Come on, Stephanie!" Trish says. "You've got to push this baby out! Get really mad!"

Mrs. Tanner just looked confused.

"Get angry!" Trish urges her again. "Show me your angry face."

Mrs. Tanner bares her teeth somewhat awkwardly. She doesn't look angry, more like she's at a dentist visit.

We go for another half hour like that, with Trish playing the role of cheerleader, urging Mrs. Tanner to get angry and "push like you mean it." Mrs. Tanner continues to push like she doesn't really mean it. Meanwhile, I'm starting to see some spontaneous, repetitive decelerations in the baby's heart rate. I'm worried that we need to get this baby out sooner rather than later.

"I'm going to call Dr. Ford," I tell Eric. "I think we need the vacuum."

"No wait," he says. He stands up from his stool so that Mrs. Tanner can see his face. I peer at him curiously, wondering what ideas the ER resident is going to have to get this baby out. "Look," he says, "I've never pushed out a baby before and obviously I never will. But my little sister gave birth recently, and she gave me a piece of advice about pushing that she said maybe I could use with patients."

Everyone in the room is staring at him, waiting to hear this piece of brilliant advice.

"She told me," he says, "you've got to push like you're having the biggest bowel movement you've ever had in your life."

Ew. Seriously, Eric.

Mrs. Tanner looks at him thoughtfully.

"Okay," she says.

Fifteen minutes later, she is holding a newborn baby boy in her arms.

And just like the birth started, it ended beautiful and perfect. There was a controlled head delivery, the perineum stretched easily, she only had mild vaginal tearing, the shoulders passed easily, the body was delivered slowly, and the baby cried instantaneously. Mr. Tanner had tears running down his cheeks as he cut his son's cord, and the baby was placed immediately on his mother's belly.

Wow, that big bowel movement thing worked really well.

———

No matter how many babies I deliver, I always have this good feeling when a birth goes well. It's like an emotional high. It can keep me going even when the caffeine runs out.

That reminds me. I need another cup of coffee.

Eric is sitting at the nursing station, writing up postpartum orders on Mrs. Tanner. Since it's his first delivery, I figure I ought to ask him if he needs any help. I walk over to clap my hand on his back.

"Nice job," I tell him. "I think you missed your calling as an obstetrician. Do you want to apply for a spot in our program?"

Eric shudders. "Don't even joke about that."

I stick my tongue out at him. "Come on, it's not that bad."

He snorts.

"Well, anyway," I say, "you'll be a good labor coach for your wife. Are you guys trying for a baby soon?"

Eric looks completely taken aback by my question. Immediately, I regret having asked it. In my line of work, it's almost automatic to ask about baby-making—it's like the third thing you ask about when making small talk, after "what's your name" and "what's the weather like." But in the real world, I recognize that it's not really an appropriate conversation topic for someone you hardly know. And honestly, I don't really want to know if Eric and his undoubtedly gorgeous wife are trying for a baby, especially when I don't even have a boyfriend.

I'm half expecting Eric to tell me to mind my own business. I'd deserve it. But I'm completely shocked by what he does end up saying.

Chapter 10

"I'm not married," Eric says.

What?

"But…" I look down at his left hand. "You're wearing a wedding ring."

Eric grins at me. "You're a doctor, not a detective, dammit."

Ha ha. I hate "Star Trek."

"I used to be married," he says. "I'm not anymore. I just kept the ring to wear at work because it stops the old women in the ER from trying to set me up with their granddaughters."

"Wow," I say. "I had no idea." Then I add, "I'm divorced too. It sucks."

Eric nods. "Pretty much."

Whoa. Eric isn't married? That's huge. That changes everything. Well, sort of.

The wedding ring still bugs me though. What divorced person still wears his wedding ring? I sure don't. I'm pretty sure David doesn't wear his. I wonder if Eric is still pining over his ex-wife. In which case, it isn't that much better than if he were actually married.

But either way, I'm not going to make a fuss about it if he flirts with me from now on.

Flirt away, cute ER resident!

———

I'm about to head to a scheduled C-section when a dark-skinned middle-aged woman whose hair is threaded with white strands approaches the nurses station. I hear her ask, "Is Dr. McCoy here?"

My first instinct is to make a run for it. This woman is too old to be a patient, which means she's the mother of the patient. I hate to generalize, but nothing good ever comes out of a conversation with a patient's mother ever. That's why I didn't specialize in pediatrics.

I try to slip away, unnoticed, but I must have pissed off a nurse at some point today, because one of them shoots a finger in my direction. "That's Dr. McCoy," she says.

Crap.

I paste a smile on my face and pretend like I hadn't just been trying to escape. "What can I do for you?"

"Dr. McCoy," the woman says, her brow knitted together. "I'm Deborah White's mother. That nice medical student Caroline says my daughter is fully dilated."

At that moment, Caroline rushes breathlessly out of Mrs. White room, still wearing her blue gloves.

"Ten centimeters!" Caroline announces triumphantly, loud enough that everybody on the floor turns to look at her. "That's fully dilated, right?"

For once, she's right.

I glance at my watch. The attending will be here any minute to start the C-section, but I can get Mrs. White started on the process of pushing. If things are proceeding quickly, maybe we can get the baby out fast before the C-section. Otherwise, I can get Jill to cover either the delivery or the section for me.

The second I reach Mrs. White room, I know something isn't right. Somehow I can just sense that Mrs. White is not ready to push yet—it's an instinct that I'm developing. And my instincts are confirmed when one of the labor nurses, a seasoned veteran named Regina, greets me by shaking her head.

"I told her not to call you over," Regina murmurs to me. "She's not fully dilated. At all."

I knew I should have run away when I had the chance.

Mrs. White, her husband, and her mother are all watching me as I glove up to check her cervix. It's not the first time that I envy the surgeons, who get to do their work while the patient is asleep, without half the family staring at them. Anyway, it's no surprise that Regina was absolutely right. Mrs. White is not fully dilated. She still two goddamn centimeters.

I remove my fingers, and face the hopeful family.

"I'm sorry," I say. "She's still only two centimeters."

Poor Mrs. White bursts into tears. I blame the whole thing on Caroline.

"How is this possible?" her mother says. She looks over at Caroline. "This girl said she was fully dilated."

"Well, she was wrong," I say. I glare at Caroline. "She doesn't know what she's doing and she shouldn't have said anything to you before she checked with me."

Caroline hangs her head.

"I'm sorry," I say again to the family. "You're just going to have to be a little patient right now. Is there anything I can do for you?"

They're quiet for a minute. Finally, Mr. White says, "Can I have a soda?"

"Of course," I say. Easy enough. "Caroline, get them a soda."

Caroline nods, eager to redeem herself. Out of everything, I think she's best at fetching sodas. Maybe she can look into that as a career opportunity if this doctor thing doesn't work out for her. "What kind of soda do you want?" I hear her ask as I storm out of the room.

"Can you get me a vanilla Coke Zero?" the husband asks.

I'm pretty sure Caroline can handle that one.

It's pathetic how I spend most of the C-section fuming over how angry I am at Caroline. Not only does she have no idea how to assess how dilated the cervix is, but more importantly, she had no business pretending like she did. You don't give patients false hope like that. Know what you don't know. That's like the most important tenet in medicine. Well, after that "do no harm" bit.

Jill has threatened Caroline with bodily harm if she so much as breathes in the direction of the call room, so the second I find a moment of downtime, I go hide out there. I need some privacy, and I'm pretty sure that Caroline would follow me into the bathroom or off a cliff or anywhere I might go.

Alone in the call room, I spend a minute just sitting on the bed and taking deep breaths. It's amazing how just sitting and breathing have become luxuries to me.

But you can only sit and breathe for so long. I find myself fumbling for my iPhone, and before I can talk myself out of it, I select David's number. Yes, I've added it to my speed dial. Yes, we have entered dangerous territory.

But if there's ever been one person that I could always call when I'm bored or pissed off, it's David.

David picks up after only two rings.

"Hey," he says, sounding surprised. "What's up, Em?"

"You sound shocked to hear from me," I tease him.

"Well," he says thoughtfully. "We just talked yesterday, so I thought…"

I knew it. I knew two calls in two days was too much. Damn.

"If you're busy, it's fine," I say. I try to sound breezy, casual. Like I couldn't care less whether he wants to talk to me or not.

"No," he says quickly. I have to admit, I breathe a sigh of relief. "That's not what I mean at all. I like hearing from you." I can almost hear him smiling on the other line. "It's a surprise, but a pleasant one."

"Good."

I'm silent for a moment. He's silent too. It's a shared silence. There aren't a lot of people I can share silence with. I really missed talking to David.

I'm the one who finally breaks the silence: "I'm having the worst day."

David laughs. "Well, that explains the phone call. What's going on?"

I fill him in on the details of how I got dragged into the room to look at a two centimeters dilated cervix, and how much I want to strangle Caroline. Even David knows that ten centimeters is fully dilated. I'm sure even he would've recognized that Mrs. White wasn't fully dilated.

I mean, how you mix up two centimeters and ten centimeters? That's a huge difference. That's an entire fist.

"I'm sure she feels worse about it than you do," David says when I finish my story.

"I hope so," I grumble.

"Don't make her feel afraid of you," he advises me. "I'm sure most of her problem is just nervousness."

I know he's trying to make me feel better, but for some reason his advice irritates me. He always seems to take the side of the other person when I'm having a conflict. No matter how much of a jerk the other person is, he always says things to suggest that maybe both of us are at fault. Why can't he just take my side? Why can't he just agree with me that Caroline is annoying?

"I've got to go," I say into the phone. "I'm being paged."

"I remember those days," David muses.

"Yeah," I say. "I'll talk to you later, okay?"

"I'm looking forward to it," David says.

As I end the call, I remove my pager from my waistband. It's completely silent.

Chapter 11

I'm worried about Marissa Block.

She's been admitted to one of the Baby City beds, and is hooked up to a monitor to watch her contractions. We're giving her magnesium to try to stop her labor, and she's received a dose of steroids. Usually 48 hours' worth of steroids are needed to help the baby's lungs mature, although if she gives birth at 24 weeks, that baby is in big trouble, steroids or not.

Marissa looks terrible. She somehow reminds me of a balloon that somebody pricked with a needle and has now deflated. It might be side effects from the magnesium, or maybe the impact of everything has finally hit her. Her hair has come loose from its bun and is in frizzy waves all over her pillow. Dark circles have formed under her brown eyes. She rolls her head in my direction as I enter the room.

"Hi, Dr. McCoy," she croaks. She doesn't even sound like herself anymore.

I walk over to her bedside, and after a moment of consideration, pull up a chair next to her bed.

"Did you Skype into your meeting?" I ask her.

Marissa shakes her head. Even just the effort of that gesture seems to be too much for her. "They're going to have to figure out a way to handle it without me. I just can't do it."

Wow, the medications must really be doing a number on her. "How are you feeling?"

"Awful," Marissa says. "Like my arms and legs are made of lead."

I reach over and check the chart by Marissa's bed, where the nurses have been recording her blood pressure. It's slightly on the high side but not enough to make me worry. "Any shortness of breath?" I ask her.

Marissa shakes her head weakly.

I listen to Marissa's heart and lungs, checking for any signs of fluid in her lungs. Then I take out my reflex hammer and check Marissa's reflexes. One sign of an overdose of magnesium is the loss of reflexes. Luckily, she's got good reflexes. She's having side effects from the medication, but she's not toxic.

"All right," I say. "Let's check your cervix."

I say little prayer as I do Marissa's cervical exam. Please God, let her still be two centimeters. But God is vengeful today or maybe just not listening. Marissa has gone from two centimeters dilated to three centimeters. The magnesium isn't working, at least not well enough.

Marissa looks like she's about to ask me if there's been any progress, but she can read the answer on my face. Her cheeks sag, and she suddenly looks far older than her age. She looks more like a future grandmother than a future mother.

"I'm going to add another tocolytic," I tell her. "We're going to monitor you closely overnight. If you dilate any further, I think we're going to need to transfer you to a facility specializing in very early preterm babies. We're not equipped for preemies younger than 28 weeks here."

"Dr. McCoy," she whispers. "Please don't let my baby die."

"We won't," I promise her automatically. But it's really an empty promise. I mean how can I promise something like that? But if it makes her feel better to hear it, I'll say it. If her baby dies, they are going to be much worse things on her mind then my broken promise.

I sit with Marissa for a short time until her eyes flutter closed. Then before I sign out to the night residents, I pay a visit to Mrs. White, whose cervix is still only two goddamn centimeters dilated. Never say there isn't any irony in obstetrics.

Chapter 12

That night, I leave the hospital in a daze. I trade a few crumpled dollar bills for a hot dog from a hot dog stand on the way home, devour it before I step through my front door, then collapse onto my bed. Next thing I know, it's morning.

I slept about ten hours and I feel pretty good, actually. My muscles are a little bit stiff, and I'm aware of the fact that I didn't brush my teeth last night, but who cares? The great thing about not having a boyfriend or husband is that you can forgo hygiene rituals in the evening when necessary.

When I get to Baby City, I find Holly in The Pit, once again collapsed into a chair, looking mildly traumatized. The second she sees me, she says, "I'm going to have an elective C-section."

"Fourth-degree tear last night?" I ask her.

Holly nods and shudders slightly.

In vaginal births, we rate tearing of the perineum based on how deep it is and where it goes. A first degree tear is the most superficial, just involving the skin of the perineum and the tissue around the opening of the vagina, but not into the muscles. These don't even require stitches. The second degree tear goes down into the muscle—this does require stitches, and usually takes a few weeks to heal. These kinds of tears are not really a big deal.

In about 5% of women who deliver vaginally, there's more severe tearing. A third degree tear extends into the anal sphincter, which is the muscle that surrounds the anus. A fourth degree tear goes entirely through the anal sphincter and into the tissue underneath it. Basically, the anus and vagina become one, if you can wrap your head around that. Obviously, this kind of tearing takes a lot longer to heal and increases the risk of bowel incontinence. I've had several patients with fourth degree tears who had to come in later for a more definitive repair of all the damage that was done.

Patients who deliver their babies vaginally usually have a much easier recovery than women who have a C-section. But if I had a choice between a C-section and a fourth degree tear, I would choose the C-section, hands down. There are just some openings that are not meant to be combined.

"I'm sure you'll push the baby out just fine," I tell Holly.

Holly snorts at me. "What are you basing that on?"

I nudge Holly's clog with my foot. "You have big feet," I point out to her. "Women with big feet always have big pelvises."

Holly holds up her feet, which are easily a size nine. Her shoes are at least an inch longer than mine. "Is that a fact, Doctor?"

"I'm writing up an article on it," I joke.

Okay, there are no peer-reviewed studies that say that women with big feet have big pelvises. But I'm pretty sure it's true.

Ted, Jill, and Eric join us for rounds. Caroline is nowhere to be seen, for a change. I look behind me, certain I'll see her standing there, but no luck. Maybe she decided to rotate at different hospital. Hell, maybe she quit medicine altogether.

"Caroline is with Mrs. White, consoling her," Jill says before I can get my hopes up.

I stare at Jill. "Did something happen to the baby?"

Jill rolls her eyes. "No, she's still only two centimeters dilated."

Our attending for the day is Dr. Shepherd, who is also our program director, and also happens to be the most terrifying person on the planet, Jill included. Dr. Shepherd never comes to the morning sign out, and only appears, like an apparition, the second she is required.

"All right," Jill says, clapping her hands together. She's always happy to be running the show. "Let's do the sign out."

With Jill leading the way, we run through the list of patients with great efficiency. There are a handful of women admitted to Baby City right now, in various stages of labor. I notice that instead of a patient's name, in one slot Holly has written only "Giant Baby." At around 4 a.m., Holly starts to get incredibly creative.

"Who is the giant baby?" I ask. "Does that refer to the fetus or the patient?"

"The fetus," Holly giggles. "That's Mrs. Kelly. Her ultrasound showed an 11-pound fetus, but we're hoping it's a little smaller than that. It feels pretty big though."

"No C-section?" I ask.

Holly shakes her head. "She insists she wants to do it vaginally. This is her second and she feels like she can push him out."

Yeah, we'll see about that.

"One more thing," Holly says. "There's a surprise in Mrs. Kelly's room."

I raise my eyebrows at her. "What?"

"I can't tell you." Holly's got this annoying grin on her face. "Otherwise it wouldn't be a surprise."

Okay then…

We run through the list of patients, ending with Marissa Block. Thank God, the board still records her as having three centimeters of cervical dilation.

"When did you get that number?" I ask Holly.

"I checked her about an hour ago," Holly says. "And it wasn't easy. I needed a pair of hedge clippers to get in there."

Jill laughs. "I know! It's like the Amazon jungle or something. I thought I was going to have to page Emily to bring in a rope to rescue me when I did her exam."

Don't get me wrong, I like Marissa. I feel incredibly sympathetic to what she's going through right now. But man, she is really hairy right now. The Amazon jungle is a pretty accurate description.

"I think I found a few new life forms in there," I chip in. "I had to fight them off with the speculum."

Holly dissolves into giggles. "Oh my God, as soon as I get home I am going to make an appointment to get myself waxed. There is no way I'm getting delivered with an Afro down there."

The three of us are stifling laughter at this point. I don't know why, but there's something about a lot of hair that is just really, really funny. I almost don't hear the loud muttering coming from my right side. When I finally look, I see that Eric is staring at us, just shaking his head. Jill notices the expression on his face, and narrows her eyes. "You got a problem, Kessler?"

Eric sits up straighter. I can actually see the anger in his green eyes and I cringe.

"Yeah, I do have a problem actually," he says. "This woman is seriously ill and her baby is in danger, and you're sitting here making fun of a little bit of hair."

Holly, who is not easily shamed, says, "Have you seen this woman? This isn't 'a little bit' of hair. We're talking Crotch Rapunzel here."

"You guys are doctors," he says. "This woman trusts you. I think you should all be ashamed of yourselves."

Even though he says it to all of us, I feel like he's looking directly at me as he says it.

"You're so full of shit," Jill says to him. "Like you guys don't make fun of the drunks and drug addicts in the ER. Don't act so holier than thou."

Eric stands up so quickly that his chair nearly falls over. His hair is still mildly damp from a recent shower, and I see a tiny droplet of water roll down his cheek and onto his neck.

"You know what?" he says. "Do what you want. I'm not going to stand here and debate this with you. But I'm not going to listen to it either."

He stalks out of the room, leaving the four of us staring at each other. Unsurprisingly, Jill seems absolutely furious. Holly looks about as embarrassed as I feel, although I suspect she's still planning to make that waxing appointment. She doesn't really need to though, because she's practically hairless below the neck.

"What an asshole," Jill says, shaking her head. "He lives the sweet life, strolling in at eight in the morning for his ER shifts, while we work our asses off down here. And then he comes in and judges us? He can go suck it."

"Here, here," Holly says.

"I agree as well," says Ted. I'm pretty sure Ted never said anything negative about Marissa. But he's apparently figured out that his best bet is sucking up to Jill. Maybe he's smarter than he looks.

Jill stares at me, waiting for my response. Like Ted, I've also learned that going against Jill is not a wise move. And anyway, we really didn't do anything wrong. We were just blowing off some steam.

"He's a total jerk," I say.

And Jill nods her approval.

———

Mrs. Kelly is the mother of Giant Baby. She's is a big woman herself, with a wide, friendly, freckled face, and orange-red hair that reminds me of a pumpkin. She's lying in her hospital bed, looking very comfortable with her epidural, her hands gently caressing the uterus housing Giant Baby. Her belly definitely looks on the larger side, but it's hard to tell from far away.

Usually I find the patient's husband at her side. But today, that husband seems to be absent. Instead, there is a chubby, freckled, orange-haired boy sitting by her bed, enjoying a blue lollipop. He seems to be just as calm as his mother.

"Hello, Mrs. Kelly," I say. "My name is Dr. McCoy."

"Hi, Dr. McCoy," Mrs. Kelly says. "This is my son, Patrick."

"I'm five," Patrick volunteers. He takes a lick of his lollipop with his blue tongue.

Granted, there are no rules about kids being allowed in Baby City rooms here. But seriously, who would want their five-year-old son around while in labor? It seems like the kind of thing that little Patrick will be describing 20 years from now in therapy sessions.

But naturally, I can't say anything like that.

"Are you feeling okay?" I ask.

"Wonderful," Mrs. Kelly says. She actually doesn't sound sarcastic.

"Dr. Park talked to me about the fact that your baby was measuring large on ultrasound," I say. "Did she explain the situation to you?"

Mrs. Kelly nods. "She did. But I think I can push him out. Patrick was a big baby and I got him out no problem."

"How big was he?"

"Nine pounds five ounces."

Well, that's a start. "Did Dr. Park tell you what the risk is with a large baby?"

Mrs. Kelly nods again. "The shoulder can get stuck."

"Right," I say. "And if we can't get the shoulder through, the umbilical cord can get squished and cut off oxygen to the baby. It can be very serious, Mrs. Kelly. Even fatal."

"I understand the risks," she says. "But I'm certain I can get the baby out. I just *know* it."

Let me tell you something: I don't believe in psychics. At all. I especially don't believe that women have some sort of magical psychic connection with the babies inside their uteruses. You don't know what your baby is thinking. And even if you did, I'm pretty sure the baby has no idea whether or not he can get through the pelvis. Newborns are not that smart.

But if I said all that, I'm sure Mrs. Kelly would take it the wrong way.

I make a move to check Mrs. Kelly's cervix, and immediately, Patrick shifts to the foot of the bed. I look over at him, then at Mrs. Kelly, who doesn't seem at all concerned.

"Um," I say. "I'm going to check your cervix now."

"Go for it," Mrs. Kelly says.

Patrick isn't budging. The kid just stands there, licking his blue lollipop. Okay, I guess I'm just going to have to do this with him watching. I've done pelvic exam before with children in the room, but usually they weren't staring quite this intently.

I get my fingers in and out as quick as I can, trying to limit how much of his mother's vagina Patrick gets to see. She's eight centimeters, so getting close at this point. I wonder if she's going to at least clear Patrick out of the room for the delivery itself. I'm scared the answer is no.

I look around the room. "Is the baby's father... coming soon?"

Mrs. Kelly shakes her head. "He had to work today. Couldn't get out of it. But luckily, I have Patrick."

You sure do.

"All right," I say. "We'll keep monitoring you and hopefully we won't need to resort to a C-section. Do you have any questions?"

"How 'lated is she?" Patrick speaks up.

I stare at the little boy in surprise. "Do you mean 'dilated'?"

Patrick thinks a moment then nods.

"Um," I say. "She's eight centimeters dilated."

"And how much 'lated does she need to be before the baby comes out?"

"Ten centimeters," I reply.

Patrick thinks another moment. "So two more?"

I look at Mrs. Kelly surprise. This five-year-old child does better math than some of our medical students. Hell, some of our residents.

"That's right, Patrick," I say. I smile down at him. "Do you have any other questions?"

"Can I have a Coke?" Patrick asks.

Why do people keep asking me for soda? I'm a doctor, dammit, not a vending machine.

"Sure," I say. "As long if it's okay with your mom."

"Oh," Mrs. Kelly laughs. "Patrick just does what he wants."

Yeah, I suppose if you can't keep your kid from looking at your vagina, you're not going to have much luck with soda.

———

I feel really guilty about how we laughed at Marissa this morning. I can't stop thinking about it. Every time I start to go into Marissa's room, I feel a flush rise up on my face. Maybe Marissa didn't hear what we said, but in a way, that makes me feel worse about it. She trusts us, like Eric said. I can't imagine what she'd think if we knew we were making fun of her behind her back.

Marissa appears to have shrunk even further overnight. She seems almost lost within the sheets and blankets in her hospital bed, and her eyes seemed sunken in their sockets. We're infusing some pretty potent medications into her. Basically, we're destroying her to save her baby's life.

"How are you doing?" I ask her.

Marissa manages a weak smile. "As of two hours ago, still only three centimeters."

"No," I say. "How are *you*?"

"Freaking awesome," Marissa says flatly.

Okay, that was probably a stupid question.

I reach out and give her hand a squeeze. She squeezes back weakly, and again, I get worried that she may be toxic on the magnesium. She is barely able to nod her consent as I pull out my reflex hammer. Her reflexes may be a little less brisk than before, but seem to be present.

"Are you going to check my cervix now?" Marissa asks. That's all she cares about now. She's just trying to hold it together for the sake of the baby.

I nod.

Overnight, the Amazon jungle has tripled. I can almost hear lions roaring in the distance and make out a monkey swinging from a vine. I'm sure there isn't actually more hair and it just looks like a lot more because she hasn't showered, but wow. It actually takes some serious effort to get through all the hair.

"Three centimeters," I announce.

Marissa lets out a breath and I let out the very same breath. I was scared somehow that Marissa might dilate further as some sort of karmic retribution for the things we said about her this morning. But it looks like we're in the clear. At least for now.

"Listen," I say as I straighten up and peel off my gloves, "if there's anything you need... food, drink, toiletries..." I think again of the conversation this morning and add in a quiet voice: "Nair..."

Marissa's eyes widen, and I almost smack myself in the head. Why did I say that? What was I *thinking*? I guess I figured maybe she was bothered by the hair too, and in my sleep-deprived brain, I thought maybe I was doing her a favor. Trying to help. After all, she wouldn't want all the residents to be making fun of her.

Goddamn Eric has officially scrambled my brain.

I want to take it back, act like it was a big joke, pretend I never hinted Marissa's overgrowth of hair might be a problem. But I can see her eyes already narrowing. She's a brilliant attorney and she can see right through me.

"Do you have an issue with my hair, Dr. McCoy?" Marissa says. Her voice has taken on a sharp edge that she had lost since she started on the magnesium.

"No! Of course not!" Except my voice is far too high and overly cheerful. I'm the worst actress ever. Even when I was in grade school, I never got good parts in the school play... I always ended up being a tree or something. I was that bad.

"Because I wouldn't want *my hair* to be causing you any emotional distress," Marissa goes on, her voice now dripping in sarcasm.

Oh God, she hates me.

"Marissa," I say, practically pleading with her now. "I didn't mean anything by that. Really… you're here to save your baby… I mean, who cares about *hair*?"

Marissa's black eyes flit over me, finally resting on my face. Her lips settle into a straight line.

"Call me Mrs. Block," she says.

Chapter 13

Mrs. White's baby is not happy.

Before I even walk into her room, I check the monitor of her baby's heart rate and see really ugly looking repetitive late decelerations and minimal beat to beat variability for 20 minutes. I hope her cervix has made some progress, because otherwise she is almost certainly headed for a C-section.

Caroline is sitting with Mrs. White when I come in. They're holding hands. It's nice she has time to sit there with her patient and hold hands while I work my ass off.

"Okay," I say. "Let's see if your cervix is dilated further."

As I do the cervical exam, Caroline talks cheerfully. She's a one-woman pep talk. "I told Mrs. White that she's going to be my first delivery," Caroline chirps.

My fingers touch Mrs. White cervix. Still two centimeters, not a millimeter more. Damn, this woman's cervix is stubborn. Her water's been broken for over 24 hours now and her baby's heart rate is not looking good. I think this trial of labor has just ended.

"Mrs. White," I say. "I'm sorry, but I'm going to contact my attending Dr. Shepherd and ask her to come in to do a C-section on you."

"Okay," Mrs. White says calmly.

Okay? Yesterday she was in hysterical tears when I announced she was still two centimeters dilated. Now she seems like she couldn't care less. I'm completely baffled.

"You're okay with that?" I say.

Mrs. White nods emphatically. "My mother told me last night that when she was pregnant with me, she was only able to dilate two centimeters and then needed a C-section. And *her* mother also only dilated to two centimeters. So I guess it runs in my family, huh?"

Wow, that's weird.

"You can call it the Two Centimeters Curse," I suggest.

Mrs. White laughs appreciatively at my joke. I feel like I'm batting a thousand, so I turn to Caroline and say, "And now you get to see your first C-section."

Caroline's already pale face whitens a few shades. "Oh, good."

That's not exactly the response was hoping for. Please God, don't let Caroline faint into Mrs. White's abdominal cavity. That's all I ask.

———

Caroline is pacing now. We're outside OR and Mrs. White is being prepped for her surgery, but we've got a good 15 minutes, at least. Caroline keeps walking up and back across the length of the room. She's making me dizzy.

It takes all my effort not to tackle her.

"Caroline," I say. "Have you ever been in a surgery before?"

Caroline shakes her head. "But I've seen a lot of them on TV."

Oh great.

"Do you know how to scrub?" I ask her.

This time, Caroline nods eagerly. "Yes, we had a class before the rotation began. You scrub each finger 200 times."

Caroline is going to be scrubbing for the rest of our lives, apparently.

I give Caroline a few pointers, then set her on the process of scrubbing, in hopes she'll be done sometime in the next five to seven years. In the meantime, I go look for Dr. Shepherd. I know she's going to want to scrutinize Mrs. White's fetal heart rate tracing, and probably make me doubt my decision to take the patient in for a section. That's what Dr. Shepherd does best.

I find Dr. Shepherd at the nurses' station, examining Mrs. White's tracing, like I predicted. Dr. Shepherd is tall. She may be the tallest woman I've ever met in my life, which makes it all the more odd that she always wears high heels, even in the OR. In another life, Dr. Shepherd could have been a model. She's tall, thin, and looks like she was probably very beautiful about a decade ago. Now she's what you'd call elegant or handsome rather than beautiful. There are fine lines around her eyes, and her dark blond hair is laced with gray. It seems somehow fitting that Dr. Shepherd wouldn't bother with hair dye and just allow herself to age gracefully. I really respect the woman, but I'm also terrified of her.

Unfortunately, she also happens to be our residency director.

"Hello, Emily," Dr. Shepherd says, without looking up at me.

"Hello, Dr. Shepherd," I say, stifling the urge to bow or curtsy for her. Or possibly salute.

I lean forward, to make sure that Dr. Shepherd is looking at the right tracing. The move causes Dr. Shepherd's dark eyes to jump up and glare at me.

"Please, Emily," she snaps. "Will you give me some breathing room?"

"I'm sorry," I say quickly. I step back a foot or two, and watch Dr. Shepherd's eyes narrow as she examines the strip of paper. I've seen enough heartrate tracings that I feel pretty confident with my decision, but of course, now she's making me doubt myself. Maybe I should tell Dr. Shepherd about the Two Centimeters Curse.

"When did her membranes rupture?" Dr. Shepherd asks me.

"About 30 hours ago."

"Okay," Dr. Shepherd says.

I cheer internally. "Okay" is the best compliment you can get out of Dr. Shepherd. A "good call, Emily" would be way too much to hope for.

I follow Dr. Shepherd to the OR, where Caroline is still in process of scrubbing. The good news is she seems to have finished scrubbing her fingers and has now moved on to her hands. Sometime a week from Tuesday, she'll probably finish her forearms.

"This is our medical student, Caroline," I say to Dr. Shepherd.

"Hi!" Caroline chirps. She waves enthusiastically, and I suck in a breath, hoping she hasn't ruined the scrubbing process and has to start over. Dr. Shepherd acknowledges Caroline with only the faintest nod of her head.

Dr. Shepherd and I start scrubbing. I have to hand it to Caroline that she finishes up at the same time as we do. She seems kind of proud of herself, and I'm almost about to pay her a lame compliment, when for reasons I will never understand, she reaches for a paper towel to dry her hands.

"What are you doing?" I scream at Caroline.

Caroline freezes in the middle of drying her hands.

"The paper towels are *not* sterile," I say to her. I want to shake her. "Now you have to scrub all over again."

Caroline cheeks turn red. "I didn't realize..."

I sigh. "Just come in when you're done, okay?"

I'm about to back into the OR, when I see something truly horrifying. Caroline is reaching into the garbage can to pull out the sponge she had just been using to scrub with. I can't even believe my eyes.

"What are you doing?" I scream again.

Caroline frowns. "You just told me to scrub again."

"Why are you taking a sponge out of the *garbage*?"

Caroline looks down at the sponge in her hand. "It wasn't in the garbage. It was *on top of* the garbage."

"There's no 'on top of' the garbage with surgical sponges," I say, disgusted. "It was *in* the garbage bin, therefore it is contaminated and garbage."

The redness on Caroline's face has now spread to her ears. "I didn't want to waste another sponge."

I sigh. "Please, Caroline. Waste another sponge."

I wonder if I need to have someone watch Caroline scrub, just to ensure that she doesn't use another piece of refuse to do it. She's just lucky that Dr. Shepherd didn't see that little performance. Dr. Shepherd has thrown medical students out of the OR for much less.

Inside the OR, we prep Mrs. White's belly with Betadine. During C-sections, you have to put pressure on the fundus of the uterus in order to deliver the baby's head. Since I am on the short side, that means I generally need to stand on a stool during all C-sections. But when I'm with an attending who is as tall as Dr. Shepherd, I end up on two stools. It sort of feels like I'm doing the surgery while on stilts.

Dr. Shepherd lets me make the incision then proceed with the section, but based on prior experience, I know that the second I do anything she doesn't like, she'll take the scalpel away from me and that will be it. I hold my breath as I cut, trying to stay extremely focused.

I'm about to cut through the uterus, when all of a sudden, Caroline bursts into the room. "I'm here!" she announces.

Goddamn Caroline.

"Hi, Caroline!" Mrs. White calls from the other side of the curtain.

I hate it when patients talk during their C-sections. I feel like there are two times when people shouldn't be allowed to talk to you. The first is when you're performing a major abdominal surgery on them. The second is when you're trying to use the toilet. I'm not sure which one is more annoying.

Dr. Shepherd assigns Caroline the job of holding the retractor. She seems to be taking it really seriously, and there's a look of deep focus on her face. At least it keeps her quiet. I think if she started having a conversation with Mrs. White, I would lose it.

Once again, I start to make the incision in the uterus. Before I can start cutting, I feel Dr. Shepherd pulling the scalpel out of my hand.

"Too low, Emily," she says.

That's it, apparently. My part in the surgery is done. I blew it.

I completely blame Caroline.

Dr. Shepherd delivers Mrs. White's daughter without further complication. The baby looks great when she comes out. We give her a nine on the Apgar. Too bad that when she gets pregnant someday and goes into labor, she's only going to dilate to two centimeters.

"Oh my God!" Caroline squeals. "She's so cute!"

I look down and I see Caroline's grip loosen on the retractor as she strains her neck to catch a glimpse of the newborn on the other side of the curtain. I'm about to yell at Caroline to pay attention when Dr. Shepherd reaches out and smacks the back of Caroline's hand with her own. Caroline's eyes widen in surprise, but she tightens her grip on the retractor and pays attention again.

And for once, her attention is actually needed. C-sections tend to be very bloody surgeries compared with most. I often leave the room splattered everywhere with blood, and I have to cover every inch of my scrubs to avoid them getting ruined. But Mrs. White seems to have a particularly vascular uterus which now has no tone due to her prolonged labor, and it is therefore bleeding like crazy. Waves of warm blood are pouring out of her, drenching my hands, and making it impossible to see. Caroline is retracting, I'm suctioning like crazy, but Mrs. White's abdomen is still a big pool of blood.

In general, when something like this happens, you have to keep your calm. Again, more so than with other surgeries, because the patient is actually awake. I can hear Mrs. White cooing over her daughter with her husband, completely oblivious to how much blood is gushing out of her. She'll be fine—we can stop this bleeding. But we don't want Mrs. White to know about any of this.

And she wouldn't have, if Caroline hadn't commented: "Oh my God, why is there so much blood?"

"It's a normal amount of blood," Dr. Shepherd says through her teeth. At least she doesn't slap Caroline again. Although I sort of wish she would.

"And it's so warm…" Caroline murmurs.

I look over at Caroline's face. All of a sudden, she's looking incredibly pale. "Are you okay?" I ask her in my most quiet voice.

She nods.

"Do you need to sit down?" I press her.

"No, you need me," Caroline insists.

I'm debating if I should force Caroline to sit down when the decision gets made for me. Almost in slow motion, Caroline's eyes roll up in her head and she drops to the floor like a rag doll.

Chapter 14

The loud clunk as Caroline drops scares me half to death. The clean scrub nurse rushes to her side, and I hear Caroline murmuring, "I'm okay, I'm okay…" I peer over the edge of my footstool tower and see blood trickling down the side of Caroline's face.

"What *happened*?" I hear Mrs. White ask from the other side of the curtain.

I look over at Dr. Shepherd, who sighs heavily.

"Emily," she says. "Don't we have an ER resident rotating here right now?"

I nod. "Yeah. Eric Kessler."

Dr. Shepherd addresses the scrub nurse. "Would you please find Dr. Kessler and have him evaluate this young lady?"

Undoubtedly, she doesn't remember Caroline's name. Which is lucky for Caroline.

It takes us a while, but we get Mrs. White stitched up again just like new. When I get out of the OR, I go to The Pit and find Caroline in a chair in the center of the room, still looking very pale, with some white gauze hastily bandaged to her forehead. Eric is leaning over her, peering into her right eye with an ophthalmoscope. He glances at me when I enter the room.

"I hear you broke the medical student," he says.

Ha ha.

"Caroline," I say. "Are you okay?"

"I think so," she says softly. I see her squeeze her fingers around a crumpled tissue in her lap, which is stained with blood and presumably tears.

Eric pulls away from Caroline and lowers the ophthalmoscope.

"She's fine," he says. "I don't think we need to bother with any blood work, considering this was clearly a vasovagal syncope. I put in an order for a head CT just to waste some taxpayer dollars, but I'm pretty sure she's okay."

I let out a breath. "Good."

"Well," Eric amends. "Except for the laceration on her forehead." He peels back the gauze, and sure enough, Caroline has a pretty nasty wound on her forehead, just below her hairline. The edges are gaping open and there's still a fair amount of blood oozing out, which has saturated the gauze. "This needs stitches."

Caroline looks horrified. "I've never had stitches before."

"It's no big deal," Eric says. "I'll do it for you right now. It'll take five minutes."

Caroline bites her lip, and looks in my direction. "Emily, could you do it?"

No. No way. I am not stitching up Caroline's forehead after everything she's put me through today.

Luckily, Eric sees the look on my face and gets the hint.

"Come on, Caroline," he says. "This is your *face*, not a vagina. You want *me* to do it. I do this like a hundred times a day in the ER."

Caroline reluctantly agrees, thank God. Eric follows me out of the room so that I can show him the cabinet where we keep the suture material and lidocaine.

"Thanks," I say to him.

"Yeah, well," he says, grinning at me. "If Caroline gets a laceration on her vagina, it's all you."

"Deal."

I rifle through my pockets and dig out the key to the cabinet. I think it's a little bit dumb that we have to keep the suture cabinet locked. Are there really suture thieves roaming the hospital? As I hand the key over to him, Eric grabs my fingers and shivers slightly.

"Are your hands always this freezing?" he asks me.

"Yes." I yank my hand away from his and glare at him.

"Your hands are, like, abnormally cold."

Yes, I have cold hands. It's probably a side effect of all the weight I've lost during residency and the fact that I no longer have any padding on my body. If I'm not wearing gloves and I touch a patient, chances are they'll scream. Or at least make some comment about "cold hands, warm heart."

I shrug. "I don't know what to tell you."

"I think you may have a serious problem with your arterial circulation," he says with a straight face. "We may need to do an angiogram."

I roll my eyes at him. "Are you done?"

"I'm going to give vascular surgery a call," he says.

Ha ha, very funny.

"Here," he says, "let me at least check a pulse."

Eric picks up my hand again and places the pad of his index finger on my wrist, over my radial artery. Except the way he's cupping my hand in his makes me think that this isn't entirely about checking my pulse. Also, it's taking him way too long. He could have taken my pulse at least three times over in the time that we're standing there, staring at each other.

I should probably take my hand back. Except his hands are so warm. And his eyes are just so green and sexy.

I'm not sure how long we would've stood there if I didn't get a page overhead alerting me to the fact that Giant Baby is ready to be born.

Chapter 15

Apparently, the Giant Baby is now crowning.

I put in a page to Dr. Shepherd to let her know she needs to stay nearby. As everyone has explained to Mrs. Kelly, the biggest risk of a large baby being delivered vaginally is shoulder dystocia, meaning the shoulder gets stuck above the pubic symphysis after the head has already been delivered. This is an obstetric emergency, and the baby can die if the umbilical cord is compressed in the birth canal because its oxygen supply gets cut off. That's why when it seems like a baby is really big, we might recommend a C-section.

But if Mrs. Kelly doesn't want a C-section, it's her choice. We can't force a woman into surgery. And anyway, now it's too late.

When I get into the room, Mr. Kelly is still absent, but Patrick is maintaining his vigil at his mother's bedside. There's no rule against him being here, but I'm not sure how I feel about having a five-year-old child in the room during a delivery.

Actually, I do know how I feel. I think it's really weird. But what can I do?

"My mom wants to start pushing," Patrick informs me. "She's ten cm, which is fully 'lated."

I'm seriously considering asking Patrick if he would like to replace Caroline. Once he learns how to pronounce the word "dilated," he'll be one step ahead of her.

"She can start pushing now," I tell Patrick (and his mother).

"When the baby is born," Patrick says. "Can I cut the 'bilical cord, please?"

I look at the nurse in the room, and she shrugs.

"I guess you can. If it's all right with your mother."

Mrs. Kelly laughs. "Just try and stop him."

Mrs. Kelly gets the hang of pushing right away. With only two pushes, the baby is fully crowning. I really thought I had more time than that. And oh my God, this baby has a very, very large head. I don't know I've ever seen a head this big before. And it's coming out slowly, which is a sign of an impending shoulder dystocia.

Trying to stay calm, I tell the nurse to page Dr. Shepherd right away.

As the head emerges, I shift the patient so that her legs are hyperflexed against her abdomen. This little maneuver is called McRoberts and it's supposed to widen the pelvis and flatten the spine in the lower back. I say little prayer as I apply suprapubic pressure. Please don't get stuck, baby. Please don't get stuck.

And just like that, the shoulder slips right under the pubic bone. And the baby's body is free.

I almost pass out from relief.

The nurse comes back into the room and looks thrilled to see the small toddler... er, newborn boy has been born. I clamp the umbilical cord, and that's when I notice that Patrick is about a foot away from me, peering over my shoulder expectantly. He was absolutely silent through the entire birth. What a great kid. Definitely mature beyond his years.

"May I please cut the 'bilical cord?" he asks.

"Of course," I say.

I smile at him as I hold out his baby brother for him to see, and the nurse hands him the scissors. Patrick looks down at the newborn and inhales sharply.

"Wow," he breathes. I'm certain he's about to say something incredibly profound, but instead he cries out, "Look at his balls!"

Well, maybe he isn't up for replacing Caroline just yet.

———

Giant Baby, also known as Benjamin Kelly, weighs in at ten pounds fifteen ounces. When I announce this to Mrs.

Kelly, she asks me, "Can I still have credit for giving birth to an 11 pound baby?"

I smile at her. "Yes, I think you can."

When I get out of the delivery room, after sewing up Mrs. Kelly's small second-degree laceration, Dr. Shepherd is waiting for me at the nurse's station. She does not look pleased. I guess that Caroline fainting in the operating room put a damper on her day.

"Were you ever planning on telling me that your patient was about to deliver?" Dr. Shepherd asks me. "Or were you waiting to see if the shoulder would get stuck first?"

I feel my face growing warm. "It happened a lot faster than I thought."

Dr. Shepherd's eyes meet mine. "Don't let it happen again."

I nod wordlessly. The last thing I want to do is piss off Dr. Shepherd.

I notice that she's been thumbing through Marissa Block's chart. Eric has been keeping an eye on her cervix for me since I've been so busy today. I'm hoping she hasn't dilated any further.

"Is she still three centimeters?" I ask.

Dr. Shepherd puts down the chart. She gives me a look like I said something worthy of Caroline.

"*You* tell *me*, Emily. Isn't she your patient?"

"Um," I say brilliantly.

Dr. Shepherd sighs. "That ER resident was on his way to Triage, but he told me he's worried she's dilated to four centimeters. If that's the case, I'd like to transfer her to a hospital that can manage very early preemies."

Oh no. I hope Marissa isn't about to deliver. I don't want her to have the baby that Jill showed her in that photograph.

"I'm sure she's fine," comes a voice from behind me.

I turn around and see Jill. Apparently, she's been listening in to our conversation.

"That resident has no idea what he's doing," she says. "She's probably still just three centimeters. We've got her on magnesium and Indocin, right?"

"You know she can still progress on tocolytics," Dr. Shepherd says sharply. "Why don't we all go see her? We need to be on the same page with this woman."

Jill is grumbling to herself as we follow Dr. Shepherd to Marissa's room. Maybe it's my imagination, but Marissa seems a little bit peppier than last time I saw her. There's some color back in her cheeks and she's even combed out her hair little bit.

"Mrs. Block," Dr. Shepherd says. "I'm Dr. Shepherd. We've met before in clinic, I believe."

Marissa nods. "Yes, I know. I remember you very well."

She sounds much more like her old self somehow.

"I'd like to check your cervix again," Dr. Shepherd says. "I know we've been checking a lot, but it's important to make sure there's no sign of impending labor."

"Be my guest," Marissa says.

Dr. Shepherd lifts Marissa's gown, and I hear Jill suck in a breath. The Amazon jungle is gone. Vanished. Harvested by foresters. I look at Marissa's bedside table, and I see a bottle of Nair and a small pair of scissors. I look over at Jill, who obviously sees it too.

Marissa notices us staring at the hair removal devices, and gives us both a pointed look.

"I wouldn't want anyone to be bothered by my hair," she says.

Oh no.

"Don't be silly," Dr. Shepherd says as she performs her exam, oblivious to the fact that Jill's face is currently turning purple. "Nobody cares about a little bit of hair."

I don't think I've ever seen Jill this angry before. And honestly, she's always a little bit angry. I feel like we need to get out of the room before she explodes into a million little pieces.

"I'm getting four centimeters," Dr. Shepherd announces, pulling off her gloves with a loud snap. "Mrs. Block, I'm going to recommend that we transfer you to another facility, one that's better equipped for handling very early preterm infants."

"That's just fine with me," Marissa says, now actively glaring at Jill and me. Oh God.

Dr. Shepherd discusses some of the details with her and fields questions for what feels like hours before we're able to escape the room. As we're sliding through the doorway, I feel Jill's nails dig into my arm. She has really long nails for a surgeon.

"I am going to kill that son of a bitch Kessler," she hisses in my ear. "I can't *believe* he did that."

Oh my God, she thinks that Eric is the one who told her.

I should probably clue her in and confess to my little faux pas, but I'm terrified to have that anger directed at me. Anyway, she already hates Eric, so what's the difference?

"I know," I murmur. "I'm… a little surprised too."

"Why did you even let him near her?" Jill growls. "I mean, I would've done her cervical checks if you were busy…"

An enraged Jill is a little bit terrifying. I'm actually sort of afraid she might kill him. We have enough scalpels lying around. Eric is bigger and stronger, but Jill will have a weapon and the element of surprise. I should probably try to calm her down.

"Look, Jill," I say. "No harm is done. Mrs. Block didn't say anything to Dr. Shepherd."

"That's just dumb luck!" Jill points out. "When he told her, she could've reported us immediately. She still can, Emily."

I have no idea what I can say that will keep Jill off the warpath. I search my brain for inspiration, but Jill has no intention of waiting around. She stalks away from me, her thin hands balled into fists.

Damn, maybe I should have told Jill that truth. Oh well, what's the worst that could happen?

———

Caroline's head CT is negative. She doesn't have a bleed in her brain or a skull fracture.

Eric has officially diagnosed her with a concussion, so we send her home early. However, Jill tells her in no uncertain terms that she needs to be at work at 6 a.m. tomorrow morning. I guess Caroline will be okay to work. I feel like a head injury can only improve her performance at this point.

Things slow down after Marissa Block is transferred out of Baby City. All the scheduled C-sections are over, and nobody's even close to giving birth. Things are so relaxed that I buy myself a bag of Doritos from the vending machine. I actually search the floor for some vanilla Coke Zero, but I can't find it. I could really use Caroline right now.

I settle down in The Pit in a chair with my Doritos. After about five Doritos, my fingertips are good and orange with artificial cheese powder. Am I the only one who thinks that licking the artificial cheese off my fingers is almost as good as the Doritos themselves? That should be a new product. Fingers that you can lick artificial cheese off of. Or maybe not.

Hey, I'm a doctor, not a marketing executive, dammit.

I've licked my final finger clean when Eric suddenly bursts into the room. He gives me a cursory glance then kicks one of the chairs in the room hard enough to send it flying. It bangs against the wall with a loud crack that's enough to make me almost drop my Doritos.

I look up at Eric's face, which is bright red. He's fuming.

"Your chief is a real bitch, you know that?"

I guess Jill managed to catch up with him. She probably screamed at him in front of everyone. Well, at least he's still alive.

I force a smile. "You knew that already, didn't you?"

Eric just stares at the wall for a minute, taking deep breaths. Finally, he does an about-face and walks back out of the room.

It's probably better he doesn't know the whole thing is my fault.

———

It's 6:05 p.m. based on the clock hung up on the wall of The Pit, and I can see Jill checking her watch for good measure. She folds her arms across her chest. "Where is Holly?"

"Um," I say. "I think she said she had an OB/GYN appointment today."

Jill raises her light brown eyebrows. "So that means she's late?"

I shrug.

"I mean," Jill goes on, "She's got the whole day to schedule these appointments now. Literally. She can make the appointment anytime from 9 a.m. to 5 p.m. Why would she not be able to make it here by six o'clock?"

I shrug again. Jill does sort of have a point, but I feel weird saying anything against Holly.

"And it's not the first time…" Jill mumbles. She looks at her watch again. "If she's going to be this late to signout, she ought to call."

Again, Jill has a point. If you're going to be late, you really should call. But I keep my mouth shut.

Jill studies my face. "Don't you think so, Emily? I mean, it's just common courtesy."

Apparently, she's not going to let me get away with pleading the fifth. I fiddle with the drawstring of my scrubs, and finally say, "Yeah, she should probably have called."

Our conversation is interrupted when Holly appears in her blue scrubs, huffing and puffing slightly because apparently, even walking short distances makes her out of breath these days. She swipes a few strands of sweaty black hair from her face.

"I'm so sorry I'm late," she gasps.

Jill raises her eyes to look at Holly. If Holly were a medical student or an intern like Ted or *Eric*, Jill would be sarcastically berating her right now. But Holly is a third year OB/GYN resident, and that commands a little bit more respect. Holly is one of us. So Jill can't play it that way—she's got to be a little more subtle.

Jill smiles sweetly. "Were you at an appointment?"

Holly nods. "Yeah, my OB/GYN."

Jill clucks her tongue. "Too bad you couldn't get anything earlier, huh?"

Holly's cheeks color slightly. "This was the only time they had to see me," she says.

"Yes, Dr. Reynolds is very busy," Jill says. She flashes that overly sweet smile one more time, the one that always makes me cringe a little bit inside. "Maybe next time, when you're going to be so late, you could give us a call just to let us know."

Holly glances up at the clock on the wall then looks back at Jill. "But I'm only five…" she starts to say, but then thinks better of it. She coughs and lowers her eyes. "Yeah, sure thing, Jill."

You could cut the tension with a knife. Where is Dr.
Ford to tell a dirty joke when you need him?

Chapter 16

For reasons that aren't immediately clear to me, Holly has a fetal scalp clip attached to her ankle when I arrive at signout the next morning.

Fetal scalp clips are what we attach to the fetuses' scalps in order to get a more accurate measure of heart rate if we need to. I watch her fiddle with it for a minute before I feel compelled to say something clever.

"You know," I say. "Your baby isn't in your ankle. I thought we reviewed this during intern year."

Holly sticks out her tongue at me. "I just want to know how much these clips hurt the babies."

"And?"

"It pinches a little," she says.

"Maybe this is a stupid question," I say, "but why didn't you put it on your *scalp*?"

"I thought it would get stuck in my hair," Holly says, pointing at her thick mane of straight black hair. "And then I'd have to get someone to cut it out for me, like gum."

"Get gum stuck in your hair a lot, do you?"

Holly smiles. "Constantly. Peanut butter doesn't get it out, trust me."

I settle into a chair while Holly continues to fiddle with the scalp clip. It takes her at least two more minutes before she realizes how silly it is and detaches it.

"Hey," she says. "Neither of us is on call Saturday. You up for margaritas?"

I hesitate. I am slightly embarrassed to tell this to Holly, but I've been hoping to have a serious talk with David on Saturday night about the possibility of my moving back to Ohio. Or at least, I was going to try hinting at it. If I can work up the nerve.

"I'm not sure…" I say.

"Please," Holly beseeches me. "I need a few stiff drinks after what Ted has put me through this week."

"You know, you can't actually drink."

Holly sniffs. "I'm allowed to have a glass of wine."

Yeah, right. Holly won't even smell alcohol, much less guzzle one of her usual margaritas or even a half glass of wine. She refuses to admit it, but Holly is very protective of her fetus. She once ate some cold cuts by accident, and I thought she was going to stick her finger down her throat and try to regurgitate it.

"Okay," I agree.

After all, how many nights out do I have left with Holly? Ten? Fifteen? I can't imagine going out for margaritas if there's a baby on her lap.

When Caroline shows up, I search her face for subtle signs of brain damage. I'm not sure exactly what I'm looking for though. Divergent pupils? An unsteady gait? I don't see any of that, although I do think she looks mildly dazed. She's got a white bandage on her forehead, and I'm kind of tempted to peek under to take a look at Eric's handiwork. I'm sure he's got to be pretty good at suturing facial lacerations. I haven't done one in years. Most of the suturing I do doesn't get seen by anyone, except for possibly a few adventurous husbands.

Dr. Buckman is the attending today, which means there's a special bargain on C-sections in Baby City. We are going be slicing through so many uteruses today, it's not even funny. There's also a VBAC who just arrived in Triage with contractions.

In OB/GYN, VBAC stands for Vaginal Birth After C-section. Most obstetricians will recommend that a woman who has already had a C-section have a second one with their next pregnancy. But for various reasons, a lot of women don't want to do that. First, the recovery time for a C-section is a lot longer than for a vaginal delivery. It's a major abdominal surgery and there are risks of developing complications. Even if there are no immediate complications, there's a risk of bowel obstructions in the future from surgical adhesions. If you want to have multiple pregnancies, it can be risky if you have multiple C-sections because the uterus could rupture.

There are other reasons why women want to try for a vaginal delivery after C-section that I don't approve of. For example, some women who have a C-section feel like they were cheated out of "the birth experience." In my opinion, the birth experience is about getting a healthy baby. If people aren't holding hands and singing kumbaya while you're birthing, I don't think that's any great tragedy.

The good news is that about 70% of women who try for a VBAC are successful. The bad news is that 2% of women who try for a VBAC rupture their uterus, which could result in their death or the death of the baby. Personally, I don't think I could take that kind of risk. With a repeat C-section by a skilled OB/GYN, you are pretty much guaranteed a healthy baby. Why would you take a 2% risk of losing your baby?

But, hey, it's their choice.

Chapter 17

Postpartum rounds are fast today. Eric and I split the ward, so it's half as many patients as usual. Most ladies are doing well and don't have too many questions about their breasts. There's one woman who has staples that are ready to come out and I forgot to bring a staple remover kit with me, so I promise her I'll be back later.

Caroline, who has phenomenal timing for a change, appears just as I'm finishing up with my last postpartum patient. She's ready to present to me on Mrs. Dugan, the woman trying for a VBAC.

"Do you think she's a good candidate?" I ask Caroline.

Caroline nods vigorously. "Definitely."

"Why?" I ask her.

"She really wants to have a vaginal delivery," Caroline explains.

I roll my eyes. "So that's the indication for a trial of labor? *Really wanting* a vaginal delivery?"

Caroline bites her lip. I feel sort of bad grilling her when she just had a concussion yesterday. But seriously, this is pretty basic stuff.

"Was her previous incision a low transverse incision?" I ask.

"Yes?" Caroline says.

"Well, was it?"

Caroline nods hesitantly. I bet anything she has absolutely has no idea.

"What was her previous indication for C-section?"

"She was breech." Breech means that instead of the baby's head pointing down, the baby was coming out foot first or butt first.

"And is she breech now?"

Caroline hesitates. "I... I don't think so."

Hopefully not. I doubt anyone would let Mrs. Dugan have a trial of labor if her baby was breech. Especially not on a day that Dr. Buckman was working.

"All right," I say. "Why don't you take out the staples from Mrs. Allen in Room 409, and then we'll head down to Labor and Delivery."

I hand over the suture removal kit that I picked up from the medical supply room to Caroline, and her eyes light up. I wish *anything* could make me as happy as picking staples out of an abdomen makes Caroline.

I watch as Caroline heads off to Mrs. Allen's room, but then she starts skipping and I have to look away. That girl is far too excited about removing staples. I'm sure she'd be equally excited about writing the prescriptions I'm about to do, but I'd like to get out of here sometime before midnight.

After I've completed a large stack of prescriptions, I notice that Caroline still hasn't returned. I have a really bad feeling that she got one of the staples stuck. If you attempt to remove the staple at the wrong angle, sometimes it can twist in the way that makes it very difficult to get out. That happened once before with a medical student and it was a real pain in the ass to pry it free. I'm sure Caroline is valiantly trying to get the staple loose.

I pop in to Mrs. Allen's room, expecting to see Caroline leaning over her belly, in her usual position for staple removal: her face about two centimeters away from the incision. However, it turns out that Mrs. Allen is all alone.

"Hi again," Mrs. Allen says to me cheerfully. "Are you going to take my staples out now?"

"Um," I say awkwardly. I'm not sure how to phrase my next question without sounding like a complete flake. "Has my medical student Caroline been in here?"

Mrs. Allen's frowns at me. "No…"

Shit. Where *is* she?

I systematically check every single room, searching for Caroline. I have absolutely no idea where she's gone.

It's like she's vanished into thin air. This will be a story in the newspapers: medical student goes to take out staples and is never seen again.

I get to the end of the hallway and I'm completely baffled. Seriously, where did she *go*? I've checked every room. I even checked the rooms of the patients that Eric saw. The only rooms I haven't checked are the rooms occupied by the patients of private attendings.

About 25% of the patients who deliver at Cadence Hospital are private patients. They are seen by private practice OB/GYNs who don't work with residents. We are not to see those patients, touch those patients, or even breathe on them. We're certainly not supposed to go peeking in their rooms.

But dammit, I've got to find Caroline.

The first private patient's door is closed, so I knock gently. I hear a voice tell me to come in and I enter the room. And I almost faint.

Caroline is removing the private patient's staples.

Chapter 18

I'm going to have a stroke. I am literally going to burst an aneurysm in my brain right now. And it will be all Caroline's fault.

I clear my throat loudly, and Caroline looks up and smiles at me. "I'm just about done," she assures me.

That's what I was afraid of.

"Caroline," I say. "Can I please talk to you for a minute?"

Caroline straightens up, and dutifully follows me out of the room. Her smile fades slightly when she sees the look on my face.

"Why are you taking out that woman staples?" I'm trying my best not to yell.

Caroline furrows her brow. "You said to take out the staples of the woman in Room 401."

I almost smack myself in the head. Or better yet, smack Caroline in the head. "I said *409.*"

Caroline's face turns a shade paler. "Oh," she says. "Oh my God…" She groans and clutches her cheeks. "She even told me she didn't think her staples were supposed to come out yet."

Great. "Did it look like her incision was open?"

Caroline just looks at me blankly.

"Did the edges stay together?" I clarify.

"I'm not sure," Caroline admits, hanging her head.

I am going to kill Caroline. I swear to God. They're going to find her body tomorrow, bludgeoned to death with a staple remover.

"Can't we just staple it closed again?" Caroline asks me.

"It doesn't work like that."

If that incision is open, the patient is probably going to have to go back to surgery. The thought of having to explain that to the patient and then to her attending makes me physically ill. And while it's technically Caroline's fault, I'm the one supervising her. Which means that the responsibility is really mine. I should've made damn sure she knew whose staples to take out.

Oh my God, I really don't want to look at that incision.

For now, I decide to play it cool, until I know how bad the situation is. I brush past Caroline and walk into the mystery patient's room. The woman looks slightly perplexed, but not particularly upset.

"Hello," I say. "I'm Dr. McCoy."

"Nice to meet you," the woman says.

"How are you feeling?" I ask. I'm pretending like I'm really supposed to be here, even though it's a sin to even be in the room. I think bullshitting patients is a skill that most residents have acquired.

"Fine," the woman says.

She looks up at me curiously. It occurs to me that I don't even know what her name is. But I think it would look pretty bad to ask her at this point.

"Listen," I say. I take a deep breath. "Can I take a peek at your incision please?"

"Well, everyone else has," the woman agrees amicably as she lifts her gown.

I say a quick prayer. *Please God, let this incision be closed. If you make sure this incision is closed, I promise that I will show my gratitude by not murdering Caroline. Even though I really want to.*

I pull the blankets away from the private patient's belly. I squeeze my eyes shut as I do it, because I'm too afraid to look. But when I open my eyes, I can see immediately that this woman's incision is closed, more or less. She'll heal fine without another trip back to the OR.

My knees almost buckle with relief. I'm never letting Caroline take out staples ever again.

———

I remove Mrs. Allen's staples myself. Obviously.

After I'm finished up on the postpartum floor, I go to Triage to see Mrs. Dugan, the prospective VBAC patient. Right now, I trust Caroline about as far as I can throw her, so I intend to take my own history.

I walk into Mrs. Dugan's room while she is in mid-contraction. She's lying on the table, her eyes squeezed shut as she clutches her hospital gown and breathes through pursed lips. I wait a minute, allowing for the contraction to subside. Mrs. Dugan's shoulders finally relax, and she smiles at me and says hello.

Mrs. Dugan is an older mom. She's 37, which makes her advanced maternal age. Anyone over 35 is advanced maternal age, which basically means that they're at higher risk for birth defects and complications of pregnancy. However, Mrs. Dugan's pregnancy has so far been uncomplicated. Well, aside from the fact that as of two weeks ago, her baby was still breech. But at the last visit, she was noted to be vertex (i.e. the baby was head down).

"Hi, I'm Dr. McCoy," I say. "I hear you want to do a trial of labor instead of a repeat C-section."

Mrs. Dugan nods. "I just felt so sick after my last C-section. It was hard to even enjoy the baby. I can't imagine going through that again, and I was told that since the last one was breech, I have a good chance of delivering this baby vaginally."

"That's true," I agree. "How did your baby flip? Did the doctor do an external version?" An external version is a procedure done by an OB/GYN in an attempt to flip the baby from breach to vertex.

"Nope," Mrs. Dugan says. She smiles proudly. "My cat did it."

Excuse me?

"Your cat?" I ask as politely as I can.

Sometimes it's hard to keep a straight face.

"Oh yes," Mrs. Dugan says. "Wally positioned his bum over the baby's head and he purred his heart out for about an hour. All the while, it felt like there was a circus going on in my belly. When he got up, she was flipped over."

Well, that's a new one. Maybe Mrs. Dugan will be willing to rent out her magical kitty to other women with breech pregnancies.

———

I don't know how Dr. Buckman talks every woman he meets into having a scheduled C-section. Dr. Buckman really loves C-sections more than any attending I've ever known. I'm guessing C-sections are better for him than women attempting labor. It's easier for him to know when he has to come in, do a quick section, and then leave, rather than risking being called in at any time to assist with a difficult birth or an emergency section.

If you ever even attempt to (diplomatically) question him about his high C-section rate, Dr. Buckman has a lot of answers ready for you. His list of indications for an elective C-section is a mile long. Aside from The Princess and her itchiness, I've seen him schedule them for a teacher who wanted to have her baby the day after classes ended, for the desire to maintain a "perfect vagina" (whatever that is), "auspicious" star signs and astrological dating, the all-encompassing "suspected cephalopelvic disproportion" (baby's head too big for birth canal... *maybe*), and basically just anyone who was tired of being pregnant and didn't have a favorable cervix.

Somehow the patients scheduled today are particularly objectionable. They all seem to have some sort of opinion about how they would like us to make their surgical incision. I can't imagine a patient having a gallbladder removed or heart surgery telling the doctor how to cut them open, so why is it that every woman thinks she can tell us where her incision should be?

For example, one patient informed us she had spent the last month at the beach. I'm sure she was quite a sight wearing a bikini with her giant pregnant belly, and the bonus was that she had tan lines. We were not to make the incision above her tan lines.

Not to be outdone, the next patient came in unhappy about her scar from her last C-section. She wanted us to remove the scar while delivering her current baby. It isn't our job to remove scars. If I wanted to do that, I would've gone into plastic surgery. I would've had a much better lifestyle and made a lot more money, that's for sure.

The long string of scheduled C-section patients comes to an end with Ms. Watson.

Ms. Watson is here for a repeat C-section. Not to be crass or anything, but Ms. Watson is huge. I genuinely think that this woman is the most obese woman I have ever done a C-section on. Her weight in the chart is recorded at 402 pounds. She's large enough that it's actually very hard to tell that she's even pregnant. When you hear crazy stories about women who don't realize they're pregnant until the day they deliver, it's more believable when you see a woman like this. I'm wondering how the hell we're going to get this baby out of her.

But of course, I wouldn't say that to Ms. Watson.

"Listen," Ms. Watson says to me. "Dr. Buckman said he would tie my tubes after the baby is delivered."

"Sure," I say.

It's not an unusual request for a woman having a C-section to ask us to tie off her fallopian tubes after delivering the baby. It takes an extra few minutes and then she doesn't have to worry about birth control ever again. Pretty good deal.

"Also," she adds. "Please don't mention I'm having my tubes tied to my fiancé."

Um, say what?

"You haven't told your fiancé that you're getting your tubes tied?" I ask her. I'm trying not to sound judgmental as I secretly judge her. This is incredibly unethical.

Before Ms. Watson can respond, there's a knock at the door. A tall skinny man enters the room, presumably her fiancé. While Ms. Watson may be the fattest woman I have ever delivered, her fiancé may be the skinniest man I have ever seen. He has long gangly limbs, eyes that bulge in sunken sockets, and an Adam's apple that's as big as my fist. Somehow I'm reminded of that nursery rhyme about Jack Sprat who could eat no fat and his wife who could eat no lean.

"This is my fiancée, Jack," Ms. Watson says. "Jack, this is Dr. McCoy."

Okay, that's just too funny.

Mr. Sprat reaches out to shake my hand. "Are we right on schedule?"

I nod. "I'm hoping to get you into the OR in about 30 minutes."

"Wow," Mr. Sprat says. He puts his hand lovingly on Mrs. Watson gut. "I can't believe in about an hour, we're going to have another little girl." He winks at me. "Of course, the next one is going to be a boy."

Odds a million to one you're wrong.

Ms. Watson smiles tolerantly as Mr. Sprat rambles on.

"Not that there's anything wrong with little girls," he says. "I've just always wanted a son. Someone to toss a football around with and go to the gym together."

Mr. Sprat is wearing a T-shirt, and by the looks of his biceps, he desperately needs somebody to go to the gym with him. I think I could easily wrap my fingers around his entire upper arm.

"I'm not so sure we're going to try for a third," Ms. Watson mumbles.

Mr. Sprat smiles confidently. "I think I'll be able to talk you into it."

At this point, I'm beginning to wonder if somebody's punking me or something. I mean, here is a guy who desperately wants another child, and I am not allowed to tell him that his future wife is about to be sterilized. I want to scream at the guy: *Your fiancé is getting her tubes tied!*

But I can't do that, of course. She's my patient and he isn't. Patient confidentiality and all that. Dammit.

As I leave the room, Mr. Sprat is already picking out names for their third child.

———

We get Ms. Watson into the OR for her C-section right on schedule. Thank God, Mr. Sprat didn't want to be in the room for the section. I don't think I could handle a running monologue from him through the surgery, where he makes plans for future children.

Dr. Buckman has probably done more C-sections than any other OB/GYN in the hospital, but even he looks intimidated as we stand before Ms. Watson's abdomen. He turns his head this way and that, like he's trying to figure out the best way to make an approach.

"This will be tricky," he says under his breath.

No kidding.

In a repeat C-section, the incision is almost always made in the same place as the last incision. You don't want to create a new location with scar tissue. But in Ms. Watson, the initial incision was made high on her abdomen, transverse, over what appears to be the thickest layer of her abdominal fat. I don't know who did her last C-section, or what on earth was going through their head. It's like they wanted to give the finger to the next person who had to do this.

"I guess we should go through her scar," Dr. Buckman finally decides.

"You don't want to go lower down?" I ask him.

Dr. Buckman thinks a little longer. For a second, I swear he's going to suggest she get out of the OR and instead have a trial of labor. But that has its own set of problems. I know from Ms. Watson's chart that her baby is measuring large and could get stuck, and it frightens me what might happen if we had to get this baby out in a hurry.

"Just go through the scar," he says again.

It ends up being one of the hardest C-sections I've ever done. We literally have to cut through about a foot of fat to get to Ms. Watson's uterus. We could definitely use Caroline here to help hold the retractor. I offered her the opportunity to come inside with us, but she just got this scared look on her face and shook her head vigorously.

The baby is a big one, tipping the scales at nine pounds twelve ounces. As soon as the newborn girl is free, we start stitching up Ms. Watson's uterus. After we're done with that, we have to tie off her fallopian tubes. I know we have to do it, but I still have misgivings. I'm not going to march off and tell Jack Sprat about it, but maybe I can make Ms. Watson see reason.

"Are you sure you still want your tubes tied?" I ask Ms. Watson, who is chatting with the nurse about her baby on the other side of the curtain.

Dr. Buckman looks up at me sharply. It's definitely not standard practice to question patients on their surgery right in the middle of it.

"Of course I do!" Ms. Watson says, as if this is the dumbest question she's ever heard. And it very well might be.

"I just thought," I babble on, despite a voice in the back of my head telling me to shut the hell up, "maybe you talked to your fiancé and changed your mind. I mean, if you want to talk to him about it first…"

I hear Ms. Watson suck in a breath on the other side of the curtain. Dr. Buckman's fingers pause mid-suture. All of a sudden, I really wish I could take back what I just said.

"For your *information*," she says, "when I had my last C-section, I spent over a month in the hospital. I got an awful infection and they thought I was going to die. I didn't want to get pregnant this time, but I couldn't tolerate the hormones in birth control. I know Jack wants more kids, but I don't want him to try to talk me out of this, and it's more important for me to be alive to take care of the kids that I have. If I make it out alive this time, I never want to go through this again." She pauses meaningfully. "So why don't you mind your own goddamn business, Dr. McCoy."

The entire room has gone completely silent. Dr. Buckman just shakes his head at me.

"I'm sorry," I mumble.

When will I ever learn to keep my fool mouth shut?

Chapter 19

I expect to get at least scolded by Dr. Buckman for what I said to Ms. Watson, but he doesn't mention it. I think he's just relieved that we managed to scoop that baby out of her. That was a rough C-section. I wouldn't be at all surprised if the incision doesn't close up quickly. There is a lot of soft tissue that needs to heal in this woman.

I guess she was right to get her tubes tied.

As Dr. Buckman leaves the OR, he says to me, "How is that trial of labor going?"

"Very well," I say.

Dr. Buckman shakes his head.

"Beware," he says. "These patients can turn very quickly. We don't want to be rushing her into the OR with a ruptured uterus."

Well, duh.

"If there's any doubt in your mind," he says, "we'll do the C-section."

"I'm comfortable with waiting," I say.

Dr. Buckman frowns at me, obviously not pleased with my answer. I think he was hoping I'd beg him to take the patient in for a C-section right now now now! A VBAC that gets converted to a C-section is like a wet dream for him.

"Maybe I should see her myself," he says thoughtfully.

"There's no need for that," I say.

"All the same," he says. "I'm going to pay her a visit."

Dr. Buckman says he needs to run to the bathroom, so I wait for him outside Mrs. Dugan's room. It's actually kind of weird that he said he needed to use the bathroom. I literally don't think I've ever experienced an attending saying they needed to use the bathroom before. I guess I assumed that after graduating residency, everyone developed a magical bladder that could hold pee for up to 24 hours at a time.

I kill some time by shooting a text message over to David: "Just got reamed by patient!"

Almost instantly, David writes back: "Well deserved?"

I'm about to text back to David a smiley face sticking out its tongue when Dr. Buckman strides over to me. He's still wearing scrubs, but his hair is neatly combed and I detect a splash of cologne. It seems like I was right about the magical bladder—he only went to the bathroom to doll himself up. Maybe he thinks he can flirt his way into a

C-section. It wouldn't work on me, but it seems to work on every other female patient.

I hope Mrs. Dugan can resist the allure of Dr. Buckman.

Caroline has pulled a chair up next to Mrs. Dugan's bed, and they're chatting like old friends. They both have their phones out and it seems like they're comparing photos of their cats. I stride over just in time to catch a glimpse of Caroline's cat wearing what appears to be a pink party hat. That girl has far too much free time.

"Hello, Mrs. Dugan," Dr. Buckman says in his most smooth, silky voice. "My name is Dr. Buckman. How are you feeling?"

Mrs. Dugan lifts her eyes from her cat photos. She doesn't swoon, which is a surprise to everyone. In fact, she looks suspicious.

"Fine," she says. "Perfect. I feel great."

Dr. Buckman looks at the tracings of her baby's heart rate and clucks his tongue. I'm not sure what he's clucking about because the tracings look perfect. But Mrs. Dugan, who presumably can't read fetal heart rate tracing as well as I can, looks worried. "What's wrong?" she asks.

"Mrs. Dugan," Dr. Buckman says. "Has a doctor had a frank discussion with you about the risks of VBAC?"

Mrs. Dugan nods. "Yes. My uterus could rupture and it could kill me and the baby."

Good girl.

"The risk is about 2%," Dr. Buckman says ominously.

"Yes," Mrs. Dugan says. "I know."

"That means for every 50 women who come in for a trial of labor after a C-section, one will have a rupture of her uterus."

Mrs. Dugan nods again. "I understand what 2% means."

Dr. Buckman squirms, looking mildly pissed off. I guess he figured he'd just march in here and convince her to let him take her straight to the OR. Meanwhile, Caroline is beaming like Mrs. Dugan is her star pupil.

"Fine," Dr. Buckman says. "As long as you're willing to accept the risk."

"I wouldn't be here if I wasn't, would I?"

Dr. Buckman looks like he has more to add, but right then Mrs. Dugan has a contraction and doesn't seem like she particularly wants to listen to him anymore. Even though I sort of agree with Dr. Buckman in theory (don't quote me on that), I really have to admire Mrs. Dugan for standing her ground. I have a feeling she's going to push out this baby no problem.

———

"Mrs. Dugan is ten centimeters dilated!"

I look up from the orders I'm writing in Triage, and see Caroline in front of me, nearly bursting with excitement. Her cheeks are all flushed and she's panting slightly. She must have run the whole way here.

"Really?" I say, raising my eyebrows to exhibit my skepticism. It's not that I don't believe her, but...

Yeah, I don't believe her.

Caroline looks sheepish. "The nurse said so."

Well, I definitely trust the nurse. Even the worst nurses here on Baby City are actually very good.

"Okay," I say. "I'm coming."

Caroline is literally skipping along beside me as I walk to Mrs. Dugan's room. Why is she always skipping? I guess she's excited because she hasn't seen any vaginal deliveries yet. Still, it's incredibly annoying. I manage to bite my tongue for the first 30 seconds or so, but then I can't stand another second.

"Caroline," I say. "Can you please walk like a normal person? This is very unprofessional."

Caroline stops skipping. She hesitates for a moment, like a baby not quite sure it can take a step. Then she starts walking again very tentatively, staying a safe five paces behind me. Having her follow me like that is even more annoying though. I almost want to tell her to go back to skipping again.

Sure enough, Mrs. Dugan is all set to go. She's fully dilated, as Caroline promised. I can easily feel the baby's head. I can just tell that she's not going to have any problem pushing this one out. I ask a nurse to page Dr.

Buckman and let him know that the VBAC is about to start pushing, but the baby could end up born before he gets here.

A nurse holds one of Mrs. Dugan's legs and her husband holds the other leg.

"You ready to push?" I ask her.

She nods eagerly.

I attempt to guide Caroline into the stool between Mrs. Dugan's legs, but it's like she's stuck. I give her another push and Caroline faces me with wide blue eyes.

"What are you doing?" she whispers to me.

"You're going to deliver this baby," I say.

"Me?" Caroline gasps, her face turning a shade paler. Please don't faint, Caroline.

"Yes," I say irritably, giving her another push in the direction of the stool.

Caroline still doesn't budge.

"I'm not *ready*," Caroline says.

I roll my eyes. "It's easy. Really."

But Caroline refuses to sit down. And right now, I don't have time to try to persuade her. I guess I'll be the one delivering this baby.

"Okay," I say to Mrs. Dugan. "Get ready to push with your next contraction."

I suppress the temptation to tell her to push like she's having the biggest bowel movement of her life.

Anyway, it's clear that Mrs. Dugan does not need any instructions on how to push. Despite the fact that she's a newbie at this, her first push is fantastic. I see the perineum stretching around the baby's head, and I'm convinced that the baby will be out within half an hour.

"Great job!" I tell her. "Keep doing it just like that!"

She gives another push and I modify my prediction: she's going to deliver in the next 15 minutes. Maybe less.

"Another one just like that!" I coach her.

"No," Mrs. Dugan says loudly.

For moment, I think I've definitely heard her wrong. I glance over at Caroline, who is frowning with confusion. "What?" I finally say.

"I don't want to push anymore," Mrs. Dugan says. "I want another C-section."

What?

Chapter 20

"Mrs. Dugan, you're doing great," I say. For some reason, my patient is freaking out and now she just needs a little pep talk. "Just a few more pushes and the baby will definitely be out."

"No," Mrs. Dugan says. She's as firm now as she was when she was insisting on a trial of labor. "I don't like this. I want a C-section."

It's almost like Dr. Buckman suddenly entered her body during labor, and now he's controlling what she says like a puppet master. Of course, that isn't really possible. *Or is it?*

"Honey," Mr. Dugan says. "You've been talking about how you don't want a C-section for your entire pregnancy. Now you've almost got the baby out. You can do this."

"I want a C-section!" Mrs. Dugan snaps at him. "When *you're* giving birth to the baby, *you* can decide how you want it delivered."

Everyone does their best to convince Mrs. Dugan to push out her baby, but she just won't do it. I can't drag the baby out of her vagina. If she doesn't want to push, we're going to have to do a C-section. Which is going to be all the more fun with the baby's head firmly lodged in her pelvis.

I call Dr. Buckman to inform him of the change in plans and he reacts with elation, throwing in an "I told you so" for good measure. There's part of me that honestly does believe that Dr. Buckman must have a voodoo doll of Mrs. Dugan in his office that he's poking with pins to make her say what he wants her to say, which is the only way I can account for this woman's bizarre behavior. Then again, you don't really need voodoo to explain the crazy things women do while in labor.

As they whisk away Mrs. Dugan to the OR, Caroline grabs me by the arm hard enough that I'm pretty sure her fingernails are going to leave indentations.

"Emily," she whispers urgently. "I don't think I should go to the C-section."

"Why not?" I say.

Caroline squirms. "You know what happened last time…"

I am seriously running out of patience with this girl.

"Caroline," I say. "That was a really bloody C-section. I'm sure you'll be fine this time."

Caroline doesn't seem quite so sure. And to be honest, I'm not *that* sure.

"I'd rather skip it," she says.

Okay, my patience has officially run out.

"Caroline, first you don't want to deliver a baby and now you don't want to go to a C-section. You realize this is an obstetrics rotation, right?"

Caroline nods timidly.

"And you don't want to fail, do you?" I press her.

"No," she whispers.

"Then I suggest you follow me to this C-section," I say.

Caroline's lower lip trembles and I'm scared she's about to start crying. But instead, she drops her head and follows me without another word. Maybe I'm being a little too harsh, but seriously, this is getting ridiculous. You can't be on an OB/GYN rotation and never see a baby get born. Going to C-sections is *not* optional.

Dr. Buckman arrives quickly at the OR, possibly afraid Mrs. Dugan might change her mind. There's part of me that wants to ask my patient again if she's really sure about this and try to talk her out of it, but that didn't go so well with the last patient. So like I said, I'm just going to keep my fool mouth shut.

Dr. Buckman positions himself on one side of the operating table holding Mrs. Dugan, and I'm on the other side. After a few minutes, Caroline shows up, having apparently reduced her scrubbing time to a somewhat manageable amount. She positions herself at my left side.

"I'm ready!" she announces, as if we were all waiting for her.

"Why don't you take the lead on this, Dr. McCoy," Dr. Buckman says to me, giving me a wink above his surgical mask. He's in a really good mood about the VBAC failing. Plus we've done nothing but C-sections today, so I guess he figures I know what I'm doing.

Caroline is given the job of holding the suction, despite the fact that there is nothing to suction yet. I figure it will give her hands something to do instead of getting in the way of my sterile field. I take the scalpel and cut along Mrs. Dugan's prior C-section incision. The least I can do is not create a new scar.

I've completed the incision when I see something flicker out of the corner of my eye. I look to my left, where Caroline is standing. I look down at her hand holding the suction, and see that she's trembling. I check her face but it's impossible to tell how she is because of her mask. All I can see is her terrified blue eyes.

"Are you okay?" I ask her.

"Yes," Caroline says.

I'm not sure I believe her. "Are you sure?"

"*Mrs. Dugan* is the patient, not this young lady," Dr. Buckman jokes. (He has no idea what Caroline's name is.)

I don't want to make Caroline look bad by explaining to Dr. Buckman that she's already fainted at one C-section. I'm about to ask her one more time if she's okay, but before I can get the words out, I see her eyes suddenly roll up in their sockets. I drop the scalpel, panicked, and manage to catch Caroline just before she hits the ground.

"Holy shit!" Dr. Buckman says.

I can't even begin to imagine what Mrs. Dugan is thinking behind that curtain.

Caroline's eyelids are fluttering slightly. Caroline is small and thin, but so am I—in about one minute, I'm going to be on the floor too. Just as I start to lose my balance, one of the scrub nurses rushes over and helps me lower her into a chair. Luckily, it's a rolling chair, so we're able to easily push it out of the OR. Caroline is half-conscious, mumbling something in her confused state.

"I'll go get some juice," the nurse volunteers.

I nod. "And Dr. Kessler," I add.

I can't believe I have to sit here babysitting her. I'm a doctor, dammit, not Caroline's mother. If Eric gets over here quickly, I can probably make it back in time to close up Mrs. Dugan.

I crouch down next to Caroline, whose eyes are cracked open. She's taking shallow breaths.

"How are you doing?" I ask her, with as much tenderness as I can muster.

"Embarrassed," she murmurs.

I would be too, if I were her.

A few minutes later, I see Eric approaching us with a cup of copper-colored liquid. I guess the nurse told him what happened. He crouches down next to Caroline.

"I want you to drink this," he says.

Caroline gulps down the drink, which is either apple juice, bourbon, or possibly urine. She avoids looking at either of us.

"No head injuries this time, I hope," Eric says, grinning up at me.

I shake my head. "I caught her."

Eric lays his hand on Caroline's shoulder. "I think we should get back to The Pit. Do you think you can walk?"

"I… I'm not sure," Caroline admits.

"No problem," Eric says.

He straightens up, looks down at her for a minute thoughtfully, then places one arm under his knee and one around her shoulders, and hoists her up in the air. He winks at me again and then purposefully walks off in the direction of The Pit.

Jill happens upon us at that moment, and appears completely baffled. She looks over at Eric and Caroline, and shakes her head. "Did I miss something?"

"Caroline fainted."

"Christ. Again? Does she have some sort of fainting disorder?"

Good question.

I just shrug. "I guess she's squeamish."

Jill rolls her eyes. "What a precious little flower."

Jill is eyeing the way that Eric is carrying Caroline across the room in his arms, like they're on some very screwed up honeymoon. I can't help but notice the way Eric's biceps bulge out under the cut of his scrub sleeves.

"Why is loverboy over there carrying her?" Jill asks.

"She was too weak to walk."

"Give me a break," Jill groans. She looks thoughtful for a moment then grins evilly. "Hey, maybe we should give Mrs. Kessler a call and tell her that her husband been carrying around cute blond medical students."

"There's no Mrs. Kessler," I say. "He's divorced."

"A nice guy like that? What a shocker." She pokes me in the arm. Her long nails scratch me, and I wince at the jab of pain. "Five bucks says he hooks up with Caroline by the end of the month."

Jill's probably right. There's some obvious chemistry going on between Eric and Caroline. Men love damsels in distress, and Caroline plays the part without even trying. He's rescued her twice in two days, and now he's *carrying* her, for Christ's sake. Plus, if I am being completely objective, she's really pretty. I can't blame him for falling for her.

Chapter 21

Mrs. Dugan gives birth to a healthy baby boy and Caroline spends the rest of the shift lying down in the resident call room. Jill is livid at the thought of someone other than an OB/GYN resident using that room, but I convince her that it would be heartless to make Caroline lie down on the floor. Eric checks on her periodically to make sure she's okay and God knows what else he does with her.

This shift doesn't end a moment too soon.

As soon as I get out of the hospital, I make a beeline for the hot dog truck. Somehow it doesn't occur to me while I'm at work that I haven't eaten in about ten hours, but the second I step out of the door, hunger completely overtakes me. I actually feel little bit weak.

I realize this is my third day in a row of eating hot dogs for dinner. I think the hot dog guy may actually feel sorry for me. When he gives me my usual hot dog with a glob of mustard and ketchup, he flashes me this concerned look. When a guy with five teeth total and dirt permanently ground into his fingernails seems to think my lifestyle is too unhealthy, I might be in trouble.

Still, the hot dog looks delicious. I'm preparing to take a great big bite when out of nowhere a hand reaches out and yanks the hot dog away from me.

I'm stunned. I've been the innocent victim of a hot dog mugging! I didn't know that could actually happen. Who would want my two dollar hot dog? How could somebody do this to me? At this point, I wish they'd taken my wallet instead.

Man, I'm really hungry.

I turn around, searching for the perpetrator of this theft. I expect to see a man dressed in black with a gun on his belt making off with my hot dog, but instead I see Eric. He's standing behind me, holding my hot dog hostage in his hand, shaking his head at me.

"You weren't really going to eat this, were you?" he asks me.

"No," I say sarcastically. "I was going to balance it on my nose like a seal." I make a grab for my hot dog, but he holds it out of reach. He's got at least six inches on me, and his arms are a lot longer.

"I saw you buying a hot dog yesterday," he says. "I can't let you eat hot dog for dinner two nights in a row. I just can't."

Actually, it was three nights in a row.

"Why not?" I retort. I've given up on trying to retrieve my hot dog for the time being. I need to lull him into a sense of false security, then I'll get the hot dog back when he least expects it.

"You know," he says, "New York hot dogs are made from rat meat."

"Then rat meat is delicious," I say.

Eric shakes his head at me again then, to my horror, he tosses my hot dog in a trashcan. I want to strangle him. For a moment, I actually consider pulling the hot dog out of the trash and eating it anyway. It's not actually *in* the trash. It's really just *on top of* the trash.

Wow, I'm even worse than Caroline.

"You asshole!" I yell at him. "I can't believe you threw away my hot dog!"

"Your stomach will thank me," he says. He puts his hand on my back and steers me away from the trashcan, possibly recognizing my temptation to take the hot dog back. "I'm going to take you to a restaurant that has the best burgers in the entire city."

I'm embarrassed to admit that I get a little tingly at the touch of Eric's hand on my back. I quickly shake it off.

"I highly doubt this place has the best burgers in the city," I say. "This is New York, you know, not Wyoming."

"I'm going to make you into a believer," Eric says.

I don't care how good these burgers are. If we don't eat soon, I may have to start devouring my clothing. After

15 blocks of twists and turns, I'm starting to get incredibly crabby. But every time I question Eric, he assures me that it's right around the corner. I am beginning to worry that he doesn't actually know where this place is.

Finally, we come to a halt in front of this tiny, hole in the wall restaurant that I would have definitely walked past without noticing. The sign on the restaurant simply says "Burgers" in plain black writing. And the "R" is partially scratched off.

I make a face. "Are you serious? This is it?"

Eric nods eagerly. "Best burgers in the city," he repeats.

The place is kind of dingy and I almost don't want to go in. Although considering I was willing to eat rat meat from a hot dog cart, I guess I shouldn't be such a diva. Eric grabs me by the forearm and pulls me inside.

And oh my God, this place is *hot*. It's easily hotter in here than it was outside, and we're talking about a humid New York August. I feel my hair frizzing up into an Afro around my ponytail. I wipe a few droplets of sweat off my forehead with the back of my hand.

There are no tables to speak of, only a counter with stools. Eric slides onto one stool and I slip into the stool next to him. A hairy, overweight man whose wife beater T-shirt is literally drenched in sweat approaches us with a notepad.

"What'll you have?" he asks us.

"Can I see a menu?" I ask.

"No menu," the guy grunts. "Only burgers."

Then why the hell did he ask me what I was going to be having?

Eric quickly intervenes: "We'll have two cheeseburgers with grilled onions, sides of fries, and two Heinekens."

The guy grunts again in understanding. As he walks away, I can see his back is covered with thick tufts of hair. I think they may have taught a gorilla to cook and wait on people.

"What if I don't want a beer?" I mutter to Eric.

"All they've got to drink here is beer," he replies.

I wipe a few droplets of sweat off my neck. I'm beginning to even sweat into my bra. I don't know how much longer I can sit in this place. I look at Eric, who doesn't seem bothered at all.

"Why couldn't you just let me have my hot dog in peace?" I say.

Eric looks slightly wounded. "Come on, give it a chance."

"Why didn't you take Caroline here instead?" I say.

Maybe I'm being a little bit catty, but I can't help it. I'm hot and hungry.

Eric laughs. "I don't think Caroline would appreciate this place."

"So what kind of place would you take her to?"

Eric shrugs. "I don't know. Why would I take Caroline anywhere?"

"Oh, come off it," I snort. "I know you guys are into each other. It's so obvious."

I have to hand it to him, Eric actually looks very surprised.

"What you talking about?" he asks. "I'm not 'into' Caroline. Why would you think that?"

"Whatever."

"I'm not," he insists.

"You've rescued her like twice now," I point out. "Men love women that have to be rescued."

Eric blinks at me. "*I* don't."

I snort again.

"Not that I don't appreciate you generalizing me into some typical male stereotype," Eric says, "but I really don't like helpless woman. I prefer a woman who is confident, who can take charge of a situation. There's nothing sexier than that."

"Yeah, right," I say.

Eric holds up his right hand. "Scout's honor."

"You were a scout?" I ask, rolling my eyes.

"I sure was," he says. He winks at me. "Scout's honor."

"Okay, fine," I say. "Prove it to me. What did your ex-wife do for a living?"

"Surgeon," he says without blinking an eye. "Well, surgery resident."

Whoa. I didn't realize that Eric used to be married to a surgeon. I'm actually sort of impressed. Of course, he *divorced* her.

Something gets jogged in the back of my memory from way back during intern year. A consult on a pregnant patient on the surgical service from a resident named Mary Kessler. I met Mary only briefly, but she seemed incredibly nice. But what was most memorable was probably how completely gorgeous she was. Mary had the typical Snow White beauty—the hair as black as coal, skin as white as snow, and lips as red as blood without the aid of lipstick. I can definitely see a guy like Eric being married to someone like her.

"Was your wife Mary Kessler?" I ask him.

Eric's eyes widen. He looks mildly alarmed. "Yes…"

"I don't know her very well or anything," I say quickly. The last thing I want to do is associate myself with his ex-wife. "I just met her one time. She seemed… nice."

"Yeah," is all he says.

"Are you guys still friends at all?" I ask him.

"Not exactly," he mumbles.

It's pretty obvious that he doesn't want to talk about his ex-wife, and I'm not going to bug him about it. I don't really want to start talking about David either.

I look down at Eric's left hand and see that he hasn't taken off his wedding ring yet. Presumably he takes it off at home. I hope. I can't help but think he may still be hung up on his beautiful ex. Not that I can throw any stones.

Fortunately, the awkwardness is broken by the gorilla plopping two plates of food down in front of us, as well as our beers. My burger looks pretty ordinary, though I have to admit it smells really good. I like the way that the onions are overflowing into the grease of the burger.

Eric grins at me. "Dig in."

I pick up the burger and take a bite. Grease dribbles down my chin but I honestly don't care. This, I have to admit, is the best burger I've ever eaten in my entire life. I was wrong about getting back together with David. I'm going to marry this burger. This burger and I are going to get a house together in Long Island and we're going to have two children and a terrier. I love this burger. I can't say that enough.

"Well?" Eric asks me.

"Um," I say. "It's okay…"

He laughs. "You're not that good an actress, Emily."

"Fine," I huff. "It's amazing, okay? God, you're so annoying."

Eric laughs again and we finish our burgers mostly in silence. I'm so starving and this burger is so good, I've devoured it in less than a minute. Eric must be hungry too because he finishes his pretty quickly. We gulp down our beers and when the check comes, Eric pays it. I figure that's fair considering he threw away my hot dog.

Even though it's got to be close to 90° outside, it feels downright nippy compared to the restaurant. I breathe a sigh of relief when we're on the street again.

"Where do you live?" Eric asks me.

I tell him my address and he raises his eyebrows.

"Do you have a death wish?" he asks.

"It's not that bad," I insist. "Anyway, I'm poor. Where am I supposed to live? Park Avenue?"

"I'll walk you home," he says.

I roll my eyes. "I'll be fine, thank you very much."

"I'd feel better about it."

Okay, now he's being really annoying again. I fold my arms across my chest, and say, "I thought you said you liked women who don't need to be rescued."

Eric turns his green eyes on me and looks at me in a way that makes my whole body tingle. Damn, that boy is really cute. We just stand there, staring at each other for a minute, possibly the longest minute of my life. A minute I don't particularly want to end.

Finally, a smile touches his lips.

"You're absolutely right," he says. He takes a step back. "Goodbye, Emily."

Eric walks in the opposite direction, and it's a least another minute before I can start breathing normally again.

Chapter 22

I wish I could say that on my day off from work I do something fantastic. I only get four days off per month so it seems like I really ought to be doing something great on those days. Or at least something healthy like going for a run. But the truth is, I mostly just sleep. I suspect about 90% of my nonworking hours are spent sleeping or at least on my bed.

I shut off my phone alarm and wake up whenever my body feels like it. Which is maybe about ten o'clock in the morning. I make myself an English muffin with butter on it and then I go back to sleep for a little morning nap. Hey, even the President gets to enjoy a day off, right?

At some point during my afternoon nap, my phone beeps with a text message. I rub my eyes and groggily fumble for my phone. My heart speeds up when I see David's name on the screen. The text reads: "bttf is on."

"Back to the Future" was David's and my favorite movie. We must have watched it a thousand times together. We sort of had this theme of '80s movies that we loved and that was our favorite. "Back to the Future" was *our* movie.

I fumble for my remote control while simultaneously calling David on my phone. He doesn't even answer with hello.

He just says, "NBC."

I flip to the right channel and relax against my pillows with the phone on speaker next to me. It makes me feel almost like David is lying next to me in bed. Is that pathetic? It sounds sort of pathetic as I'm saying it.

"You haven't missed much," he says.

On the screen, Doc Brown is explaining to Marty McFly how he stole plutonium from Libyan terrorists. Were there really a lot of terrorists from Libya in 1985? I guess so.

"You know what I don't like about this movie?" David says.

"Nothing?"

David laughs. "I just think it's annoying that this movie switches back and forth between how things that Marty does in the past change the future and things he does in the past explain the future."

"No, it doesn't."

"Sure it does," he says. "For example, the future is different when Marty returns to it. Like, his parents are successful and skinny. So in that sense, he changes the future."

"Right," I say. "So there you go."

I know exactly where David is going with this. He actually runs through this routine almost every single time we watch this movie.

"But at the same time," David goes on, "Chuck Berry hears the song 'Johnny B. Goode' only because Marty was playing it at the dance. So in that sense, the past *explains* the future."

"You're right," I say. "I guess time travel really isn't possible."

"I'd be really sad if that were true," David says.

We chat for the rest the movie, David continuing to point out all the inconsistencies. And then the movie ends and we continue talking. For hours. It's like we have a million things to say to each other, just like in the old days. A few times, I just get lost in the sound of David's voice. I really do miss him.

At some point, I glance at my watch and realize with a start that I'm meeting Holly in less than an hour and I haven't even showered yet.

"I've got to go," I tell him, accidentally cutting him off midsentence.

"Oh," David says. "Sorry. Um, do you have a date?"

He sounds so awkward asking me that. I want to reach through the phone and give him a hug.

"No, nothing like that," I say. "I'm just meeting my friend Holly for dinner and drinks."

"Oh, okay," he says. He sounds distinctly relieved.

"I'm not seeing anyone right now," I blurt out. Then I quickly add, "I mean, nothing serious." David is quiet, so naturally, I continue babbling on. "To be honest, I've been thinking about leaving New York entirely. There are some great fellowship programs in Detroit, like at Beaumont, and that's less than an hour away from my parents in Toledo. I'd really like to live close to home again."

David is silent for what seems like an eternity. I'm squeezing my hands into fists so hard that my fingernails are biting into my palms.

"That would be awesome, Em," he finally says. "You should definitely come back."

I inhale sharply. "You think so?"

"Definitely," he says. He adds softly, "I didn't think you should've left in the first place."

Yeah, my bad.

We say our goodbyes, but I can tell something has changed between me and David. Before it was all just speculation, but now it's obvious that he wants me to come home. He wants me back. And I want him back too.

I mean, I'm pretty sure I do.

———

It's no surprise that when I get to the Mexican restaurant ten minutes late, Holly still hasn't arrived. Holly is chronically late to social events. Usually when we say we're going to meet at a certain time, I tack on about 15 minutes to that time in my head. She's so consistently late, that it's almost like she's on time. But when she has her baby, I may have to do some adjustments. I'll probably end up having to add like three hours or something.

Holly arrives about 18 minutes late, and I've already been seated at our usual table. She's wearing a black maternity top that shows off how excited she is to finally have big breasts. I haven't seen her in anything but scrubs in a while, and it kind of surprises me how big she's gotten. Holly is seriously pregnant. Not that it should come as any surprise because I've done ultrasounds on her myself, but it's just weird to see my friend with a big belly like that.

Holly plops herself down across from me and sighs dramatically.

"I'm out of breath," she announces. "I have literally walked for two blocks and I am out of breath." She pauses. "Isn't that the most pathetic thing you've ever heard?"

To be honest, Holly is a somewhat whiny pregnant lady. Even though her pregnancy was planned, she doesn't seem to be enjoying any aspect of it. First it was the nausea, which was so bad that she had to take medications for it, and one day she vomited so much that we had to hook her up to an IV and give her some fluid so she could finish her clinic. Then she started complaining about back pain shooting down her right leg. And now she's all about the shortness of breath.

It's possible that I haven't been the most sympathetic friend in the world. It was her choice to get pregnant during residency, after all. Plus, when you're a single, 30-year-old female who doesn't even have a boyfriend, it's hard to look at your pregnant best friend who has a fantastic, doting husband, and say, "Oh, poor you."

But I'm feeling so good about David right now that I'm willing to be as sympathetic as Holly wants me to be.

"That sucks," I say.

Holly, encouraged by my comment, puts her sandaled foot on the chair between us.

"And look at this," she says. She pushes her thumb into the skin of her ankle. When she pulls away, you can see the indentation she's left behind. "I have pitting edema!"

"Pretty soon your feet won't even fit in your sandals," I say.

"I'll have to wear paper bags to work," Holly says.

We share a giggle at the idea of Holly working through her shift in Baby City with two brown paper sacks tied to each ankle. It seems like the kind of thing she might do.

The waiter comes by to take our order: a strawberry margarita for me and water for Holly. I don't think I've ever seen Holly drink plain water before.

"Not even a Coke?" I ask her.

"I read a study that caffeine in late pregnancy can contribute to colic," Holly says. "I figure I better stick to water, just to be safe."

"So are you subsisting solely on water now?"

Holly points to her belly. "You think I got this ginormous by drinking only water?"

Okay, I wouldn't say it to her face, but Holly has definitely gained a little too much weight. She's always been a bit on the chubby side, and it's obvious she put on more weight than she should have. It's going to be a bitch for her to lose it later.

But you never, ever say that sort of thing to your best friend.

Our drinks arrive and I take a long swig of my margarita. I've already decided I'm going to order a second tonight. I do have to work tomorrow, but these margaritas are pretty weak. I'll be fine.

"So," I say to Holly. "Are you busy on September 15th?"

Holly suppresses a smile. "Why do you ask?"

"No reason," I say coyly.

We both know that I am planning a baby shower for Holly. As the best friend, it's basically my job. We are both so busy these days that there's really no way to completely surprise her. So she's pretending not to know, and I'm pretending it's not completely obvious that she knows.

"I'm free," Holly replies. "The whole day. No plans at all."

"Okay, great," I say. "I just wanted to make sure that your social life is as pathetic as mine."

Holly sticks her tongue out at me. "Oh, stop it, Emily. You could have a boyfriend anytime you wanted. You know that."

"That is definitely not true." I shake my head. "And anyway, I don't want just any guy."

Holly's ears perk up. "Is there someone in particular you have in mind?"

I bite my lip. I usually tell Holly everything, but I've been avoiding telling her about David. I mostly was worried that it would work out, and I didn't want to look pathetic if it didn't. I mean, there's nothing worse than trying to get your ex-husband back and failing. But now that things are going so well, I guess it's okay.

"There is sort of someone," I tell her.

Holly's whole face lights up the way it always does when she's about to hear a new piece of gossip. Holly doesn't have a pregnant glow, but right now she is definitely glowing.

"Emily Lauren McCoy! Tell me the name of your young gentleman caller!"

I take a deep breath. "David."

Holly's heard enough about David that she immediately knows who I'm talking about. And I'm not thrilled about the way her face falls.

"You mean your ex-husband?"

I nod.

"But…" Holly furrows her brow. "You didn't even *like* him."

I frown at her. "What are you talking about? Of course I liked him. I *married* him, didn't I?"

"And then you divorced him," Holly points out.

"Yeah, and that was a mistake," I say.

"Through our entire intern year, you kept talking about how relieved you were not to be married to him anymore."

Did I really? I don't remember that.

"You're exaggerating," I say, rolling my eyes. I take another long sip of my margarita. "David is interested in getting back together and I think I want to also."

Holly starts to say something else, but before she can, I add, "And if you were a supportive friend, you'd be happy for me."

I don't point out the obvious, which is that it's easy for Holly to be judgmental when she has everything.

Holly lifts her chin. "As long as you're happy, I'm happy for you."

And that's what best friends are for.

Chapter 23

I start out the next morning by having a fight with the patient. Always a good sign of things to come.

Mrs. Morgan is 13 weeks pregnant. She showed up to Triage complaining of cramping, but no bleeding or spotting. She's completely freaking out over this fairly benign symptom, which makes me think that the next 27 weeks are going to be rough. For us.

"I don't know what to say," I tell her. "You're not having any contractions, at least not here. The baby's heart sounds fine. Your cervix is closed. And you said there's no bleeding, right?"

"There's something wrong," Mrs. Morgan insists tearfully. "I know my body, Dr. McCoy."

I hate it so much when patients say "I know my body." Guess what? Nobody knows their body that well. That's why we have all these tests to monitor the pregnancy. Women have no idea when their baby is in distress.

"We can get an ultrasound," I offer.

Mrs. Morgan looks somewhat mollified. "Right now?"

I brace myself. "The hospital doesn't do them on Sundays. You can come in first thing tomorrow morning though."

Those lucky bastards in ultrasound get Sundays off. I wish I were an ultrasound tech right now.

"But that will be too late!" Mrs. Morgan exclaims.

I shrug helplessly. "I don't know what else to say…"

"What about an hCG level?" Mrs. Morgan asks.

"That wouldn't really tell us anything," I explain.

Mrs. Morgan sniffs. "Well, it would tell us if the pregnancy was progressing."

No, it wouldn't.

"The test isn't really informative at this point in your pregnancy," I try to tell her. "The hCG level declines at a completely variable rate during second trimester."

And that's when the fighting begins. I patiently try to explain to Mrs. Morgan how unhelpful an hCG level would be, but she becomes completely obsessed with it. The more I tell her how useless it would be, the more she wants the test. I don't know why she can't trust my judgment.

"Please, Dr. McCoy," she begs me. "Just order it and I'll never bother you again."

I don't believe that for a second, but if getting the hCG level will make her happy, I don't know why I'm fighting it. I've ordered far more useless tests than that.

When I get back to The Pit, I find Jill chewing out Caroline, who apparently just arrived, nearly an hour late. Caroline is nearly in tears, but not quite.

"This is completely unacceptable, Caroline," Jill is saying.

Caroline sees me enter the room, and looks in my direction for help.

"The subway got stuck," she explains. "I was trapped in a car for over an hour."

Jill rolls her eyes, as if this excuse is completely unbelievable. I believe it, only because I don't think Caroline is capable of lying. Besides, subways do get stuck.

I cock my finger at Caroline.

"Come with me," I say. "I've got a patient I'd like you to see."

Caroline hurries after me, relieved to be freed from her confrontation with Jill. At least this time she walks next to me instead of five paces behind.

"The subway really did get stuck," she says.

"I believe you," I say.

"About ten minutes in, I realized I was standing in a puddle of urine," Caroline adds. A detail I definitely did not need to know. "And the worst part is that you know it must've been *human* urine. Because dogs aren't allowed on the subway."

"Great story, Caroline," I say.

She smiles. I think she may have missed the sarcasm.

I stopped with Caroline in front of Triage Room 3, which contains Ms. Ingram. I had flipped through Mrs. Ingram's chart earlier, and the second I saw the bipolar diagnosis, I decided this was a patient for Caroline. If this woman is bipolar and pregnant, she is almost certainly off her medications. And therefore completely batshit crazy.

And therefore a great patient for Caroline to deal with. She has the time to hold the hand of a crazy pregnant woman and I don't.

I leave Caroline at the door to Ms. Ingram's room, and return to The Pit. Jill is updating the board with current information about each patient's progress in labor. Nobody seems close at the moment, so we've got a little bit of breathing room.

"Is Eric coming in today?" I ask her.

Jill shakes her head. "The ER residents rotating here are capped at 60 hours a week, if you can believe that."

Wow. I can't remember the last time I worked less than 60 hours in one week. I think I work more hours than that during my vacation weeks.

Jill continues writing on the board.

"By the way," she says. "I got a call about Marissa Block."

My heart speeds up a notch. "What about her?"

It would probably be too much to hope for that Marissa gave birth to a totally healthy baby.

Jill lowers her voice. "The baby died."

"Oh my God," I say.

"Yeah," Jill says.

We're both quiet, sharing a moment of mutual silent mourning for the baby. We make it through about 30 seconds of silence before a nurse comes in to grab one of us. Back to work.

———

I'm still thinking about Marissa when Caroline returns to report back on Ms. Ingram, the bipolar lady. Caroline is clutching her little notebook, which is about 50% of the size of her hand. Why did she buy such a small notebook? She could've bought one twice that size and still fit it in her white coat pocket. She looks about six years old playing detective when she's writing in that tiny notebook.

"Okay," I say. "Tell me about Ms. Ingram."

Caroline starts talking in her annoyingly chipper voice: "Ms. Ingram is a 39-year-old woman with three kids and a history of bipolar—"

"Tell me her gravida and para," I say.

Caroline looks at me like I just said something in Latin. Which I guess I sort of did. But still, she's been here a week. How does she not know this? She should've known gravida and para the first day.

"You don't know what gravida and para mean?" I ask her.

Caroline bites her lip. "Not... exactly."

"You're kidding me, right?"

Caroline is not kidding me.

"Short version," I say. "Gravida is the number of pregnancies, and para is the number of babies delivered. The long version you look up sometime today and know it cold by tomorrow. Got it?"

Caroline nods solemnly.

I pull the story out of her in several long, painful pieces. Ms. Ingram has an extensive history of difficult to control bipolar disorder combined with heavy menstrual bleeding. For this reason, plus the fact that she already has three little kids, she decided to get a uterine lining ablation. Basically, this means she destroyed the lining of her uterus, even though it's not technically a sterilization procedure. And somehow, against all odds, Ms. Ingram got pregnant again.

Fortunately or unfortunately, at 16 weeks gestation, Ms. Ingram is starting to bleed. Because of her procedure, she's at very high risk for miscarriage. I'm concerned that this is what we're seeing.

"Do you think she'll lose the baby?" Caroline asks, her light brown brows knitted together.

"It's possible," I say.

I can't help but think of Marissa Block.

Caroline chews on her lower lip. "By the way," she says. "There's an outpatient clinic tomorrow and I was wondering if I could go. I really want to get practice doing Pap smears."

I sigh. "Caroline, you haven't even seen a baby get born yet."

Caroline frowns. "I know, but—"

"I promise you, you'll get plenty of clinic exposure during this rotation," I say. "Just be patient."

Caroline nods, although I suspect patience is not one of her virtues. Her biggest virtue right now seems to be finding patients bottles of vanilla Coke Zero.

Ms. Ingram's examining room is a zoo. Caroline told me that she had three children and she has brought all three of them along with her today. Ms. Ingram has flaming red hair and freckles, and all three of her kids have the same identical red hair and freckles. It would be cute if the little monsters weren't destroying the examining room. One of them is unraveling the white paper cover for the examining table all over the floor, a second is pulling out all the supplies from one of the drawers, and the third is pulling paper towels out of the dispenser and tossing them haphazardly onto the floor. And Ms. Ingram isn't doing a thing to stop any of this.

I clear my throat when I enter. The kids look up for a second, determine I'm nobody important, and continue on their path of destruction.

"Hello," I say. "I'm Dr. McCoy."

Ms. Ingram simply grunts in my direction. Her second tallest child, an adorable little redheaded girl with pigtails, throws a speculum at my head. It narrowly misses.

"I hear you're having some bleeding," I say.

"Body's rejecting the alien species," Ms. Ingram explains.

Okay then.

"What do you mean?" I ask carefully.

"I had my uterus wiped out, but I still got pregnant," she says. "So it ain't no human baby. Pretty sure it was an alien that knocked me up."

I flip through her chart, mostly for show.

"The baby looked human during your last ultrasound."

I act like this is something that was specifically noted: *Baby appeared human during sonographic assessment.*

"Well, 'course it would *look* human," she snorts.

Of course.

I need to check on how the fetus is doing. I start pulling out the Doppler from the upper cabinet, which thankfully the little monsters have not been able to reach. Ms. Ingram's eyes widen when she sees it.

"Oh no," she says. "You ain't getting those x-rays near me."

"It's not x-rays," I explain patiently. "This is the Doppler to listen to the baby's heart. It works by using sound waves."

"It's all the same thing," she says. "I'm not going to fall for that."

This lady is completely nuts.

"Are you taking any of your medications for your bipolar disorder?" I ask her.

"I can't on account of the alien baby," she says.

Okay, no surprise there.

"What medications were you on before?" I ask.

Ms. Ingram starts ticking off medication names on her stubby fingers. "Lithium, Depakote, Zyprexa, Tegretol…"

Whoa. If she was on all those medications at once, she must have pretty severe bipolar disorder. And now she's just running free, unmedicated, having outright delusions about alien babies, while simultaneously caring for three small children. This is frightening.

"Would it be all right if I do a pelvic exam?" I ask.

Ms. Ingram nods. Without asking her kids to turn their heads or go to the corner of the room like some women do, she just starts pulling off her underwear. She's wearing a maxi pad and I can see that it's completely drenched in blood. This is definitely not a good sign.

It's hard to even see much with the speculum because there's so much bleeding. I do a manual exam and her cervix is three centimeters dilated. At 16 weeks, Ms. Ingram's fetus is far too young to survive being born right now. It seems likely that she's going to miscarry at this rate. I can't even tell for sure if the baby is alive anymore, considering she won't let me check the heart with the Doppler.

Miscarriages are incredibly common. By some estimates, about a third of pregnancies end in miscarriage. But most of those miscarriages happen very early in the pregnancy. Ms. Ingram is in her second trimester, which means the miscarriage is a much bigger deal. She's already obviously lost a lot of blood and there's the potential for hemorrhage. I can't let Ms. Ingram go home while she's bleeding like this.

"I'd like to admit you to the hospital," I tell her.

"The aliens won't like that," Ms. Ingram says. "It's harder to get to me in the hospital."

"Why do they need to get to you?" I ask.

"To take the baby back to their home planet," she replies, like I'm an idiot for even asking. I sort of feel like an idiot for asking.

I glance at Caroline, who is amazingly managing to keep a straight face through all this. I turn back to Ms. Ingram.

"Don't worry," I say. "We have our own hospital spaceship that protects the hospital and all the patients in it from alien threats."

Ms. Ingram's eyes narrow at me. "You do?"

I nod solemnly.

"What's your spaceship called?"

"The, um…" I bite my lip. "The Starship Enterprise."

Ms. Ingram looks at me suspiciously. "You ever been on this spaceship?"

"Oh, sure," I say. "Lots of times."

"Dr. McCoy is the main physician for the Starship Enterprise," Caroline speaks up. "If you don't believe us, you can check that out on Internet, if you'd like."

Actually, I really hope she doesn't do that. Because I'm pretty sure any investigation into the Starship Enterprise will reveal that Dr. McCoy was actually a man named Leonard.

But somehow this seems like enough to satisfy Ms. Ingram. I even manage to extract a promise from her to call the kids' father to come get them. And hopefully keep them for the remainder of her pregnancy.

Chapter 24

Dr. Shepherd's our attending today and she's not pleased with me right now. As we talk on the phone, I can almost feel her irritation.

First, I admitted Ms. Ingram with three unsupervised children in her care. That's bad enough.

Second, she seems flabbergasted when I tell her that Ms. Ingram has not permitted us to monitor her pregnancy in any way.

"So you don't even know if the fetus is still alive?" Dr. Shepherd asks incredulously.

"No," I admit. "She won't let me check."

Dr. Shepherd sighs her "if you want to do something right, you've got to do it yourself" sigh. I've disappointed her yet again.

"I'll be down in a few minutes," she says.

Dr. Shepherd trusts us about as far as she can throw us. Actually, she could probably throw us pretty far. So she probably trusts us less than she could throw us.

About five minutes later, Dr. Shepherd is striding onto the ward. As usual, she's wearing heels, despite the likelihood that she may have to go into the OR today and also the fact that she's about a million feet tall even without the heels. With the heels on, I have to really crane my neck to look up at her.

"Where is Ms. Ingram?" Dr. Shepherd asks.

I point in the direction of the room where Ms. Ingram is staying. My heart sinks when I see that the three little monsters are still in the room with her. Moreover, the nurse must have given them cups filled with ice, because there is ice literally over every inch of the floor and every surface of the room. I have to walk carefully to avoid slipping and Caroline is holding onto furniture. Dr. Shepherd with her heels is likely in mortal peril.

Ms. Ingram gets that suspicious look on her face as soon as she sees the new visitor to the room.

"Who are you?" she asks.

"My name is Dr. Shepherd," she says in a voice that makes you feel like everything is under complete control. Dr. Shepherd is nowhere near as terrifying to patients as she is to us. "I'm the attending on Labor and Delivery today."

Dr. Shepherd pulls a Doppler machine out of her white coat. I hold my breath, expecting Ms. Ingram to protest. But to my complete surprise, she doesn't. I guess when you command the kind of authority that Dr.

Shepherd has, everyone does what you want. Even the psychotic patients.

I watch as Dr. Shepherd positions the Doppler over Ms. Ingram's belly. Caroline is watching also, her blue eyes as wide as saucers. Dr. Shepherd adjusts the sensor, searching all over the uterus, in every possible location. Finally, she shuts off the machine.

"No heartbeat," she announces. "I'm sorry."

I'm expecting Ms. Ingram to say something about alien babies, but instead she just nods and says, "Thank you."

Maybe somebody slipped her some lithium since I last saw her.

"I think," Dr. Shepherd says to Ms. Ingram, "the best thing to do at this time is to surgically remove the fetus from your uterus. If we don't do that, you're at risk for infection."

Ms. Ingram nods. "I understand."

"Emily," Dr. Shepherd says to me. "Set up the OR for a D&E, and get Ms. Ingram's consent."

D&E stands for dilatation and evacuation. It's a nice way of saying that we're going to dilate Ms. Ingram's cervix and suck the fetus out of her.

Dr. Shepherd strides out of the room and I'm left to face Ms. Ingram, who is now staring thoughtfully at her slightly swollen belly. "Do you have any questions for me?" I ask her.

Ms. Ingram slowly lifts her head.

"Yes," she says softly.

She's acting so serious compared to how she was earlier. If this is a question about whether fetuses go to heaven, I'm not sure I can handle that.

"I want to know," she says, "if you can get my kids more ice. I think they're all out of ice."

You've got to be kidding me.

Caroline, jumping at the chance to be useful, raises her hand. "I'll get more ice!"

I want to beg her not to, but she's already gone. I don't know what the hell we're going to do with these kids when Ms. Ingram is in the OR. But either way, I definitely don't think they should have more ice.

"Is their father coming soon?" I ask as gently as possible.

As annoyed as I am about this situation, I need to be nice to this woman. She just lost a baby.

Ms. Ingram shrugs. "He says so, yeah. But he ain't so reliable."

"Is there anyone else you can call?" I press her.

She shrugs again.

I wonder how Caroline's babysitting skills are.

I've almost finished discussing the procedure with Ms. Ingram, and I'm about to leave the room for consent forms when Caroline returns, clutching three cups filled to the brim with ice. She races into the room, obviously completely forgetting that the floor is already covered in ice. Almost in slow motion, her legs slip out from under her, and then she is flat on her back on the floor.

The kids think this is the funniest thing they've ever seen. Actually, it's a little funny. I'm worried by the end of this rotation, Caroline is going have some real brain damage.

I kneel down beside Caroline, who is thankfully still conscious. "Are you okay?" I ask her.

Caroline nods yes, but I can see that her eyes are filling up with tears. As inconspicuously as I can, I help her get to her feet and lead her out of the room. She's limping slightly as we make our way to The Pit, which is empty for the moment.

The second she gets in a chair, she drops her face into her hands and starts to sob. I put my hand on her shoulder, silently wishing that Eric were here today.

"Are you hurt?" I ask her. "You need to go to the ER?"

Caroline shakes her head.

"I'm okay," she whimpers. She looks up at me with red rimmed eyes. "I'm just sad about the baby."

That was the last thing I expected her to say. "You are?"

Caroline nods. "Aren't you?"

Well, no. I'm not. I guess I would be, if Ms. Ingram had been. Or maybe I still wouldn't be. It's sad when there's a fetal demise, but I have to admit, it's not something that I would ever cry about. Neither would any one of the residents. Dr. Shepherd certainly wouldn't.

But maybe we're all just heartless.

———

The D&E on Ms. Ingram is uneventful. Needless to say, Caroline sits this one out. I ask her if she wants to go and she shakes her head, and I don't push her. Picking Caroline up off the floor twice in one day is too much for me.

On the plus side, Caroline does help out the nurses to watch Ms. Ingram's three children during the procedure. When I come out, the kids are all eating fistfuls of saltine crackers. One of them is trying to eat six saltines in a minute. (Which is impossible. I've tried it.)

We have a quiet moment on the floor, so I hide in The Pit. I take out my phone and start doing a search for local funeral services under the name Marissa Block. After clicking through a few websites, I find it. Memorial service tomorrow for Megan Block, one day old. I'll be working through the entire thing.

I jot down the address of the funeral parlor, and then find the name of a florist. I dial the number, not sure what to say. I've honestly never ordered flowers for a funeral before. Actually, I'm not sure I've ever ordered flowers for *anything* before. If I ever needed flowers, I generally just bought them from one of the dozen stores selling them on the street.

"Miriam's flowers," a chipper woman answers the phone.

"Hello," I say. "I'd like to buy flowers for... a funeral."

"Oh, of course." The woman's voice takes on a more somber tone. "Which parlor is it held at?"

I read off the name of the parlor and tell her the name Megan Block.

"Oh, yes," the woman says. "That's the newborn."

"Yes," I say softly. I clear my throat. "I'd like to send a flower arrangement." Obviously.

"What you have in mind?" asks the woman.

"Um," I say. "What do you have? I mean, what's appropriate for a funeral?"

"Would you like small or large arrangement?" the woman asks.

"Small," I answer right away. Hey, I'm poor and live in the ghetto.

"Perhaps a spring arrangement of purple violets and yellow begonias," she suggests.

A spring arrangement? That sounds a little bit too cheerful. "Is that appropriate for a funeral?"

"Oh, absolutely," the woman assures me.

Okay then. A spring arrangement it is.

"And what would you like the card to say?" the woman asks me.

Card? I have to think of something to write on a card? Christ.

"Um," I say, "what do people usually write?"

The woman doesn't know what to say, probably because I asked a very stupid question. But what am I supposed to say? *Sorry your daughter died. Sorry we couldn't save her. Sorry we bullied you into being admitted and then she died anyway. Sincerely, Dr. McCoy. P.S. Sorry that I hinted that the hair growth in your genital area was unacceptable.*

"Um," I begin. "Write 'Dear Marissa, I am so sorry for your loss. Condolences, Dr. Emily McCoy.'"

Maybe I shouldn't have thrown the 'doctor' in there. But I just imagine her seeing the flowers and wondering who the hell Emily McCoy is.

"Great," the woman says.

Wonderful, she approves.

"How much will that be?" I ask.

The woman pauses, presumably looking up the numbers.

"With delivery, that will be $87."

I nearly choke. That sounds like a lot of money for a small arrangement of flowers, although I'm sure the woman thinks I can afford it now that I announced I'm a doctor. I can't remember the last time I bought anything for myself the cost that much. But somehow I feel I owe it to Marissa Block, so I read off my credit card number and resign myself to many nights of Ramen noodles and hot dog cart dinners.

———

You can always tell by looking at Caroline when she has something to say. She stares at you, and then opens her mouth several times and has several false starts. That's how I know as we're gathered for our evening sign out that Caroline had something to say to Jill. I can't imagine what, considering Caroline is obviously terrified of Jill. It must be something important.

"Um, Dr. Brandt?" Caroline says finally. I'm actually a little bit proud of her for working up the nerve to say something. Even though she probably shouldn't.

Jill lifts her eyes. She's fiddling with her phone again. I'm pretty sure that whatever she's trying to do with her phone is something that Eric could help her with, but she'll never ask him again in a million years. She's especially furious with him that he gets Sunday off while everyone else has to work.

"What is it?" Jill snaps.

"Um," Caroline begins, "so Tuesday is my mother's birthday."

I don't like where she's going with this. I try to send her psychic vibes to stop talking now, before it's too late.

"Happy birthday to your mother," Jill says flatly.

"The thing is," Caroline continues, even though she really should just shut up, "I bought tickets to a show on Broadway a month ago. I didn't know I'd be on this rotation and have such late hours. The show starts at six, so I was just wondering…"

Jill's eyes fill with rage. "So you were wondering if you could leave early?"

"Well, yes," Caroline confirms. She folds her hands together and sits up straight, maybe trying to be a model of a medical student who is allowed to go home early one day. She's definitely not hearing my psychic message.

Jill looks over at me. "Emily, when is the last time you got to see your mother on her birthday?"

"Years ago," I reply truthfully.

"I just didn't know I would be on this rotation," Caroline explains quickly.

Jill nods. "Yes, but you knew that you would be in *medical school*, right? You knew you would be a third-year on clerkships. So you knew there was a decent chance you might have responsibilities on the night of the show. Right?"

Caroline is intently studying her lap. "I guess so."

"So why should I make an exception for you?" Jill says.

Somehow Caroline doesn't realize that this is a rhetorical question. She says, "It won't happen again. I promise."

"It won't happen this time," Jill snaps. "Signout is at 6 p.m. and I expect you to be there. You're going to be a doctor soon. You can't just cop out because it's your *mother's birthday*. It's completely irresponsible."

Caroline looks like she's blinking back tears. I suppose I could say something to support her, but the truth is, I agree with Jill. Leaving early for your mother's birthday? What kind of bullshit is that? I don't even get to leave early for my own birthday.

"I'm sorry," Caroline mumbles.

Jill just shakes her head.

———

When I get home that night, I just barely have the energy to boil some water to pour into my cup of noodles. I'm pretty sure that the salt content of the cups of noodles that I eat for dinner with alarming frequency will probably contribute to my stroke at some point in the future, but I can't worry about that now. I'm poor and I'm hungry.

I settle onto my bed with my cup of noodles, being careful not to spill it and give myself another second degree burn on my stomach. I reach for the remote control, and flip on the television. It's amazing how there are so many more channels now than there were when I was a kid, yet there's still the same garbage on. I flip off the television, and stare at the wall for a few minutes while I chew on my soggy noodles.

And then, even though I tell myself I shouldn't do it, I find myself dialing David's number on my phone. This is becoming a nasty habit.

I find myself disappointed when he doesn't answer after the first two rings. After the fourth ring, I start to feel alarmed. Then his voicemail picks up. For a moment, I contemplate leaving a breezy message about how I'm out with friends and having a great time or something less pathetic than sitting in my apartment eating noodles, but then decide against it. Too bad I can't erase the fact that I called. Surely his cell phone will rat me out.

It's a Sunday night and David isn't picking up his cell phone.

Of course, there are lots of good explanations for that. Maybe he's in the bathroom and he didn't take his phone with him (although unfortunately, I know that he always takes his phone into the bathroom). Of course, maybe he took the phone, but didn't want to talk to me while on the toilet, which I completely respect. Or else, maybe he just had the phone in his pocket and didn't hear it ringing.

I don't know why my mind keeps chiming in with the possibility that he might be out on a date.

Maybe because David is 30 years old, good looking, nice, smart, and romantic. The clothing company where he works has tons of single, young women who are probably just waiting to snap him up. They were probably giving him a respectable grieving time after our divorce before they descended on him.

The point is, if I spend my time twiddling my thumbs, trying to decide if David is the right guy for me, it might be too late.

Chapter 25

Every time I see Holly at work, she looks little bit more exhausted than the day before. When I arrive at the hospital on Monday morning, she really looks beaten-down. There are bona fide purple circles under her eyes, and she's sitting in a chair, holding her belly. I feel a twinge of concern.

"Are you okay, Holly?" I ask.

Holly nods. "Just trying to catch my breath. I'm fine."

I'm not entirely sure I believe her, but I decide to let it go. Holly's a big girl. She can look out for herself.

"Has Caroline delivered any babies yet?" Holly whispers to me.

I shake my head. "It's like she's cursed. Every patient she follows ends up needing a C-section." And of course, we're all too scared now to let Caroline into the room during C-sections.

Eric arrives wearing green scrubs, which is essentially giving the middle finger to Jill, but also makes his green eyes look really sexy. He flashes Jill a big grin when he comes in, and she doesn't return it.

"You look well rested," Jill sneers.

Eric stretches his arms dramatically. "Oh yeah, it was great having the whole weekend off."

I know he's trying to goad Jill specifically, but he's actually making all of us sort of hate him right now.

Dr. Ford is our attending for the day. He peeks into our signoff, gives Ted a quick high-five, then disappears. Nobody is going to give birth imminently, so he's got a little breathing room.

Jill assigns Caroline to follow Mrs. LeClair, who is currently four centimeters dilated. Caroline skips off in the direction of Mrs. LeClair's room, and I can see Jill roll her eyes. It's pretty certain that Caroline will not be getting a good evaluation from Jill.

"So," Eric says to me, after Jill has left to see a patient in Triage. "Did you go back to the burger place?"

"No," I reply.

I really haven't been back there. But only because yesterday after work, I searched an entire square mile radius around the hospital, looking for it. I was starving, but I really needed those burgers. I feel like I must have passed the place or something. Or maybe it's some kind of sci-fi thing where the burger place only appears to certain people.

By the end of my search, I was practically in tears. But in my defense, I was very hungry.

"Well," Eric says, "if you ever want to go back, just let me know."

"Where is it again?" I ask, as casually as I can muster.

"It's a little hard to explain how to get there," Eric says vaguely.

It's like he's holding the burger place hostage. Why can't he just tell me where it is? Damn him.

I may actually have to go with him for burgers again today.

———

The postpartum patients are particularly unpleasant today. I understand that they're in pain, their hormones are shifting, and that they're dealing with new babies, but I can only tolerate so much. Besides, I'm pretty sure that I'm still getting less sleep than any one of them.

Mrs. Everly, who is two days postpartum, is in tears when I enter the room. She's holding her newborn baby daughter and sobbing her brains out. Of course, this isn't that unusual. Everybody worries about postpartum depression, but the changing hormones after delivery can make most women pretty emotional.

"What's wrong?" I ask her.

Mrs. Everly wipes her face with the back of her hand. "This is an outrage, the way they treat people here."

"What do you mean?" I ask carefully. I think the postpartum nurses are excellent, but every once in a while, patients have complaints.

Mrs. Everly gestures at her baby, who is sleeping peacefully in her arms. "Just look at her!"

I peer closely at the baby. She looks like a totally normal, ordinary, happy newborn. Her head is a little bit squashed, which is totally normal for a first vaginal delivery.

"Um…"

"Look at the bow in her hair!" Mrs. Everly cries.

There is a little pink bow somehow attached to her baby's head. I'm not a huge fan of the bows, but I guess they're pretty cute. I've seen them on many of the female newborns. Anyway, I don't think there's anything horribly wrong with it.

"It's so ugly!" Mrs. Everly complains, wiping tears from her cheeks.

It is? It seems like a pretty normal pink bow. How many varieties of newborn bows are there out there?

"I asked the nurse this morning if she could get a new bow for Sophie," Mrs. Everly continues, "and she said she *couldn't*. That these were the only kinds of bows she has. Can you imagine?"

Yes, I can imagine only having one kind of newborn bow. What I can't imagine is thinking it's appropriate to complain to your doctor about it.

"I'm so sorry," is what I end up saying.

"You guys need to stock other kinds of bows," Mrs. Everly advises me.

"Maybe you should write a letter to the hospital about it," I tell her.

"I think I will," Mrs. Everly says.

I wish I could be the one to read that letter.

"Anyway," I say. "You're all cleared to be discharged today. Do you have any questions for me about anything?"

Mrs. Everly nods. "Before I go, can you have my baby blanket laundered for me?"

Is she serious? I think she is.

"I'm afraid not," I say.

"But it's dirty!" she cries, bursting into tears all over again.

This is going to be a long day.

Chapter 26

When I get back to the Baby City ward, I find a young man waiting for me at the nurse's station. By the looks of the anxious expression on his face, I would bet the farm that he's a father-to-be. The new dads always look the same: bewildered, frightened, and excited all at once.

"Dr. McCoy?" the man asks me, wiping moisture from his forehead with the back of his forearm. His dark hair is glistening with sweat that's dripping down into his shirt collar.

"Yes," I say.

"I'm Neil LeClair," he says. "My wife Donna is in labor."

Right. Donna LeClair. That's the woman who Caroline has been following. The one I'm hoping will give birth today so that Caroline can finally see a baby get born.

"Yes, of course," I say. "You have a question?"

Mr. LeClair nods. I notice he's got large pit stains on his T-shirt. They need to keep the Baby City rooms a little bit cooler.

"I was just wondering," he says.

"Yes?"

"When do you think that Donna is going to have the baby?" he asks. "She's four centimeters dilated right now."

I see how nervous he looks and I take a little bit of pity on him.

"I think she'll have the baby today," I say. "Or maybe during the night."

Mr. LeClair wrings his hands together. "Do you think it will take that long?"

"It's hard to predict these things," I say patiently.

Mr. LeClair sighs loudly then nods again. "I understand."

He turns away and shuffles back to his wife's delivery room, presumably to report back that he had no idea when she's going to have the baby. I hope she goes easy on the poor guy.

———

The second I'm alone in The Pit, I start texting David about what is shaping up to be a pretty awful shift. Fortunately, he's awake and texts me back. We're deep into a conversation, consisting mostly of suggestive emoticons, when I hear a voice above my head:

"Who are you flirting with, Dr. McCoy?"

I slip my phone into my pocket before Eric can get a closer look. He's standing above me, his hands folded across his chest, an amused expression on his face. I'm pretty sure he didn't see anything.

"Nobody," I say innocently.

Eric rolls his eyes. "Yeah right."

I jut out my lower lip. "As if I would tell you."

"How about this?" Eric says. "You tell me who you're texting, and I'll take you back to the burger place this week."

Oh man, he's figured out my one weakness. I want to tell him to go to hell, but even more, I really want those burgers.

"Fine," I say. "But you have to promise not to judge me."

"I can't promise that," Eric says, plopping down into a chair next to me. He folds one long leg over the other. "In fact, if you're asking me not to judge you, I'm almost positive that whatever you're going to tell me is something I won't approve of, and therefore I will definitely judge you."

He is so annoying. "Then I'm not telling you."

"I'll tell you what," Eric says. "I can't promise I won't judge you, but I can promise that I won't *say* anything judgmental to you."

"No deal."

"Oh well," Eric says with a shrug. "I guess you never get to eat those burgers again."

Damn him.

"Fine!" I say. "The guy I was texting was my ex-husband, David." I pause. "The truth is, we're thinking about getting back together."

Eric's green eyes widen and he sucks in a breath. "Okay…"

I glare at him. "You said you weren't going to say anything judgmental."

"I *didn't* say anything judgmental," he insists. "I just said 'okay.' What's wrong with that?"

"But you were *thinking* something judgmental."

He shrugs. "Well, that wasn't part of my promise, was it?"

I bite my lip hard. "You think I'm making a mistake, don't you?"

Eric stands up from his chair and looks around the room. "I'm hungry. Is there anything to eat around here? Or do I have to raid the vending machine?"

"You know," I say, ignoring his fake hunt for food. "David is my best friend. We're meant to be together."

Eric stops looking around the room and folds his arms across his chest. "Come on, Emily. That's bullshit and you know it. He's not your best friend."

"How do you know?"

Eric sits back down in his chair so he can look me right in the eyes. "Because you don't divorce your best friend."

Something about the way he says that makes all my previous reservations about David come flooding back. Three years ago, he wasn't my best friend. I resented him... I almost hated him. I honestly believe something has changed since then, but... has it really? David still has zero career ambition. I still am completely focused on my career.

Oh God, am I really making a terrible mistake?

"Would you ever consider getting back together with your ex-wife?" I ask Eric.

"Absolutely not," Eric says. But there's a hesitation in his voice. It's slight but I can hear it. Mary Kessler is a beautiful woman, and I can't blame Eric for still being a little hung up on her. I get the feeling that Mary was the one who ended their relationship, and I can't help but wonder what her reasons were.

I lower my voice a few notches.

"Can you tell me what happened?" I ask. "I mean, between Mary and you?"

Eric's cheeks flush slightly. "You really want to hear this?"

"Of course I do," I say.

He nods slowly. "Okay."

Chapter 27

Eric opens his mouth as if to say something, but before he can get any words out, there's a knock at the door to The Pit.

"Dr. McCoy?" a nurse says. "Someone would like to speak with you right now at the nursing station."

Crap.

It bothers me tremendously when patients' family members come to the nursing station, asking to speak with the doctor right away when it's clearly not a real emergency. Do they think I'm just sitting around with nothing to do but rush over to speak with them? Granted, at the moment I don't have much to do. But the family member doesn't know that. Anyway, I'm having an important discussion with Eric right now. He's about to tell me why his wife left him.

"Just a minute," I tell the nurse.

Obviously, I could come out right away. But it's just the principle of the thing.

I turn back to Eric, but it's obvious from his face that if he was about to confess something to me, the moment is lost.

"I better go," I say. *Unless you want to tell me really quick?*

He nods, looking very relieved. "Go ahead."

"We'll talk later," I promise.

"Sure," he agrees.

But I can tell he's lying. Whatever he was going to tell me, I'm pretty sure he's changed his mind.

I head out to the nursing station. My heart speeds up when I see a thin, gray-haired woman standing there, waiting for me. She's wearing a navy blue suit, and for a second, I'm scared she's about to serve me with a lawsuit or something. Can you get sued as a resident? I can't imagine what they'd try to take from me. I live in a single room in the ghetto. Are they going to sue me for the frozen pizzas in my refrigerator?

"Dr. McCoy?" the woman asks me in a clipped voice.

"Yes…" Oh my God, maybe she really is going to serve me with a lawsuit. I wish I hadn't kept her waiting.

But she doesn't. Instead, she holds out her hand to me, and I shake it. "I'm Mrs. LeClair," she says.

I'm fairly sure this woman could not be married to the young man who came out here asking about his wife. Plus she's clearly not in labor or even pregnant.

"I'm Donna LeClair's mother-in-law," she explains, probably seeing the confusion on my face.

"Oh, nice to meet you," I say.

I swear to God, if my mother-in-law is with me when I am in labor, somebody better remove her. Not that I don't like David's mother. It's just that there's a time and a place for mother-in-laws, and that time and place is not when you're pushing an eight pound baby through your vagina.

"So the nurse says that Donna is now five centimeters dilated," the elder Mrs. LeClair says. "When do you estimate the baby will be born?"

Wasn't it only an hour ago that Neil LeClair came out here asking the exact same question? Apparently, they didn't trust his answer.

I shrug. "Hard to say."

"Can you take an educated guess?" she pushes me.

I made a guess for Mr. LeClair, but I'm not feeling quite so generous right now. "I really have no idea."

"No idea," Mrs. LeClair says, turning the words around in her mouth as if she can't believe I would say such a thing. Well, believe it.

"Sorry," I offer.

"Do you think the epidural she got is slowing things down?" Mrs. LeClair asks.

"No, I don't," I say. Mrs. LeClair doesn't seem satisfied with that answer, so I add, "We could turn it off if you'd like."

And then I feel mean. Poor Donna LeClair has enough to deal with without threatening to take away her pain medications.

"I'll talk to Donna about it," Mrs. LeClair says. "What about giving her some patossium?"

Patossium? What the hell is that?

"To augment her labor," Mrs. LeClair adds, so I know this wasn't just a word she'd made up.

"Do you mean… Pitocin?"

"That's what I said," Mrs. LeClair says.

"There's no indication for it," I say. Although I suspect somewhere out there might be a textbook which lists one of the indications for Pitocin as "pushy family members." Maybe one written by Dr. Buckman.

We go back and forth a few times, arguing about the necessity of Pitocin, until my pager goes off. I say a quick thanks to the pager gods. About 99% of the time, my pager goes off at the most inconvenient moment possible. Usually when I'm on the toilet. But every once in a while, I get lucky.

"Sorry," I say to Mrs. LeClair. "I've got to get that."

For moment, I'm worried that Mrs. LeClair is going to follow me to a phone, and wait for me to be finished so we could keep discussing the benefits of "patossium." But thankfully, she goes back to her daughter-in-law's room without further fight.

———

The page actually came from Eric, who was seeing a patient in Triage while I was arguing with the elder Mrs. LeClair. He wants me to come see a patient who is 34 weeks pregnant. He's concerned that she may have HELLP.

HELLP is considered an obstetric emergency. It stands for hemolysis, elevated liver enzymes, and low platelets. It can cause horrible complications, including stillbirth, seizures, kidney failure, massive bleeding, and even death of the mother. It's not something to mess around with. If this patient has HELLP, she needs to be admitted to Baby City. Unfortunately, the only cure is delivering the baby, so we would need to induce her ASAP.

"Why do you think she has HELLP?" I challenge him, when I meet him in Triage. Despite the fact that Eric has proven himself competent and trustworthy, this is the first case we've seen since he's been here.

"We see it sometimes in the ED," Eric explains. "She's got right upper quadrant pain, her blood pressure is sky high, and her urine dip is positive for tons of protein."

"Okay," I say. He does appear to know what he's talking about, although the differential diagnosis for those symptoms also includes just plain preeclampsia. The distinguishing factors would be seen in the lab values. "Why don't you order some labs?"

"Got 'em back already," he says. "Her LFTs are through the roof and her platelets are 50. I just called Dr. Ford to let him know about the patient."

"Oh," I say. I frown. "Then how come you paged me to help you? It sounds like you did everything."

Eric grins at me. "I thought you might need help escaping from that old lady out there."

He's completely right. If he hadn't called me over here, it would've been difficult to extract myself from her.

"Thanks," I say grudgingly.

"Besides," he says, "the cafeteria closes in ten minutes and I haven't seen you eat so much as a cheese doodle since you've been here. Go get lunch."

I look up at the wall of charts for Triage patients, which has filled up in the last 20 minutes or so. Sometimes that happens—one minute you're bored, then the next you're overwhelmed. We need to start working our way through this backlog.

"Can't," I say. "Too busy."

Eric rolls his eyes. "Emily, I think your patients can wait five minutes for you to grab a turkey sandwich." I start to reach for the first chart and he says, "I checked every chart. There's nothing up there that can't wait. Come on, when is the last time you ate something?"

I don't know why Eric is so obsessed with making sure I receive proper nutrition. He's a doctor, not my mother, dammit.

"I can go a long time without eating," I tell him. "I'm an OB/GYN resident. We're like camels."

Instead of laughing at my little joke, Eric gets this really weird look on his face. He looks incredibly sad all of a sudden.

"What's wrong?" I ask him.

"That camel thing," he says quietly. "Mary always used to say…" He looks down at his sneakers for a minute then he shakes his head and looks up again. "You've got to eat," he says with new resolve.

I shrug. My nonchalance is somewhat undermined by the fact that my stomach growls loudly at that moment. Stupid stomach.

"I'm going to go get us both lunch," Eric decides.

Without waiting for a response, Eric jogs off in the direction of the cafeteria. While I watch him leave, I wonder if I should page Mary Kessler and let her know that her ex-husband is still in love with her.

Of course, I suspect she may already know.

Chapter 28

You know how people say you should eat spicy food or have sex or something like that in order to go into labor? Well, if you *don't* want to go into labor, you should get seen by Caroline. It's like she has some magic touch, where every time she sees a patient in Triage, it turns out that they are not really in labor. Whereas every patient that Caroline *doesn't* see needs to be admitted to have a baby.

It's almost creepy.

While working our way through the massive backlog of patients in Triage, I get a page from the operator. Pages from the operator usually mean somebody is calling from an outside line. It's pretty rare to get pages from outside lines on rotations in Baby City, since there's a nurse who triages possible labor patients who call from home. I can't imagine who else would be calling.

I call back the operator, and they tell me to hold for an outside call. When I hear someone pick up on the other line, I say crisply, "This is Dr. McCoy."

"Hello," a tinny voice says on the other line. Sounds like a cell phone with a bad connection. "This is Mrs. Rhodes."

I search my brain unsuccessfully. Who the hell is Mrs. Rhodes? There is nobody admitted to Baby City right now with that name.

"Yes…" I say tentatively.

"I'm Donna LeClair's mother," the woman says.

Oh. Great. I really hate the operator for putting this call through.

"How can I help you?" I ask.

"Well," Mrs. Rhodes says. "Donna has been in labor all day. We're just wondering when you think the baby will be born?"

"I don't know," I say through my teeth. Jill has mouthed off to patient's family members before and it's never a good idea. But man, I see the temptation.

"You must have some idea," Mrs. Rhodes presses me.

"I'm sorry," I say. "I really don't."

Mrs. Rhodes sighs loudly. "Maybe I should come there."

Oh, please don't. "You're welcome to if you'd like."

There's a pause on the line, followed by a muffled discussion between Mrs. Rhodes and presumably her husband about whether they should go see her daughter. Finally, Mrs. Rhodes gets back on the line.

"Do you think you could give me directions to Cadence Hospital?"

"Sure," I say. I really don't have time to sit here and give her directions, but it's easier than trying to predict exactly when her daughter will give birth. Maybe this will get her off the phone. I attempt to call up a subway map of New York into my tired brain. "Where are you coming from?"

"Memphis," Mrs. Rhodes says.

"*Tennessee?*"

"Of course."

Oh, for Christ's sake.

"I'm sorry," I say again. "I don't know how to get here from Tennessee."

"You don't?" Mrs. Rhodes sounds astonished.

"Sorry."

(I'm a doctor, dammit, not Google Maps.)

"Well, can you transfer us to somebody who can give us directions?"

I have no idea how to transfer a call. And even if I did, I can't imagine who could give directions to the hospital from Tennessee.

"Sure," I say cheerfully.

"Thank you, sugar," Mrs. Rhodes says.

I gently lay the receiver back in the cradle. Whoops, dropped call.

It's been a really long day.

When I finally get back to The Pit after we clear out Triage, I feel like my ankles are about to give out from under me. I remember when I first started medical school, having to stand for long periods of time was one of the hardest things. At the end of a long surgery, my feet and ankles would feel like they were on fire. I'm not sure if my foot muscles have gotten stronger, but I can stand a lot longer these days without difficulty. But there are some times when the amount of hours I spent on my feet catches up with me.

I feel worse for Holly though. She says that by the end of her shift, her shoes don't fit her anymore.

I collapse into a chair, and slide my feet out of my clogs for one glorious minute. Even comfortable shoes stop being comfortable after a certain amount of time.

"Emily?"

I look up and see Caroline standing at the door to The Pit. She's clutching her little notepad in her hands, her eyebrows knitted together.

"What is it now?"

That came out just a little bit harsher than I intended, but dammit, I need a minute to myself right now.

"Well," Caroline begins, "I was just in the room with the LeClairs and…"

I sit up straight. Is she fully dilated finally? I wonder where her mother is en route from Tennessee to New York.

Caroline says, "The family was just wondering when you think the baby will be born. She's six centimeters dilated."

I feel my hands ball into fists. I can almost sense my skin turning green like The Incredible Hulk.

"Caroline," I say in a low growl. "Every single person in this hospital has asked me when that baby will be born, and every single time my answer is the same: I. Don't. Know. Do you *see* a crystal ball in my hands?"

Caroline shakes her head.

"Do you think I have some psychic ability that I haven't shared with you yet?"

Another shake of the head.

"The next time that they ask when the baby is going to be born, why don't you use your brain and tell him that the baby will be born when it's freaking ready to be born."

"Okay," Caroline says in a tiny voice.

And now I feel guilty.

I sigh and drag myself to my feet. Mrs. LeClair isn't progressing fast enough, at least not enough for her family.

"Let's go break her water," I say.

"Really?" Caroline asks, sounding like I just asked her if she wanted to go to Disneyland.

"Yeah," I say. "That will probably move things along."

Caroline hurries after me down the hall to Mrs. LeClair's room. It's a room all the way at the end, which sadly has not prevented her family from bothering us. When I get inside the room, I see Donna LeClair, a small woman with mousy brown hair, lying comfortably in bed, hooked up to monitors revealing that her babies heart is going at 120 bpm (normal). Her husband and mother-in-law are pacing across the room, both of them on their respective cell phones. There's another man in the room (father-in-law?) who is sitting by the window, reading a newspaper.

The second I walk inside, the elder Mrs. LeClair snaps her cell phone closed and says, "Oh, thank God. Are you here to deliver the baby?"

Everyone in the room looks at me expectantly.

"No," I say regretfully. "I'm just going to break her water."

"Is that okay?" the younger Mr. LeClair asks. Except he's not looking at me. He's looking at his mother. The woman who thinks Patossium is an actual medication.

"I don't know if that's a good idea," the elder Mrs. LeClair says. She put her hands on her hips.

"It will help the labor progress," I explain.

The younger Mr. LeClair and his mother appear to be conferring together. I glance over at Donna LeClair.

"Do it," she says.

"You're the boss," I say, mostly for the benefit of everyone else in the room.

I'm hoping that Donna LeClair will command her in-laws to leave the room for this intimate procedure, but maybe she's just used up all the willpower. In any case, the elder LeClairs stay put. For the record, if I am ever in labor and my water needs to be broken, I want my in-laws out of the room before my legs get spread apart, for Christ's sake.

I break Donna LeClair's water using a sterile hook. Caroline is watching over my shoulder, close enough that I'm worried she might get splashed in the face by amniotic fluid. I expect the usual gush of normal, clear fluid that I've seen a thousand times before.

But unfortunately, there's nothing usual about Donna LeClair's amniotic fluid.

Chapter 29

A newborn's first bowel movement has a medical name: meconium. Since fetuses don't eat meals, the meconium is made up of all sorts of things that were swallowed over the course of the pregnancy, including hair, skin, etc. Usually it's dark, sticky, and pretty disgusting. (In general, once the meconium is gone baby bowel movements are not that disgusting until they start eating solids.)

In some cases, the baby passes its first bowel movement before it is born. In a practical sense, this means that the baby has a chance of inhaling the meconium. As you can imagine, inhaling your own feces is bad. It can cause pneumonia in the newborn. Usually if we see any signs of meconium when we rupture the membranes, we make sure to have the newborn suctioned immediately after birth.

It's clear that Donna LeClair's baby has already passed his meconium. But this isn't any normal meconium. This is the thickest, darkest, stickiest meconium I have ever seen. And the fetus has been surrounded by it.

Almost on cue, an alarm goes off. The baby's heart rate has dropped to the 60s.

"What's wrong?" the elder Mrs. LeClair asks me.

"Let me just reposition her," I say.

I pull off my gloves, which are soaked in meconium, then grab Caroline by the arm.

"Hey," I say to her in a low voice. "Send in Mrs. LeClair's nurse. And page Dr. Ford and tell him to come down here. Now."

Caroline nods and hurries off. For a second, she slips on some amniotic fluid, and I'm scared she's going to be flat on her face again. But she manages to right herself, and then off she goes.

The nurse and I work together to get Mrs. LeClair repositioned. I place a clip on the fetus's scalp, to get a more accurate heart rate. It is still very low. I think the LeClairs are going to get their wish. This baby is going to get born right away.

I explain to the LeClairs the need for emergency section and quickly obtain their consent. As soon as the OR is ready and Dr. Ford arrives, we're going to do the C-section. Considering everything that's happened, things are going smoothly. But we've got to get the baby out of Donna LeClair ASAP.

As I come out of the room, I see Caroline standing at the nurses' station.

"Dr. Ford says he'll be here in two minutes," she says.

"Great," I say with a sigh of relief. I look down and see Caroline's hands are trembling slightly. I guess this was nerve-racking for her as well. I decide to throw her a bone. "You did a good job."

Caroline smiles wryly. "All I did was call Dr. Ford."

"Still," I say, even though she's right. I bite my lip. "Are you going to scrub into the C-section?"

Caroline shakes her head. "I probably shouldn't. I'm bad luck."

"Who told you that?" I ask. I hope it wasn't me.

"I overheard the nurses say it," Caroline says.

"You probably misunderstood."

"They said, 'That medical student Caroline is bad luck.'"

"You have to have thicker skin than that," I say. "Come on, come to the C-section."

Caroline just shakes her head.

And to be honest, I'm relieved. That girl is bad luck.

———

Donna LeClair's baby is delivered by C-section without further incident. The baby is a little bit blue when he comes out, but then lets out a great big scream, and his Apgar score at five minutes is a respectable nine. I fully expect a hundred calls in the next few days about when mother and baby will be going home.

There is a wonderful cool breeze in the air when I get out of the hospital. Considering how muggy it usually is, I feel like I need to savor this rare burst of good weather. I rip out the elastic holding my hair in a ponytail, and shake my dark hair free, letting the wind run through the strands. I close my eyes for a moment and just enjoy the feel of it all.

Unfortunately, when I open my eyes, Eric is standing in front of me smirking.

"What you doing?" he asks.

"Nothing," I say quickly. I feel a rush of heat flow into my cheeks. Never underestimate my ability to make myself look like an idiot in front of a cute guy.

He cocks his head at me, looking thoughtful.

"What?" I say, feeling mildly irritated.

"I like your hair down," he says with a grin. "It's sexy."

I can't even manage to meet his eye as I quickly pull my hair back into a ponytail. I'm not even sure why I do it exactly, especially because it only makes Eric laugh at me.

"Burgers?" he asks, raising his eyebrows.

As much as I've been craving those burgers, food is the last thing from my mind right now. My conversation earlier with Eric has made me all the more resolute to work things out with David. I've decided that as soon as I get home, I'm going to tell David that I'm moving back to Ohio.

Before I can change my mind again.

"Not today," I mumble.

"Oh." His face falls. "Okay. Maybe… tomorrow then?" When I hesitate, he adds, "Or this weekend?"

Oh my God, is he asking me out? Is that what this is?

Not that Eric isn't incredibly cute and even apparently available, but this just isn't the right time. I've made a decision about David. I'm not going to start over with somebody new right now.

Noticing the expression on my face, Eric quickly says, "I mean, I know you love those burgers. I don't want to deprive you or anything."

I smile at him. "Yeah, maybe tomorrow."

Eric really isn't a bad guy. As soon as things are settled with me and David, I fully plan to call Mary and talk to her about him. It's so obvious that he still in love with her, and it's not fair that he should be pining like this over her. Maybe I can help them get back together. It would be good payback for letting him take the fall for the Nair incident.

———

Despite the fact that I haven't eaten anything since the turkey sandwich Eric brought me for lunch, I have zero appetite when I get home. All I can think about is the phone call I need to make to David. I can't even think about food, even frozen pizza, until I talk to him.

Losing your appetite is a sign of love, right?

I flop down on my bed to make the call. After three rings, I nearly lose my nerve, but then he picks up. His voice sounds so sweet and familiar. This is the guy I fell in love with a decade ago. And I still love him, really. We're going to make this work. I won't blow it this time around.

"Hey, Em," he says. He sounds thrilled to hear from me. "I… I was hoping you would call."

"Then I'm glad I did," I say. I try to smile, but somehow it feels forced. I wince as my stomach churns.

I hear David inhaling a breath on the other line, which is something he always does when he's nervous. I know him better than anyone in the world.

"Listen," he says. "There's something I want to talk to you about. Something important."

My heart starts pounding in my chest.

"Me too," I say.

"Yeah?" He sounds pleased. "What is it?"

"You go first," I say. David always likes to be the one to make the first move. I don't want to take that away from him. I figure I know exactly what he's going to say, but it turns out I don't.

"So the thing is," he begins, "last night, I got engaged."

What?

Chapter 30

"You... got engaged?" I must have heard him wrong. David can't be engaged. On Saturday night, we were flirting together. We're about to get back together. How is he *engaged*?

"Her name is Rebecca," David says. "She's a new receptionist at the company. We met last year and started dating, and things have just been going really well. So... it just seemed natural..."

I feel like throwing up.

"It just seems a little bit fast," I say. My head is spinning.

"Maybe a little," David admits. A tiny flash of hope. "But it also seems *right*. You know what I mean?"

"Yes," I mumble.

"Anyway," David continues, "I was really glad that you and I reconnected so that I could tell you about it myself. Becky and I talked about it, and we would love for you to come to the wedding."

David is getting married. *David* is getting married. David is *getting married.*

Holy shit.

"I think this marriage is a bad idea," I sputter.

I can't believe I just said that. I know I'm supposed to act happy for him. I know the exact words I'm supposed to say, and I can't believe the actual words that are coming out of my mouth. For a moment, I feel like I'm floating above, watching myself act like an idiot. And I'm powerless to stop it.

"You do?" David sounds very surprised. "I thought you'd be really happy about it."

"Why would you think *that*?" I snort.

"Because *you* left *me*," David reminds me. "This way you don't have to feel guilty about it anymore."

His words make me feel a little bit more in control. I get it now. David hasn't stopped loving me—this is all about revenge. David isn't marrying this Becky girl because he loves her. This is all about *me*. He wants to get back at me for ending our marriage.

I realize now what I've got to do. I've got to swallow my pride and tell David how I really feel.

"David," I say. "I made a terrible mistake. I realize that now. You and I are meant to be together."

David is quiet on the other line for a long time. "Em?"

"I want to move back to Toledo and give it another try," I say. "I still love you, and I think you love me too."

There's another long silence on the other line. It's so quiet that I can hear my heart beating. I've always been a competitive person, and right now this seems like the most important competition of my life. It's me versus her. I can beat her. I've known David since he was 19 years old, and he's been in love with me for the last decade. How can she compete with me?

She doesn't really have a chance. I'm the love of his life and he knows it.

"Emily," he says quietly. "I still care about you... maybe I do still love you even. But I don't think we're meant to be together. I mean, we want completely different things out of life. That's why you left."

My stomach sinks. No. I'm not going to lose him to a *secretary*.

"I want the same things as you," I insist weakly. "I want a house, kids, all that stuff."

"When we have kids, Becky is going to quit her job and stay home with them," he says.

I feel like he just slapped me in the face. "And that's what you want? That's all that's important to you?"

"Come on, Em," he says. "That's not all that's important to me. But it *is* important. I want to be with somebody who will put her family first."

The thing is, I know that's what David always wanted. He loved me, so he was willing to try to make it work. But it was always a sacrifice on his part. He knew that I would always be a career woman, that I would never quit my job to stay home with the children, that work would often take priority. And I knew that he hated it.

"You'd really like Becky," David says. "She's really nice."

"I'll bet," I mumble. I sound like a bitch, but I don't care.

"Don't hate me," he pleads.

And that's when I feel really pathetic. I was the one who left him, and now I'm begging to get him back. Eric was right all along. I should've just kept my dignity and moved on.

"I don't hate you," I say quietly.

And I don't. When I get an invitation in the mail for David and Becky's wedding, I'll at least send a gift. But there is no way in hell that I'm going.

———

That night, I discover David changed his Facebook status to "engaged to Rebecca Kramer." Naturally, I can't stop myself from clicking on Rebecca Kramer, and I'm immediately sorry I did. She only graduated from college two years ago (Ohio State), which makes her around 24, six full years younger than me. She sort of looks like me, but she's actually much prettier. She's a prettier, younger version of me.

David did pretty well for himself.

I spend way too long browsing through Becky Kramer's photos. So as you can imagine, I don't get a great night sleep. I drag myself to work the next morning, feeling like I got run over by a truck.

When I get to The Pit, Holly is sitting in a chair, clutching her stomach. I watch her as she breathes through pursed lips, squeezing her eyelids shut.

"Are you okay?" I ask her.

Holly opens her brown eyes.

"I'm fine," she says quickly. She looks me over, taking in my rumpled appearance. "Are *you* okay?"

"You don't *look* fine," I say, trying to ignore her question. I definitely don't want to talk to her about David right now. She won't say "I told you so," but I'll see it in her eyes.

"You don't look fine either," Holly retorts.

We stare at each other for a minute, at some sort of impasse. Whatever discomfort Holly was having a minute ago seems to have subsided.

"I guess we're both fine then," I say.

"Guess so."

I'm sure Holly is okay. She's an OB/GYN resident, after all. If she were having contractions—like serious contractions—she'd know. She wouldn't just keep doing her job, like it wasn't happening.

I mean, I'm pretty sure she wouldn't.

———

I'm really not in the mood to work today. Pretty much every baby is going to remind me of the babies that David is going to have with Becky. And about how Becky is going to stay home with them, and be this model wife and mother. A model that I could never possibly live up to.

Let's face it. I'm probably never going to get married and have kids. David was my one shot and I blew it.

My only consolation is that Caroline appears just as dejected as I do. She's been here nearly two weeks and has yet to deliver a baby. And she's fainted during two successive C-sections.

"We need to find a baby for Caroline to deliver," Jill says to me when signout is over. "She was going on and on about it this morning, and it was getting really annoying."

Jill has a point. But it's not really fair to a patient about to deliver to bring in a random medical student and say she's going to be delivering the baby. But every patient that Caroline has followed from admission has ended up with a C-section.

"I'll do my best," I promise.

At least maybe Caroline can have a good day.

I am not in a good mood today.

I keep trying to tone down the bitchiness, but it isn't easy. There are so many great opportunities to snap at people in the course of my day. I even end up yelling at a few nurses, which will undoubtedly come back to bite me.

Caroline gets the worst of it. Partially because she's the one person who doesn't have any power over me whatsoever. And partially because she is so. Freaking. Annoying. Even if I were in a good mood, it's hard not to snap at a person who follows you everywhere you go like a little shadow. I feel guilty when I'm yelling at her, but there's part of me that believes maybe it will do her some good.

As penance, I find a perfect patient for Caroline to deliver. Mrs. Oliver is pregnant with her sixth child. Honestly, by child number six, it's not even clear why she bothers to come to the hospital. You'd think she'd just deliver the baby at home, in between folding laundry. (I would imagine that with five children, she would be constantly doing laundry.)

"She said her last delivery happened really fast," Caroline reports to me, unable to suppress a smile. "She said she barely made it to the hospital in time."

"Okay," I say. "Let's deliver this baby."

Caroline's enthusiasm is almost infectious.

The attending on call today is Dr. Reichert, a petite woman who tends to be very hands-off. She'll pop in at the last moment for the delivery, and keep her hands folded in the back. I intend to let Caroline do everything.

Sure enough, within an hour, Mrs. Oliver is fully dilated and ready to start pushing. Caroline and I gown up and prepare to enter the room.

"Are you feeling okay about this?" I ask her.

Caroline only nods, apparently too nervous to even speak. I say a quiet prayer that she doesn't slip on ice or amniotic fluid, she doesn't faint, and that Mrs. Oliver doesn't end up with an emergency C-section.

Chapter 31

Dr. Reichart shows up to join us just before we go in to Mrs. Oliver's room. Dr. Reichart is one of those women who is so tiny, it's almost hard to believe she's the same species as the rest of us. I mean, I'm short, but this woman is on an entirely different level of short. And her pixie cut only makes her look tinier.

She smiles pleasantly up at Caroline, who is at least a head taller than her.

"I hear this is your first delivery," she says in her sweet little voice.

Caroline nods again.

"Good luck." Dr. Reichart pats Caroline on the back. "You'll be fine. Emily here is one of our best residents and she'll tell you exactly what to do."

Mrs. Oliver is on her back in bed, and her tired-looking husband is standing next to her, holding her hand. She didn't bother with an epidural, but she doesn't look particularly uncomfortable. She really does look like she might be able to manage a load of laundry right now, or at least within the hour.

I help hold one of Mrs. Oliver's legs and the nurse holds the other leg. Caroline positions herself in a stool, in prime baby-catching position. I can see that her hands are trembling.

Mrs. Oliver gives her first push. Even from my position, I can see the baby is crowning. Just a few more pushes should probably do it.

"Make sure to support the head when it comes out," I warn Caroline.

Caroline looks up at me. "How should I do that?" she asks.

As she's asking the question, Mrs. Oliver is giving another push. Little did either of us know, this would be the final push. Usually the head emerges with one push and the body with another. But this time, the baby slides out in its entirety in one fluid movement. And unfortunately, Caroline is looking up at me when it happens. She doesn't see the baby slip out of the mother and fall. If I had blinked, I would've missed the whole thing.

"Caroline!" I scream, my heart slamming my chest.

I can't believe that just happened.

Somehow I am frozen. Dr. Reichart races forward as fast as her tiny little legs can take her. By some miracle, the baby has not hit the floor, and instead has fallen into the pocket of the plastic drape meant to catch the bodily fluids. Glaring at both of us, Dr. Reichart snatches the baby out of the drape, and looks like she's going to faint with relief when the baby starts to cry.

"It's a girl," Dr. Reichart announces.

She's totally acting like nothing just happened, like the medical student didn't let the baby almost fall onto the floor.

I look over at Caroline, who is hanging her head. She looks miserable over what just happened. As well she should. The two of us are going to get reamed.

———

Caroline and I spend the next half hour getting screamed at by Dr. Reichart. I can't believe such a tiny little person like Dr. Reichart could be capable of such a rampage. And that she could be so *loud*. The whole thing is Caroline's fault. But I was the one supervising her, so technically, it's really my fault. But who knew she was going to look away just as the baby was popping out?

In any case, by the time we get to signout, things are pretty subdued. Every time I look at Caroline, I sort of want to strangle her. More than usual, that is.

"Only two patients currently in labor," Eric reports to Holly and Ted. Holly is sitting in a chair, clutching her belly again. Maybe it's my imagination, but Holly looks really pale.

"Are you sure you're okay?" I murmur to her as Eric tells Ted about the two patients.

"Shh," Holly says to me, keeping her eyes pinned on Eric. "I need to hear this. Ted always forgets everything you guys tell him the minute you leave."

I'm beginning to feel like Holly is avoiding answering my questions. I wonder if I can pressure her into at least letting me check her blood pressure. Maybe I can follow her next time she goes to the bathroom and surreptitiously dip her urine for protein.

"Emily?"

I feel a tap on my shoulder. Caroline is *touching* me. This girl needs to disappear. Right now. "What is it, Caroline?"

"It's Tuesday," Caroline says.

"Thanks for the update," I say and turn away from her. Hopefully, she'll get the hint and leave me alone.

"It's *Tuesday*," Caroline says again.

She didn't get the hint. "So?"

Then I remember Caroline's request from a couple of days ago. It's her mother's birthday today and she was supposed to go see a play with her. She wanted to leave early or something. But she couldn't be asking about that again, could she? It's already too late.

"There's outpatient clinic on Wednesday morning, right?" Caroline says. "Do you think I could go?"

I feel a pulse start pounding in my temple. Caroline is asking to go to outpatient clinic when she hasn't even successfully delivered a baby yet. She's *almost* delivered one, and she *dropped* it. She's got some nerve asking to skip out to have a cushy morning in clinic.

"No," is all I say.

"But I really need to learn how to do Pap smears," Caroline says. "I heard that in family medicine, one of the most important things is—"

"Caroline," I say sharply. "You're barely participating in this rotation as is." I feel my voice rise several notches. "I told you that you would get plenty of time to go to clinic, didn't I?"

"Yes, but…"

"As a third-year medical student, you need to learn how to do what you're told." My voice is just short of shouting now. "You don't get to leave early because it's your *mother's birthday* or some bullshit like that! You come in, you do your job, and you don't drop any goddamn babies!"

It isn't until I finish my little tirade that I realize that everyone in the room has stopped talking. And they're now staring at me. Like I've completely lost my mind. Caroline's blue eyes are wide like saucers.

This is so unfair. Jill throws a tantrum on practically a daily basis and nobody blinks an eye. But now I'm the crazy one? Caroline deserves to get yelled at. She *dropped a baby.* This has nothing to do with me what happened with David last night.

Absolutely nothing.

Finally, I sink down in my seat.

"Go to clinic tomorrow," I mumble to Caroline.

"No, that's okay," Caroline says. "You're right. I'll stay on Labor and Delivery all day tomorrow."

"Just go," I manage.

And then I flee from the room before anyone can see me break down.

Chapter 32

I don't cry.

I've never been much of a crier. Sometimes I'll go with Holly to some sad movie and she'll be pulling out tissues while I'm completely dry-eyed. I just don't get crying. If I have a baby someday, I definitely won't be the kind of mom who cries during the ultrasound or the birth. Not that I'm ever going to have a baby ever.

Even though I don't cry, I sit in the call room and hyperventilate for a few minutes until my fingers start to tingle. I hide in there until I'm certain the coast is clear then I slip out of the hospital. I'm not in the mood for the third degree from any of my co-residents.

I determine that hunger was at least partially responsible for my outburst, so I go to the nearest hot dog cart and get myself a hot dog with the works. I walk a respectable distance from the cart so it doesn't look like I'm being creepy around hot dog guy, and then I sit on the stoop of a random building and start eating.

I've made it through about 75% of the hot dog before Eric plops down on the stoop next to me. At first I think he's going to criticize my dinner choice, but then I realize he's got a hot dog of his own, piled high with ketchup, mustard, and sauerkraut. He takes a big bite, and for a while, the two of us sit there in silence, chewing our rat meat.

"So what was *that* all about?" Eric finally asks me.

It was too much to hope for to be able to sit in peace.

"Caroline dropped a freaking baby," I say irritably. "And *I* got my ass handed to me."

"That doesn't explain your mood the entire day," he points out.

There's another minute of silence while Eric polishes off the remainder of his hot dog. I bet his breath stinks, but so does mine. I consider denying his accusations, but then he turns his green eyes on me and my resolve weakens.

"David is engaged," I say. "To someone else."

"Mazel Tov," Eric says with a crooked grin. He quickly adds, "Sorry."

Asshole. I glare at him then stand up to leave. Eric quickly stands up too and follows me. He has to jog a bit to catch up. But he likes to jog.

"I'm sorry," he says again. "But you must realize this is for the best."

"Maybe," I mumble.

"For sure," Eric says. He sounds so confident that I can almost believe him. "I can tell David wasn't the right kind of guy for you."

I cock my head at him. "Oh really? And what *is* the right kind of guy for me?"

"Well," Eric says thoughtfully. "He should be in a profession that can understand the pressures of your career. Another doctor preferably."

I roll my eyes. "Anything else?"

"He needs to have flexible hours," Eric says. "So that he can work out a time to see you even when you're really busy. Like an ER doctor maybe."

"I see. Anything else?"

Eric grins at me. "He should have green eyes and be six feet tall."

I raise my eyebrows at him. "Excuse me?"

"Okay," he concedes. "Five foot eleven. And a half."

I have to admit, Eric's flirting is working on me. It didn't as much before, but now that David is out of the picture, it all takes on a whole new meaning.

"So where do I find a guy like that?"

"They're pretty hard to find," he says.

I smile at him and he smiles back. I feel his hand slip gently into mine, and I let him keep it there. Eric hand is warm and surprisingly calloused. I would think that a guy who's spent most of his life in school would have softer palms than that. His hands feel more like the hands of a hard laborer. It's something I'll have to ask him about later.

Eric and I walk back to my apartment in comfortable silence. Every once in a while, he'll give my hand a squeeze and I'll feel this pleasant tingling through my whole body. And every once in a while, we'll exchange excited smiles. It reminds me how very long it's been since I've been out with a guy that I really liked.

When we reach my building, I feel mildly embarrassed. Holly, who is a native, always says that there are two kinds of buildings in Manhattan: those that have a doorman and those that don't. Mine doesn't, to say the least, but I really think that there are other echelons within the doorman-less buildings, and mine is in one of the lower ones. There's a tiny green awning that sticks out and it's pretty much shredded to bits, like some angry cat was up there at some point. It takes me three tries to punch in the correct key code to get inside because all the buttons stick. That and the fact that my hands are shaking.

Eric doesn't comment though. For a moment, I wonder if he's just going to kiss me goodbye at the door to the building. But then he follows me inside, and as I climb up the three flights of stairs to my apartment, he's right behind me.

And that's when I get really nervous. Am I supposed to let him come in? I've barely known the guy two weeks. I'd like to think I could hold out longer than that.

When he sees me hesitate, Eric raises his eyebrows at me. "Aren't you going to invite me inside?"

"I don't know," I say. "You could be a rapist."

"I don't need to be a rapist," he says.

I snort. "Confident, aren't you?"

Eric is quiet for a minute. Finally he says, "I think we could both use this."

I swear, I really wasn't planning to invite him in. But something about what he says changes my mind. Maybe it's the way his voice breaks slightly on the word "both." Just like me, Eric has been through a lot lately.

"Okay," I say.

Before we can even quite make it through the door, Eric presses his lips against mine. He laces his fingers into my hair, which falls loose from the messy ponytail I had tugged it into this morning. As he pulls me closer, his five o'clock shadow grazes my chin.

The one kiss lasts for hours, or possibly more like five minutes. But it feels like hours. When we separate for breath, I hear him whisper in my ear: "I've been wanting to do that since the first day I met you."

He kisses me again, this time running his hand along the small of my back, up my spine, and between my shoulder blades. I allow my own fingers to slide along his upper arms, up to his shoulders. I have to admit, Eric may be lanky, but he has some really solid muscles in his arms and chest. David was never much for the gym, and at the end of our relationship, he was getting downright doughy. These nice hard muscles are something new and exciting. And sexy.

I find my right hand snaking under the hem of Eric's blue scrub top. My fingers thread into the hair leading from his belly button up to his chest, and before I can stop myself, I'm clumsily attempting to lift his shirt over his head. He pulls away for a split second, looking some combination of surprised and pleased.

"You want me to take my shirt off?" he asks.

"Yes, please," I say breathlessly.

Eric doesn't have to be told twice. He rips his shirt off, practically splitting the seams in his eagerness. His chest is… well, it's sexy. Lean and muscular—an athlete's chest.

"Now you," he says. He adds, "It's only fair."

I pull my own scrub top over my head, and I hear Eric suck in a breath. He kisses me again, even more deeply this time, and I'm vaguely aware that we're drifting in the direction of my bed. Or maybe we're not drifting. Maybe he's leading me. Or maybe I'm the one leading him. It doesn't really matter at this point.

I think we could both use this.

———

Here's my confession:

Up until today, I had only been with one man. Just David. I met him early in college and he was my first. And then after we broke up, I never liked anyone enough to get past the kissing phase. Even the kissing phase was kind of rare.

So David is all that I'm used to and all that I know. Honestly, that was something that used to bother me when things weren't going well with David. Sex with him was so *routine*. He never wanted to try anything new or different. I felt resentful of him for keeping me from all these exciting sexual experiences I thought I might have with other men. But then after our divorce, I missed the familiarity of being with him. We knew each other so well. He knew all the places I liked to be touched, and I knew what he was going to do before he did it. There's something very comforting and lovely about that.

Eric doesn't know me nearly as well. But what he lacks in familiarity, he makes up for with enthusiasm. Eric definitely gets an A+ for enthusiasm. Actually, he gets an A+ for a lot of things.

"Oh my God, that was great," Eric says as he lies next to me in bed after it's over. He's just staring at me, a happy, dopey expression on his face.

I nod. I'll agree with him verbally as soon as I can catch my breath.

"Really great," he says again. He props himself up on one elbow. "Can I confess something to you?"

Oh no. He's about to ruin it somehow. I hope he's not going to confess that he, like… dresses up in women's clothing or wants me to pee on him or something. I don't think I could be okay with that.

"Um, okay…"

Eric smiles crookedly. "That was my first time since… you know, since Mary."

I almost let out a sigh of relief. "Me too," I admit.

Eric's eyes widen. "You were with Mary? Wow, that's hot."

I smack Eric in the arm and he laughs. Truthfully, it's hard to imagine why Mary would've left him. He's great. I think she made a big mistake. Well, her loss.

David was always the kind of guy who would roll over and go to sleep after we were done, but Eric seems to have sudden boundless energy.

"I'm starving," he says to me. "Are you hungry? I'm really hungry." He thinks for a minute. "I'm going to make us dinner."

Before I can stop him, Eric slips on his boxers and heads towards my tiny kitchenette. He looks at my crappy stove in absolute amazement for a moment, before throwing open the cupboards and refrigerator. I just admire his lanky but muscular chest from afar. He really does have a sexy chest. For some reason, I find it strangely adorable that he has freckles on top of his shoulders.

"Emily," he says. "You have no food."

"I have food," I protest.

"You literally have no food," he says. "What do you *eat* every night?"

"I have pasta in the cupboard."

"Right," he says, shaking his head. "But you have no sauce. What are we supposed to have on the pasta? Ketchup?"

I stick my tongue out at him. "What's wrong with pasta and ketchup?"

Eric bounces back towards me. He kisses me on the lips, possibly a little more deeply than he had initially intended.

"I'm ordering a pizza," he decides. "And then on Saturday night, I'm taking you out to dinner. Someplace amazing."

I bristle slightly at his presumption. "What if I have plans for Saturday night?"

"Are you on call?"

"No."

Eric grins. "We're going to have a great time."

I don't doubt that. I haven't been quite this enamored with a guy in a long time. Even if he is incredibly annoying.

Chapter 33

Eric stays for a few more hours, eating pizza with me in bed, followed by another session of getting hot and heavy. It's pretty awesome. I'm hoping that by Saturday I can still walk, if you know what I mean.

We'd both love to have a slumber party, but the same time, we both have to be up very early tomorrow. So just before midnight, Eric bids me a very reluctant goodbye. We're both going to be dead tired the next day.

Despite everything, Eric looks incredibly chipper during signout in the morning. Even though I feel like crap, his enthusiasm makes me feel little bit better. Because it's obvious that the reason he's feeling so good is because of me.

"Mrs. Owens has been six centimeters dilated forever," Holly is saying. "I'm pretty sure she's going to be six centimeters dilated at her funeral. That baby is never ever coming out of her."

It looks like Holly had another rough night.

"I think we can get that baby out of her," Eric says. He winks at me. "Emily has a few tricks up her sleeve."

Holly looks between the two of us, and then suddenly her eyes grow wide. So much for keeping things on the down low between me and Eric. Not that I could ever keep a secret from Holly. She has ways of making me talk.

Holly just barely manages to keep her mouth shut for the duration of signout, although I can tell she's about to burst. As soon as everyone is gone, she grabs me by the elbow.

"Oh my God, Emily!" she cries. "Are you hooking up with a married man?"

"No!" I say. I lower my voice a few notches. "He's divorced."

A smile spreads across Holly face. "So you *are* hooking up?"

I hesitate for a moment then I nod.

Holly actually squeals. It's sweet that she's so happy for me.

"That's awesome!" she says. "He's so cute!"

I shrug, trying to play it cool. "He's okay."

Eric is on the other side of the floor, talking to a nurse. For moment, his eyes wander from the nurse's face, and as he catches my attention, he grins at me. I wonder if he realizes Holly and I are talking about him.

"If he's not married though," Holly says, "what's up with the wedding band?"

"He says it makes the female patients leave him alone," I say.

Although as the words come out of my mouth, I realize that it sounds kind of like bullshit. The truth is that Eric didn't take off the ring the entire time he was at my apartment. I'm not sure he *ever* takes it off. I tried not to let it bother me, tried not to think about it because we were having such a great time. But now that Holly brought it up, I can't help but be bothered by how weird it is.

"That makes sense," Holly says.

I want to agree with her, but I still can't shake the persistent feeling I've had entire time I've known Eric—that he might like me, but he's still in love with Mary Kessler.

———

Grace Miller was nine centimeters dilated and 100% effaced as of sign out. Holly assured me that Mrs. Miller will be okay with Caroline delivering her baby. It is her third, and she is pretty laid back about the whole thing.

Unfortunately, the second Caroline picked up the patient, things started to go wrong. First Mrs. Miller had a few decelerations on her heart rate tracing, but those seemed to resolve with repositioning. Then her contractions started to look funny.

"What's wrong?" Caroline asks me, leaning over my shoulder as I look at the strip monitoring the contractions. I feel her breath on my neck—she had eggs for breakfast.

"She's camel humping," I say.

Caroline looks properly horrified. I guess that sounds kind of dirty if you think about it.

"That means she's doubling up her contractions," I explain. "It's a sign of posterior presentation." I pause. "Do you know what that means?"

Caroline shakes her head no. She hasn't been able to answer one question I've asked her on the entire rotation. So why break the streak?

"You know how the baby usually comes out looking down toward the floor?" I say. Or at least, she would know that if she had ever successfully delivered a baby. "Posterior presentation is when the baby comes out looking up at the sky. It's usually a tougher delivery."

Caroline's face falls. I think she can smell another C-section coming.

"Don't worry," I say. "Mrs. Miller has had two vaginal deliveries before. We'll get this baby out of her."

When I go to see Mrs. Miller, I'm struck first by how uncomfortable she looks. She had an epidural, but she's still clearly having pain. I hope she's fully dilated and can start pushing soon.

And then the second thing I'm struck by is how young Mrs. Miller looks. I check her chart and discover that she's a year younger than I am. And she's having her *third* child.

"How are you doing?" I ask her.

Mrs. Miller winces. "Not great, Dr. McCoy. It's like the epidural isn't helping that much. I didn't feel this way with my other two."

"It's because the baby is posterior," Caroline speaks up.

Mrs. Miller stares at her.

"The baby usually comes out looking down toward the floor," Caroline explains. "Posterior presentation is when the baby comes out looking up at the sky. It's a normal variation." She adds, "It's usually a tougher delivery."

I have to hand it to Caroline. She did a really good job regurgitating what I just told her a minute ago.

"Oh," Mrs. Miller says. She brightens slightly. "That makes me feel better. I thought maybe something was wrong with the baby."

I check Mrs. Miller's cervix. She's fully dilated and the baby is low in her pelvis. She's ready to start pushing. I position Caroline between her legs, despite my misgivings after what happened yesterday.

"Don't look away for a second," I caution Caroline. Because it seriously needs to be said.

Caroline nods solemnly.

For a multip, Mrs. Miller has a hard time pushing. She looks intensely uncomfortable, and it's keeping her from getting many good pushes in. Our attending today is Dr. DeAngelis, who has always been a favorite of mine. Whenever I say something to Dr. DeAngelis, she actually sounds like she's listening to me and taking my opinion seriously.

After about half an hour of watching Mrs. Miller push unsuccessfully, Dr. DeAngelis cocks her finger at me and I rush over.

"What's wrong?" I ask.

"Maybe we should cut an episiotomy," Dr. DeAngelis says.

I wince. A lot of women don't have any tearing at all with their third delivery. I'd hate to cut Mrs. Miller on purpose.

"Let's give her a little more time," I say. "Her strip still looks good."

Dr. DeAngelis nods and smiles at me. And that's why I like Dr. DeAngelis. She actually trusts me to make a decision.

And it turns out to be the right decision—Mrs. Miller's baby starts to crown a few minutes later. Caroline is in position to catch the baby, and when the newborn emerges, sure enough, she is staring straight up at Caroline with wide blue eyes.

Caroline doesn't drop the baby this time. She lifts the newborn out expertly, and for a moment, the baby just stares at all of us with those blue eyes that actually look a lot like Caroline's. Then the tiny baby lets out a tremendous wail and turns a healthy bright pink color.

"That was so amazing," Caroline breathes. She's got a big grin on her face and she's tearing up.

It's just a baby being born. Honestly, you'd think she was the one who had just given birth.

———

In the early afternoon, I get a page from the ER. When you're on Baby City, a page from the ER is usually not a good thing. The best I could hope for is that it's a woman in normal labor who got confused and went to the ER instead of Baby City. But usually they just ship those ladies up to us in a wheelchair.

"This is Dr. McCoy," I say, when I reach the ER. I brace myself instinctively.

"Emily," a familiar voice says. "It's Hillary."

Hillary Freeman is my one friend down in the ER. Hillary and I were interns at the same time and we rotated together on the medicine service. We bonded big-time, although it's hard to remember the last time Hillary and I have gone out for drinks. I think the last time I saw her socially was at her wedding a year ago.

"Hey, Hillary," I say. "What's going on?"

"This patient Elise Cooper came in at 14 weeks gestation," Hillary says. "She was in a fender bender and is now having some back pain and spotting. I can't find a heartbeat. The patient says everything was normal at her OB/GYN appointment two weeks ago."

Crap. I hate second trimester miscarriages. They're always heartbreaking.

"Okay," I say. "I'll be down soon."

"You're the best," Hillary says.

I'm about to hang up the phone when a dangerous thought suddenly occurs to me. Before Hillary can disconnect, I call out, "Wait!"

Miraculously, Hillary hasn't hung up yet. "Yes? What's up?"

I grip the phone a little tighter. "You know Eric, right? Eric Kessler?"

I assume that since they're both ER residents, she must know him fairly well. I know I shouldn't do this. I know I shouldn't ask her about him. But dammit, I'm only human. This is way too tempting.

"Of course I know Eric," Hillary laughs. "Why you ask?"

"He's rotating here on Labor and Delivery this month," I explain, trying not to betray anything in my voice.

"He's adorable, huh?" Hillary says. I almost start smiling, then she adds, "Stay far, far away, my dear."

Oh no.

Chapter 34

"Oh my God, he's *married*, isn't he?" I nearly scream into the phone.

My heart sinks in my chest. I knew he was too good to be true. Someone that cute and charming had to be married.

That rat.

"I knew it!" I rant. "I *knew* that asshole was lying!"

Except obviously I didn't know. I completely fell for his lies. I'm such a gullible loser. And now I'm an adulterer. I've broken one of the Ten Commandments. Isn't that, like, the worst thing you can do?

I better not build any false idols.

"Um," Hillary says. "I'm getting the feeling that it's a little bit late for any warnings."

"He swore to me that he wasn't married," I say miserably.

Oh God, what if Mary Kessler confronts me in the hospital? That would be so mortifying. Maybe I should call her and apologize preemptively. And bust Eric's cheating ass. He deserves it for flirting with me and sleeping with me and tempting me with those delicious burgers.

It's not my fault. It was the *burgers*. They clouded my judgment.

"Calm down, Emily," Hillary says. "He's not married."

"He's not?" I feel my pulse slow down slightly.

This is a good thing. But it doesn't explain her ominous warning.

"No. He's not."

"Well, that's okay," I say. "I don't mind that he's divorced. I am too."

"He's not divorced either."

I frown, confused. "He's separated?"

Hillary sighs. "You really don't know?"

Yeah, I think it's pretty obvious that I don't. "Know what?"

Hillary lowers her voice several notches.

"Emily," she says. "Eric's wife *died*."

What?

"Are you serious?" I squeak. "Mary Kessler is dead?"

"Yes," Hillary says, still speaking in a hushed tone. "About a year and a half ago."

Holy shit. Actually, that explains a number of things.

Now that she says it, the dead surgery resident story does ring a bell. I think I was away on a rotation at another hospital and heard it through the grapevine. I never did hear the resident's name.

"What happened to her?" I ask.

Hillary lets out a breath. "It was super sad. Eric and Mary were one of those couples that you sort of hate because they're so into each other. They did practically everything together. They even dressed alike. Well, I guess they had to because they both wore scrubs, but there was definitely some color coordination going on. I'm sure of it."

I know what she's talking about. I hate couples like that. And I can just imagine Eric being half of one of those couples.

"Mary was really into doing all this charity work," Hillary continues. "She used to volunteer at the free clinic all the time and she even went to Haiti to help out there after the earthquake. We used to tease Eric about it... we called her St. Mary. He knew she overdid it a lot though, and he used to laugh about it too. Anyway, the two of them were running this marathon for some kind of charity. I don't know what it was—I think Mary bulldozed me into donating a few dollars, but I wasn't really paying attention. Something about kids and leukemia maybe?"

"Yeah, maybe," I say. I had forgotten Hillary's tendency to babble. I have to bite my lip to keep from yelling at her to get to the part where Mary dies.

"Anyway," Hillary says. "So Mary and Eric are running this marathon, and about at the halfway point, Mary collapses. Sudden cardiac death."

I clasp my hand over my mouth. "That's awful…"

"It really was," Hillary says softly. "Apparently, Eric did CPR on her on-site. They had an AED and he hooked it up, but she didn't have a shockable rhythm. He was the one who intubated her and rode with her in the ambulance, and they brought her right here. But by that point, she was already getting cold." Hillary's voice breaks slightly. "Eric looked terrible when they got here. He was crying and… it was very hard to watch. We kept working on Mary for a little while, even though she was dead, mostly for his sake."

"Did they figure out why she collapsed?" I ask. It's probably not appropriate to ask, but I can't help myself. Doctors always want to know how someone died.

"Hypertrophic cardiomyopathy," Hillary says. "The most common cause of sudden cardiac death in young athletes, right? Not much comfort though."

"Guess not," I say.

"Anyway," Hillary says. "Long story short, Eric was never the same after that. Mary was actually scheduled to go on this six-month trip to Bolivia, where she was supposed to be helping out at a free hospital. Eric went in her place, and he spent nine months there. I think he ended up helping to build a new hospital with his bare hands."

Well, that explains the calluses on his palms.

"Then when he came back," Hillary says, "he was just a lot different. Eric was always a lot of fun before, always joking and up for a good time. But when he came back from Bolivia, he was sort of acting... well, kind of like Mary. Really judgmental, very serious, spending every free minute he had helping out at the free clinic. Some people started calling him St. Eric behind his back."

Hillary's story is ringing true, at least somewhat. I can't help but remember how guilty Eric had made us feel about the things we said about Marissa Block. But he's lightened up since then. Of course, that was only a couple of weeks ago.

"I feel bad saying all this," Hillary says. "I mean, Eric is a really nice guy, and I don't want to jeopardize any... potential relationships of his. But you're my friend too, Emily, and I really feel like he's got pretty deep-seated issues that he hasn't worked through quite yet."

"What you mean?" I ask. Even though I already kind of know what she's going to say.

"He's still in love with Mary," she says.

Yeah, that's pretty much what I figured.

"That's why he still wears his wedding ring," she says, "even though she's been dead a year and a half. He can't seem to get over it."

I don't know what to say. I manage, "Oh."

"Maybe in another year or two," Hillary says.

"Yeah," I mumble. "Listen, I've got to go. I'll be down to see that patient soon."

"Great," Hillary says, although her usually chipper voice is subdued. "Sorry, Emily…"

"Yeah," I say again, before I hang up the phone.

I just sit there in The Pit for a few minutes, simultaneously feeling sad and pissed off at Eric. I honestly can't decide. On the one hand, he's been through a lot. I can't imagine what it must be like to see your wife drop dead right in front of you. It's definitely much worse than going through a divorce, especially a relatively amicable one like mine.

On the other hand, I feel like an idiot for believing his lies. Just because his wife died, that doesn't give him an excuse for playing me. He seduced me under false pretenses.

I haven't quite gotten it figured out when Eric comes bounding into the room. His face lights up when he sees me, and at that moment, it doesn't seem like he's in love with another woman. He seems to really like me. More than any man I've met since David. Maybe the best thing to do is just play it cool, pretend like it's no big deal.

Eric stops short when he sees the look on my face. "What's wrong?"

"You lied to me," I blurt out before I can stop myself. So much for playing it cool.

Eric's face falls. "Oh," is all he says. He doesn't even try to deny it.

"You told me you were *divorced*," I say.

His "oh" doesn't appease me. I want him to admit that he lied.

"No, I didn't," he says weakly. "I just said I wasn't married anymore."

"You've *got* to be kidding me."

Eric sinks into the chair across the room for me. He closes his eyes for a second. When they open again, they look so startlingly green. I remember the first time I saw them, how I thought they looked like fresh grass.

"Who told you?" he asks.

"Hillary Freeman," I say. I feel irritated that he hasn't yet offered an apology.

Eric groans. "Hillary is worse than my *mother*."

"She was honest with me, at least."

"Look," he says. "I'm sorry I didn't tell you. But really, it isn't that big a deal."

"That isn't what Hillary said."

"Hillary doesn't know what she's talking about. What did she tell you?"

I fold my arms across my chest. "That you're still in love with Mary. You're not ready to move on."

"That's not..." He shakes his head. "That's not true. I swear."

I gesture over at his left hand. "If it's not true, take off the ring."

My heart is pounding as Eric looks down at his left hand, at that gold band on his fourth finger. A really sad look comes over his face. He flexes his fingers then opens them again, all the while staring at his hand.

"I can't," he finally says.

Of course he can. I've seen a few women who were pregnant and had so much swelling that they literally could not remove their wedding ring. Sometimes we had to cut it off in order to revive circulation to the finger. But Eric doesn't have that problem, presumably.

"You mean you *won't*," I correct him.

He doesn't have anything to say to that.

I stand up. I can't have this conversation anymore— I've got to go down to the ER and see this consult. As I leave the room, I look back at Eric, whose head is drooped down, just staring into his lap. I think we both recognize that our short-lived affair is over.

———

My trip down to the ER could not be more depressing. Aside from the fact that I've just ended a relationship with the one guy I really liked since David, now I have to tell a poor woman that she lost her baby.

Well, maybe she didn't. Maybe Hillary is just completely incompetent at finding a fetus's heartbeat. But I suspect that's not the case.

I take the elevator down to the ER, and as the doors open, a blast of heat hits me like a punch in the face. It's even worse down here than it was in the burger place that Eric took me to. I suspect it may be a few degrees warmer than Hell down here.

It's not just me who's uncomfortable. I see nurses walking by, fanning themselves with order sheets. One patient is in the hallway on a stretcher, and he is lying in what appears to be a puddle of sweat (I hope). In the center of the ER, where the computers are kept, there are a couple of large fans rotating. I quickly positioned myself in front of one of them, and scan the room for Hillary.

I finally spot her near one of the computers. Hillary always sort of reminded me of a chipmunk in her appearance. She's small with these big round cheeks and two front teeth that jut out just a bit. When she sees me, she wipes sweat from her forehead with the back of her hand and waves to me. I hesitate, reluctant to leave the path of the fan, but I figure seeing this consult is the only way I'm going to get out of here.

"Oh my God," I say to Hillary. "It is really hot down here."

"Tell me about it," Hillary says. "The A/C is broken. I'm about to pass out."

I feel my hair starting to stick to the back of my neck, and I adjust my ponytail. "Okay, where's this patient?"

Mrs. Cooper is in Room 8B. She was rear ended earlier today, but not seriously injured. However, because of her pregnancy and the fact that she had some spotting, she went to the ER to get checked out. Hillary brought in the ultrasound machine and found the fetal sac, but was unable to locate a heartbeat.

"She's pretty upset," Hillary says.

Surprise, surprise.

When I get into Mrs. Cooper's room and shut the door behind me, I almost gasp. I thought it was hot in the ER, but without the benefit of a fan or even a window, the heat inside this room is unbearable. It's so hot, I feel like I almost can't breathe. I have to reach out and grab onto the wall for support.

When I face Mrs. Cooper, I see she's already crying. She's young, only 24, and she's sitting with a man, presumably her husband, and he's holding her hand and crying too. It's almost more than I can take right now.

"Hot in here, isn't it?" I say in a stupid attempt to lighten the mood.

Mrs. Cooper smiles weakly. "Yes, a bit."

A bit? I feel like I'm about to spontaneously combust. But it would probably be insensitive to complain any further. Considering she lost her baby and all.

"Let's just take a look," I say to Mrs. Cooper.

Before I even lay the ultrasound probe on her abdomen, I know what I'm going to find. Mrs. Cooper's uterus just seems empty to me. I don't know how I know—I just do. But even so, I make a real effort to find a heartbeat, while the Coopers watch me with wide eyes, clutching each other for dear life. Her uterus is completely silent.

"I'm sorry," I say finally. "I can't find a heartbeat."

Mrs. Cooper starts to really sob now.

"I'm so sorry," I say again. What else can I say?

Mrs. Cooper shows no sign of calming down. I lower my head, unsure if I should give her a moment alone with her husband or try to comfort her. What eventually decides it for me is the fact that the room is so goddamn hot.

"I'll give you a moment to yourself," I say and gracefully exit the room.

I page Dr. DeAngelis and fan myself with an index card while I'm waiting for her to return my page. I explain the situation to her on the phone, and she tells me she'll come over to confirm my findings, but it sounds like the best course of action, since Mrs. Cooper is only spotting, is to perform a dilation and evacuation.

I swear to God, I sweat off about ten pounds while I'm waiting for Dr. DeAngelis to meet me in the ER. The first thing she says when she sees me is, "My, it's hot."

"It's really hot," I agree.

I can see her cheeks starting to flush with the heat. A fetal demise is a delicate situation, but I can tell she'd like to get out of here as soon as possible. As soon as she confirms that there is no heartbeat, instead of clarifying the situation to the patient, she turns to me and says, "Emily, you can handle this yourself, can't you?"

"Yes," I say, although the words are hard to get out at this point because my throat is so parched. I'd like some water, although it seems entirely possible that all the water in the ER has evaporated.

"Handle what?" Mrs. Cooper asks.

"Dr. McCoy will explain," Dr. DeAngelis says, and then she is gone baby gone.

The Cooper's both stare at me, waiting for an explanation. Maybe they think I have some miracle up my sleeve that will save the baby. I don't, obviously.

As gently as I can, I explain the procedure and how it's necessary to prevent infection. Mrs. Cooper intermittently sobs through my explanation, but I finally get their consent.

The procedure won't be done today. I checked Mrs. Cooper cervix and it's closed. I'll need to put in the cervical dilator and have her come back tomorrow. When hopefully this procedure can be done anywhere besides the ER.

So all I need to do now is insert the cervical dilator. Then I can send Mrs. Cooper on her way.

Unfortunately, as soon as I'm sitting on a stool, between Mrs. Cooper's legs, the heat starts to become truly unbearable. It's like Mrs. Cooper's groin contains a heating vent. My hands start to shake, and I'm honestly not sure I can think straight anymore.

I look up at Mr. Cooper, who is watching us anxiously. "Mrs. Cooper?" I say.

"Yes, Doctor?" she asks, with such hope in her voice that I'm worried she thought I was going to tell her that I discovered the baby was okay.

"Would you mind if I opened up the door? It's really hot in this room."

The couple exchanges looks.

"Go ahead," Mrs. Cooper says. "It *is* a little bit hot, I guess."

Despite how hot it is in the ER, there's a fan pointed in the direction of the room, and that does provide a little bit of relief. It's still suffocatingly hot, but perhaps not quite as bad as it was a minute ago.

I'm about to insert the dilator, when a sharp voice makes my hand freeze midair.

"What do you think you're doing?" the voice demands to know.

My hand jerks back. I whirl around and see the face of an angry woman wearing scrubs. She's built like a bull, with her grayish blond hair formed almost into a mullet. I glance down at her ID badge and see the title of Leslie, nurse manager.

I look down at the dilator in my hands and back at the patient. What did I do wrong? Did I "pull a Caroline" and am doing the procedure on the wrong patient somehow? Maybe this woman was never pregnant and that's why I couldn't find the goddamn heartbeat.

"You need to close the door," Leslie barks at me. "You're violating the patient's privacy."

I feel my blood pressure rising.

"It's a million degrees in here," I snap back at her.

"It doesn't matter," Leslie says.

"I won't be very long," I say.

"I'm not going to stand here and argue this with you," Leslie retorts. "Close the door right now."

I push back the stool and rise to my feet. A little voice in the back of my head is telling me to apologize, close the door, and just get this done with. But I have put up with far too much today and I'm far too hot to take any shit from this nurse. She's just a nurse, for Christ's sake.

"I am the one doing the procedure," I say through my teeth. "The patient said it's okay, and the door is going to stay open. It's not your decision."

I look at the Coopers for confirmation, but they're just kind of staring at me like I've completely lost my mind. I feel like I've been getting a lot of that lately. Oh well.

Leslie looks me up and down, sizing me up. Finally, she says, "Who is your attending?"

"She's not here right now," I retort.

Leslie gets this smirk on her face. I really don't like this woman.

"She will be," Leslie says. And she shuts the door to the room with a loud thump.

Shit. I probably should've just apologized.

I can't stop fuming as I complete the procedure on Mrs. Cooper, which takes twice as long as it should because my hands are still shaking. I'm certain I was right, but the world of medicine isn't exactly fair. It's a relief at least that Dr. DeAngelis isn't waiting for me when I get out of the room. I scribble a note for the patient and get the hell out of the ER. The real relief, actually, is getting away from that stifling heat.

I need a shower. If only there were time.

———

I spend the rest of the day on edge. Eric and I are very noticeably not speaking to one another. When we pass each other, he looks at my face, then quickly look away. At one point, I come into The Pit while he's sitting inside, and he immediately gets up and leaves.

Jill notices and seems incredibly pleased.

"Did you finally recognize what a self-righteous prick Edgar is?" she asks me.

"Eric," I mumble.

"Whatever," she says with a shrug. "Only two more weeks of that guy and we'll be rid of him. Why bother learning his name?"

I watch Eric sitting down at the nurses' station, staring absently at the heart rate tracing. I still think he's really cute. I know I can't get involved with a guy like him, that he has way too many issues. But it's very hard to just turn it off.

Jill studies my face for a minute. "Emily," she says. "Nothing happened between the two of you, did it?"

"Of course not," I snip at her.

Jill looks like she has more to say, but luckily for me (sort of), at that moment Dr. DeAngelis shows up. Dr. DeAngelis has always been one of my favorite attending and I secretly thought she might have felt the same way about me. And maybe she'd stand up for me against that mean ER nurse. But now I can see the deep crease between her eyebrows and I'm pretty sure that I'm in trouble. Stupid ER nurse.

"Emily," Dr. DeAngelis says. "May I have a word with you?"

I'm definitely in trouble.

Chapter 35

Jill raises her eyebrows at me and I just shake my head. I get up and follow Dr. DeAngelis out of The Pit, and then out of Baby City entirely. Apparently, we're on our way back to her office. That is not good news for me. The more private setting we're going, the worse I'm likely going to get yelled at.

While we're waiting in the elevator, I venture to look at Dr. DeAngelis's face. She definitely does not look happy.

"It was really hot in the ER," I offer weakly.

"We'll talk about this in my office, Emily."

Great.

Dr. DeAngelis is a relatively new attending and her office is correspondingly small. There is barely room for a single chair in front of her used wooden desk. I find myself practically smacked in the face by Dr. DeAngelis's family portrait: Dr. DeAngelis, her handsome husband, and two little girls with identical blonde curls. It feels like she's taunting me. But I guess it's not her fault that her family is beautiful.

"I assume you know what this is about," Dr. DeAngelis says to me with that crease still between her eyebrows.

I nod. "It wasn't my fault though," I say. "You know how hot it was down there. Even the patient was uncomfortable."

"It doesn't matter," Dr. DeAngelis says. "The nurse told you it was a violation of patient privacy and she was right. This was a very sensitive procedure."

"I was just dilating her," I say. "It wasn't a big deal."

"Emily," Dr. DeAngelis says in a firm voice. "You were wrong. You have to understand that. You were *wrong.*"

I feel my cheeks growing hot. I know the best thing now is to do what I should've done in the first place: "I'm sorry."

Dr. DeAngelis leans back in her chair. "I'm going to have to put a letter in your file because the nurse lodged a formal complaint."

I feel tears pricking my eyes. This is the worst day ever.

"I understand," I say.

Dr. DeAngelis narrows her eyes at me. For a moment, I wonder if she's going to ask me how I'm doing, if there's anything wrong. I'm not sure if she asked me that if I would tell her. As much as I like Dr. DeAngelis, I don't know if I want to confide the problems with my love life to a woman with such a beautiful family.

But it doesn't matter. Before Dr. DeAngelis can say anything else, my pager goes off. You can't stay away from Baby City very long.

————

When I arrive on Baby City the next morning, Ted pulls me aside before I can get to The Pit. He looks concerned.

I haven't had that many interactions with Ted yet during residency. He only started just over a month ago, and all I really know about him right now is that he nearly cut off a baby's penis during a circumcision. I'm not sure what sort of thing would concern him. Possibly having cut off another penis, I don't know.

Ted furrows his unibrow. "Listen," he says. "I'm really worried about Holly."

I raise my eyebrows at him. "What do you mean?"

He bites his lip, as if he's unsure he should even be telling me this. He's probably a little bit afraid of Holly. She seems sweet sometimes, but when she's angry, she can be a real bitch.

"She doesn't look good," he says. "I keep seeing her holding her belly and making this wincing face."

"Wincing face?"

"Yeah," Ted says. He squeezes his eyes shut and crinkles up his nose. "Like that."

"Did you ask her if she's having contractions?"

Ted nods. "She told me to mind my own business."

"Let's go talk to her," I say.

I find Holly in The Pit, sitting on a chair, her legs propped up on another chair. She's holding her belly, but doesn't look particularly uncomfortable. Still, we need to know if she's having real contractions. If nothing else, because if she went into labor at night and Ted was left all alone, it would be really bad.

"Holly," I say.

Holly sits up straight when she sees me and Ted standing there as part of her personal intervention. She purses her lips together little straight line and narrows her eyes at us.

"I'm fine," she says.

"Ted says he thinks you're having contractions," I say.

Holly glares at Ted. "Oh, did he?"

"I didn't say that," Ted says quickly. "I just said you were holding your belly and making a funny face."

"I'm going to make *your* face funny," Holly says to Ted. Whatever that means.

"Holly," I sigh. "Look, there's nobody in Triage right now. Just let me hook you up to the monitor and make sure you're not having contractions. We'll all feel a lot better."

"I'm not having contractions," Holly insists.

I hold out my hand to Holly to help her rise to her feet. She takes it reluctantly.

"This is a waste of time," she grumbles.

"I love wasting time," I say.

Holly absolutely will not allow Ted in the room when I hook her up to the monitor. I don't blame her. I wouldn't want Ted looking at my naked belly either. I get the feeling that he really might be a bit of a pervert. I'm not sure why... just a feeling I get.

"I'm just having Braxton-Hicks contractions," Holly says as I'm fiddling with the machine. "No big deal."

Braxton-Hicks contractions are irregular contractions that don't signify labor. (Dr. Ford calls them Toni Braxton-Taylor Hicks contractions and we all pretend to laugh.) Usually they are not painful and wouldn't cause you to make a "wincing" face.

"Probably," I say.

Almost immediately, the first contraction appears on the screen. Holly and I both see it. "Did you feel that?"

Her eyes widen slightly. "No..."

We don't speak. The two of us just stare at the monitor, waiting for the next contraction. It happens two minutes later. And then two minutes after that. She is having real, regular contractions.

"How many weeks are you?" I ask Holly.

"Thirty weeks," she whispers, her eyes still pinned to the monitor. She shakes her head. "Shit."

"Who is your OB/GYN?" I ask.

"Reynolds," she says. Dr. Claudia Reynolds is one of the private OB/GYN who delivers our hospital. I guess Holly wanted somebody who she could trust, but she didn't want somebody she worked with touching her lady parts. I can't blame her.

"Do you want me to call her?"

Holly shakes her head. "I'll call."

On a whim, I reach out and put my hand on top of Holly's. She turns her hand over and gives me a squeeze back.

"Thanks, Emily," she says.

I force a smile. "Just take care of yourself."

———

Today Caroline is following a patient having a natural delivery. Of course, I see many natural deliveries, and most of them have convinced me that I don't want a natural delivery. It might be okay if you've had several babies before and the baby's position is perfect, but I've seen too many women in horrible pain, screaming for an epidural when it is way too late for an epidural.

When I get to the hospital in labor, the first thing I'm going to say is, "Where is my epidural?" And they're going to give it to me, because there's *no* evidence that I'm more likely to have a C-section if I get it early. I'll bring the article proving it tucked into my pants pocket, so I can whip it out if I need to.

Of course, I don't see myself in any position to be going into labor in the near or far future.

Mrs. Talbot has chosen to have a natural delivery, and to make absolutely sure she will not change her mind, she's brought her own labor coach. These people are called *doulas*. A doula supports the laboring woman, giving emotional support and suggestions about positioning. I can see how if you're in labor, it would be nice to have a person there whose job it is to support you at all times. I've met quite a few doulas and many of them are very nice, but others can be very bossy and annoying.

I can tell as soon as I walked into Mrs. Talbot's room, her doula is the latter. Mostly because the first word she says to me are, "Lindsay does not want an epidural."

"Um," I say. I look at Mrs. Talbot. "I'm Dr. McCoy. I'm the resident working with Caroline today."

"Hi, Dr. McCoy," Mrs. Talbot says. "This is my doula, Nicole."

Nicole is probably skinnier than I am, which is saying a lot. She has wavy brown hair that goes well below her waist, and she's wearing what looks to me to be a green sheet, but I guess it's probably a dress.

"She doesn't want an IV either," Nicole says.

"Got it," I say. "No epidural, no IV."

Nicole looks at me suspiciously, like I might whip out an epidural and throw it in her patient's spine while Nicole has her back turned.

She nudges Mrs. Talbot. "Give it to her."

I frown while Mrs. Talbot fumbles in her handbag and finally pulls out three sheets of typed pages. I read the title at the top, which says, "Lindsay Talbot's Birth Plan."

I skim the list, growing increasingly irritated:

No Hepatitis B vaccine

No Vitamin K shot

Do not administer antibiotics

No antibiotic ointment in newborn's eyes

No Electronic Fetal Monitor unless necessary to save my child's life

Please do not ask me if I want pain medication, I wish to give birth without medication

Only test my dilation when I am completely comfortable and ready

Do not clamp the cord until after I have birthed the placenta and the cord has stopped pulsing

Do not suction my child unless it is necessary to save his/her life

Please immediately lay the baby on my chest so I may connect with my baby

We will take the placenta and cord home with us

It goes on and on for three full pages, single-spaced. At some point, it starts talking about what sort of stitch we should use in case of an emergent C-section. All I can think about is where I'd like to shove this birth plan.

"Sounds great," I say cheerfully. "But, just a few things I should tell you… the antibiotic ointment drops are useful for—"

"Lindsay does not have any STDs," Nicole snaps at me. "That's what they're for, aren't they?"

I take a deep breath. "Can I show this to my attending?"

Mrs. Talbot nods. "Of course. Please show it to everyone. I've given copies to all the nurses."

When I get out of the room, I'm tempted to text Holly and see how she's doing, but I don't want to bother her. Also, if she doesn't text me back right away, I know I'll get really worried. Better just leave her alone.

She'll call me if there's something to know. I'm sure of it.

Chapter 36

Through incredibly strategic planning and a little bit of luck, I manage to avoid Eric all morning. Mostly it's thanks to Jill. She sent him up to see the postpartum patients, and apparently it's a particularly needy bunch today. It takes him forever to see them all, and then she sends him in for a scheduled C-section. I don't know whether she's doing it because she doesn't want to see him, or she senses something happened between the two of us. Maybe a little bit of both.

I don't mention to anyone the fact that at about one o'clock, I find a turkey sandwich in The Pit. There's a note on it with my name on the front. The scrawl inside the note simply says, "You've got to eat." It's not signed, but I can guess who it's from—there's only one person here who would get me a sandwich. I eat the whole thing because I'm starving.

At around two o'clock, Mrs. Talbot is fully dilated and ready to push. Our attending for the day is Dr. Ford, so I call him and then go into the room to assist Mrs.

Talbot. Caroline, Nicole and Mr. Talbot are already inside with the nurse. The three of them are surrounding Mrs. Talbot's bed like an entourage, telling her what a strong, powerful goddess she is. If it were me, I'd want one of them to leave. Maybe all three of them.

As soon as I step inside, I can see how uncomfortable Mrs. Talbot looks. There is something beyond just the usual labor pain here. I start to check her cervix, but then remember her birth plan.

"Can I check your cervix please?" I asked as politely as I can.

Mrs. Talbot nods breathlessly.

I can feel the newborn's head, and I can tell right away that the head is transverse, meaning it is sideways. Mrs. Talbot looks intensely uncomfortable, and I'm starting to worry that it may be difficult for her to push, that she's in too much pain. I want to say something, but I have a feeling that this crowd will not be very receptive to it. So I join Team Talbot, and help her to push.

―――――

Two hours later, Mrs. Talbot is going nowhere fast.

My initial impression was right: she is in too much pain to give effective pushes. She has tried every position imaginable and nothing has worked. And now on top of that, she's exhausted. Everyone in the room looks ready to give up. Except for Nicole, who just needs a pair of pom-poms to complete her cheerleader act.

Even though the baby isn't close to coming out, I drag Dr. Ford into the room for help. When Nicole sees Dr. Ford, she looks incredibly mistrustful. But I don't remember anything on the birth plan about "no pervy fat guys allowed in the room," so Dr. Ford stays.

"Mrs. Talbot," Dr. Ford says to the patient. "I'd like to try a pudendal block. I think it would help you with your pain and help you to push more effectively."

"No pain medications," Nicole snaps.

Mrs. Talbot, however, seems to feel differently. "Do you really think it would help, Doctor?"

"Lindsay," Nicole says, before Dr. Ford can answer. "Do you really want a big needle going *down there*?"

Mrs. Talbot pales. "I think I'll pass on the needle."

If it were a choice between a needle and labor pain, I'd pick a needle hands down.

Dr. Ford goes to bring out the vacuum. Nicole starts to protest, but then he explains that the vacuum is just being used to rotate the baby so she'll come out easier. There's no way to use a vacuum extractor to drag the baby out anyway. It doesn't work that way.

The vacuum helps a lot. An hour later, Mrs. Talbot gives birth to a baby girl. The newborn is bruised, floppy, and blue. As soon as the newborn starts to emerge, Dr.

Ford calls for the NICU team stat. I think the baby will be spending some time there.

"Can I hold her?" Mrs. Talbot asks in a small voice. Mrs. Talbot looks just as bad as her newborn does—pale, sweaty, and exhausted.

Dr. Ford shakes his head. "She's on oxygen. We really need the NICU team to take a look at her right away."

Caroline reaches out and squeezes Mrs. Talbot's moist hand. "She's beautiful. Congratulations."

We let Caroline deliver the placenta after the NICU team whisks away the baby. As it emerges, Nicole speaks up, "Don't throw that away. We're going to take it home."

Dr. Ford looks so shocked that it's almost funny. "What on earth for?"

"I make vitamin pills out of them for the mother," Nicole explains. "It's very effective for treating hormone imbalances after delivery."

Dr. Ford starts to laugh. It's a big belly laugh, dispelling the tension of the last hour of this delivery. Nicole's face turns red, but she doesn't say anything.

"I've got to remember that one," he comments as he wipes tears from his eyes. He yanks off his gown and gloves and wanders out of the room, still chuckling to himself.

———

At five o'clock, I walk by The Pit and see Holly and Jill standing inside. It's a relief to see Holly here considering I was scared that she'd be admitted to the hospital by now. But the fact that she's here an hour before her shift begins doesn't indicate good news. Plus Jill does not look happy. And Holly looks miserable.

There's a voice in the back of my head telling me I should probably not get involved, but I can't help myself. I peek my head into the room.

"Hey," I say. "What's going on? Are you all right, Holly?"

Holly ducks her head down, as Jill answers the question: "No, she's not all right."

Holly sinks down into a chair, carefully steadying herself so she doesn't land with her usual plop.

"Dr. Reynolds said that I'm not in labor," Holly says. "But she's concerned about the contractions. She put me on restricted duty."

"40 hours a week," Jill snorts. "She's not even *dilated*, for Christ's sake."

Holly lowers her eyes.

"I mean," Jill says, "what are we going to do with only 40 hours? Emily and I are both working over 80 hours a week as it is. There are only 168 hours in a week total, so that's kind of the maximum."

"I'm sorry," Holly mumbles. "It's not like I planned this."

"Well," Jill says, "you planned your pregnancy, didn't you?"

Holly winces, as if Jill had physically struck her. But it's true. She *did* plan the pregnancy.

"And it's for nothing," Jill goes on, waving her arms a little bit now. "You're not even in labor. It's just a few contractions. Just drink more water or something."

Holly is looking down at her hands, as if they contained the answer to life, the universe, and everything.

"I'm going to page Dr. Reynolds," Jill decides. "I want to see how necessary this is. I'm sure you were really laying it on thick in there, Holly."

"No, I wasn't," Holly protests weakly.

But it's too late. Jill is already having the operator page Dr. Reynolds to Baby City. Even though Jill announced she was going to do it, Holly looks shocked that she actually went through with it.

"I can't believe you're doing this," Holly says to Jill.

Jill shrugs. "I'm the chief resident. It's my responsibility."

Holly looks at me. "Can you believe this, Emily?"

Oh great. Now both Jill and Holly are staring at me, waiting for me to take sides. The thing is, even though I think Jill is being a huge bitch right now, I get it. I'm already working most of my waking hours. It seems cruel that I should have to take on even more because of Holly.

"Look, Holly," I say. "You knew something like this could happen when you decided to get pregnant. Now you have to deal with that."

A satisfied smile curls across Jill's lips as Holly stares at me.

"What are you saying, Emily?" Holly says softly.

"I'm just saying you can't expect people not to get upset," I say. "It isn't like this is an emergency appendicitis. You planned this pregnancy and now there's a complication. And everyone else in the program has to pay for it."

As the words are coming out of my mouth, I realize how it sounds. My voice has taken on an edge of bitchiness that I can't entirely control. I don't exactly mean it that way. Not really.

But it's true that ever since Holly has gotten pregnant, it's been all about her. About her feet hurting, being out of breath, being dehydrated, and now this emergency with the contractions. It's always *something*, for Christ's sake. It's like everyone else isn't important anymore. Our whole lives have to revolve around this stupid pregnancy. Obviously, there's nothing in my life that's as important as this baby, so why shouldn't I have to work every day and every weekend? You can't even compete anymore.

It's just not fair.

"I'm sorry that I'm *inconveniencing* you," Holly hisses at me. "Maybe I should just give the baby up for adoption, so I don't have to inconvenience everyone by taking maternity leave."

Actually, that would be a lot easier on all of us.

"Holly," I start to say, but I get interrupted by the phone ringing. It's Dr. Reynolds, returning the page.

I only hear Jill's end of the conversation. Jill starts grilling Dr. Reynolds about labor statistics, whether she did a fibronectin test, which is a predictor of labor. I can't hear exactly what Dr. Reynolds says in response, but it sounds like she's not happy. By the end of the conversation, Jill can't seem to get a word in edgewise. Finally, Jill slams down the phone.

"Ridiculous," Jill says, shaking her head.

I'm reminded of when Jill came into the room and frightened Marissa Block with a photo of a sick preemie. Jill has put her career in jeopardy several times in order to protect the lives of unborn babies and would probably sooner handcuff a pregnant patient to a hospital bed than let her go to work while having active contractions preterm. I've always said she cared about those babies more than anyone else.

Maybe I was wrong.

"Sorry," Holly says, not sounding very sorry anymore. It's like my words have energized her.

"I don't know what the hell we're going to do," Jill says. "Forty hours. And no nights! Why don't you just go on maternity leave now? This should count, you know. If you're only working 40 hours, that doesn't get to count as full-time residency."

"What about Eric?" Holly says. "He could pick up some shifts by himself. He's just as good as any OB/GYN resident, from what I've heard."

Jill snorts. "He's capped at 60 hours. Almost as useless as you."

At that moment, Eric must've felt his ears burning or something because he comes into The Pit, his brow furrowed. As soon as he walks in, I recognize how all of this is going to sound to him and how unreasonable we're being to Holly. I'm embarrassed he has to hear this.

"What's going on?" he asks. "Are you talking about me?" He smiles wryly. "All good things, I assume."

Jill seems to take great pleasure in recapping the whole situation.

"Holly has been put on restricted duty because she's having contractions," she explains. "I was just telling her that you can't pick up any of her hours because you're capped at 60."

Eric frowns. "I'll work more than 60."

Jill folds her arms across her chest. "Yeah, I'm sure you will."

"Of course I will," he says. "I'll work as many hours as you need me."

"You will?" Jill says flatly.

Eric shakes his head. "Whatever you need. I don't want Holly to go into labor too early, for Christ's sake."

Holly looks up at Eric and smiles for the first time since we started this conversation. "Thank you," she says.

Yeah, thanks, St. Eric.

"I need to look at the schedule," Jill says irritably. "It's not that easy. Everything has to be redone."

Eric shrugs. "If it has to be redone, that's just the way it is, right? It's not like it's Holly's fault."

Jill just glares at Eric, like she wants to reach out and strangle him with her bare hands. The way he's looking at her, it's obvious that he knows it. And he's not particularly bothered by the idea.

As for Holly, she won't even look at me. I probably deserve that.

Chapter 37

When I arrive in The Pit next day, Dr. Shepherd is waiting.

Immediately, I am scared I'm going to piss my pants. Dr. Shepherd looks really angry—she's got a flush in her high cheekbones and her lips are squeezed together into an angry little line. When your program director shows up looking furious, it's time to freak out.

Plus I'm the last person here. Eric, Jill, Holly, and Ted are sitting in The Pit, like they've been there for hours. The only person who isn't here is Caroline. I glance at my watch nervously, making sure I'm not late. The display says I have five minutes left, but I'm still apprehensive. Was there some sort of daylight savings time that I wasn't aware of?

"Have a seat, Emily," Dr. Shepherd says to me in that sharp voice of hers.

I scramble to sit down, grateful that I don't have to sit next to Holly or Eric. Damn, there are a lot of people on this rotation that I'm not on speaking terms with.

Dr. Shepherd gets up from her own seat and shuts the door to The Pit, plunging the room into silence. When she addresses us without sitting down again, I feel my stomach sink.

"It's come to my attention," Dr. Shepherd begins, "that Holly has been put on restricted duty by her OB/GYN. Is this correct?"

Holly nods. Dr. Shepherd looks at Jill, who also nods, somewhat reluctantly.

"It's also come to my attention," Dr. Shepherd continues, "that the appropriate accommodations are *not* being made for Holly. And that some of the residents have been giving her a hard time about it."

Oh God. Dr. Shepherd is looking right at Jill. Jill's face turns bright red.

"That's not true!" Jill sputters. "I just told her that I needed a little time to adjust the schedule."

"That's unacceptable," Dr. Shepherd snaps. "We don't want to do anything to put Holly's baby in danger. We are OB/GYNs after all, and we're also her colleagues."

Jill's face is so red, it's almost purple.

"Since you can't seem to handle it, Jill," Dr. Shepherd says, "I have taken the liberty of rearranging the schedule for the rest of the rotation." She looks over at Eric. "It's my understanding that you have offered to pick up extra hours, Dr. Kessler?"

Eric nods.

Dr. Shepherd looks back at Jill. "Do you feel that having Dr. Kessler on call with only one other resident would be sufficient?"

Jill glares at Eric. She doesn't want to admit that he kicks ass as a resident, but it's obviously in her best interest to do so. "Yes," she says.

Dr. Shepherd considers the group of us.

"Here's what we're going to do," she says. "The night and day shift were supposed to switch next week, but I'm going to continue with Emily on day shift with Holly. Eric will also stay on day shift to pick up any of Holly's missed hours. Jill and Ted, you'll be on nights for the rest of the rotation, starting tonight."

I don't know how to feel about this change. Night shift is quieter than day shift, so I'd been looking forward to that change. But at the same time, I hate working the night shift. I always feel like I'm in a daze, and I'm never sure when to brush my teeth.

"Holly," Dr. Shepherd says. "You were on call this Saturday night with Jill, right?"

Holly lowers her eyes. "Yes."

Dr. Shepherd looks at me and then at Eric. "The two of you will take this Saturday call. Jill will stay in the hospital tonight, so that Holly can be excused."

I groan inwardly. I *definitely* know how to feel about *this* change. Saturday call is my least favorite of all the weekend calls. If you're on call on a Friday night, at least you have all of Sunday free. If you're on call Sunday night, you've got Saturday. But when you're on call Saturday, the entire weekend is ruined. Needless to say, I will be working far more than 80 hours this week.

I guess it turns out that Eric and I couldn't have had our date after all.

"From now on," Dr. Shepherd says, "Holly will do a total of three shifts per week."

Jill lets out a gasp. "That's only 36 hours!"

"Yes, it is," Dr. Shepherd says.

I can see Jill's hands ball into fists. "Will this time off count as part of Holly's maternity leave?"

Dr. Shepherd stares at Jill for a moment before answering, "No, it will not."

I can see the words at the tip of Jill's tongue. *That's not fair.* But she doesn't say it. It probably takes all her self-restraint not to do so.

Dr. Shepherd looks at each of us, one by one, until she feels satisfied. Finally, she says, "Holly, you can go home now."

There are daggers in Jill's eyes as Holly and Ted leave the room, followed by Dr. Shepherd. The next words Jill says are murmured under her breath—I'm pretty sure I'm the only one who hears them.

"I had three miscarriages this year," Jill breathes, "and I didn't miss *one minute* of work."

I'm not sure I was meant to hear that. But I do. And it takes a long time to stop thinking about it.

When I get up to leave, I see Caroline waiting at the door to The Pit. Like a little doggie that was locked out of the house. She gives me a concerned look.

"Is everything okay?" she asks me.

"Just a few scheduling changes," I tell her.

"What?" Caroline asks.

I bite my lip to keep from telling her it's none of her business.

"Eric and I are going to stay working days," I say. "And Jill and Ted will be doing the night shift starting next week."

Caroline looks crestfallen. "You're not going to be doing nights next week?"

"No," I say.

Caroline juts out her lower lip in a pout. "But *I'm* going to be doing nights next week. I thought you were going to be there."

"I guess everything isn't about you," I snap at her.

Caroline's face falls and I immediately feel guilty. Although I'm honestly still kind of psyched about not working with Caroline anymore.

"Sorry," I mumble.

"Maybe I can ask to stay on days too..." Caroline muses.

"No!" I say a little too quickly. I clear my throat. "I mean, I think it's important for you to experience Labor and Delivery at night. It's a lot different."

Caroline sighs and nods. "Yes, you're probably right."

And just like that, I am rid of Caroline.

———

"It's not fair!"

Usually Jill doesn't want to leave Baby City for even a minute to get food, but today Jill insisted that the two of us go to the cafeteria together at lunch time. I agreed to go (not that Jill gave me much of a choice), although it makes me sad to know that Eric won't be slipping me a sandwich today. Still, hot lunches are a rarity to me, so I'm not going to pass up the opportunity.

Plus I know that Jill really needs to vent.

"I mean," Jill says, as she shoves her way past patients and ancillary staff members. "I get that she needs to work fewer hours. Fine. But it doesn't seem fair that her 36 hour weeks should count the same as our 100 hour weeks."

I just nod. I figure if I start trashing Holly behind her back, it isn't going to help revive our friendship.

"Totally and completely unfair," Jill says as she picks a cold chicken sandwich off the rack.

The line for warm meals is long, but I'm determined to get something hot if it kills me. On a hospital cafeteria scale of one to ten, our cafeteria would probably rate a three at best. And that's on a *hospital cafeteria* scale. The food usually looks semi-congealed and all the sauces are mostly water. I mostly just come here for coffee, but sometimes I'll see the same dish served on Friday that was there on Monday, and I'm fairly sure that it's leftovers. So getting a hot meal may *literally* kill me. But it's still better than something cold or microwaved or from a hot dog cart.

After deliberating for several minutes, I pick out the tortellini in a white sauce. It's somewhat disheartening to realize the tortellini is fused into giant clumps. It's still better than hot dogs though. Probably.

By the time I pay for my food, Jill is already sitting next to another resident named Alice. I can tell that Jill had already filled Alice in on most of the details of what had happened today. Alice loves gossip and is clearly eating it up.

"That's so unfair!" Alice exclaims.

I see Jill has reached the conclusion of her story.

"I just can't get over that she *told* on us to Dr. Shepherd," Jill says, shaking her head. "That's the worst part. What a loser."

"I don't think she did," I speak up. Jill raises her eyebrows. "It doesn't seem like the kind of thing Holly would do, does it?"

Jill looks at me thoughtfully. "You're right." She frowns for a minute, and her eyes widen. "Holy crap, I bet *Eric* told Dr. Shepherd."

I nod. "That's my best guess."

Alice looks fascinated. She takes a big bite of her own sandwich. "Who's Eric?"

"Eric is the ER resident rotating with us this month," Jill says, making a face. "He's an ass. Although I think Emily here may be in love with him."

"Shut up," I say.

"It's true," Jill insists. "Whenever he's nearby, there's a little puddle of drool under Emily's chin. I almost slipped in it the other day."

"Whatever," I mumble, averting my eyes.

Alice giggles. "Is he hot?"

Jill shrugs. "I suppose he's not completely hideous."

I wish they would change the subject. I take a bite of my tortellini. The noodles are mushy on the outside, and the cheese inside tastes stale and a little bit crunchy. The sauce is watery. I put down my fork.

"Wait a minute," Alice says. "Is it Eric Kessler?"

"Uh huh," Jill confirms, crinkling her nose. "Have you had the pleasure of meeting him?"

Alice nods vigorously. "Oh, yes. I have to agree with Emily here. He's really hot. Sad about his wife though."

Jill cocks her head to the side. "What about his wife?"

Alice looks between the two of us. "You mean you don't know?"

Jill frowns and I have to look away. Of course, I know exactly what Alice is about to tell us.

"She was a surgery resident here and she died suddenly," Alice says. "She had a cardiac arrest. I heard he went kind of nuts afterward and spent like a year in Brazil, living in a teepee."

I think Hillary had said he was in Bolivia. But I'm not sure about the teepee. Seems possible.

"Seriously?" Jill says, her eyes widening. "Wow, that's hard to believe. I guess that explains why he's so…"

She doesn't complete the sentence and just trails off, deep in thought. Either way, it's obvious that this new bit of information has changed the way she thinks about him. And I can see why maybe that's not something he would have wanted.

Chapter 38

Saturday call is just me and Eric. No buffer between us.

I had been sort of nervous about how awkward it would be, but when Eric greets me in The Pit the next morning, it's surprisingly not awkward. It's like nothing ever happened between the two of us. Maybe I shouldn't be so surprised though. Mary is the one he really cares about. I'm just a random chick that he banged.

When Jill signs out to the two of us, she doesn't sneer at Eric like she usually does. Or make a comment about how ER residents are lazy. She's actually quite civil to him. I guess she feels bad for him. Or maybe she's worried he's going to go nuts in the middle of the shift, leave, and go live in a teepee.

"We'll split the postpartum patients," I say to Eric, after Jill and Ted have left.

"I can see them all," he volunteers.

I raise my eyebrows at him. "You don't have to."

He shrugs. "Actually, I kind of like it. I'm not sure why you and Jill seem to hate the postpartum patients so much. They mostly seem really happy."

Oh God, maybe he's right. Apparently, I've become so bitter that I can't deal with seeing women who have just had a new baby.

Or maybe it's just the fact that the postpartum women don't want to start whining to a male resident about their leaky breasts.

"Just a matter of preference, I guess," I say.

Eric heads up to the postpartum floor, and I hit Triage to see the woman who just showed up in labor. I flip through for chart before I come in, and note that Mrs. Green had a pretty unremarkable pregnancy to this point. Well, unremarkable aside from the fact that she's 49 years old. She's possibly the oldest person I've ever seen here.

"I know, I'm ancient," Mrs. Green says to me, the second I walk in the room. She looks every bit her 49 years, or possibly older. Her brown hair is threaded with gray and she has bags under her eyes. There's a permanent crease between her eyebrows.

Her husband looks even older. He's all gray, including his beard. These two look much more like grandparents than parents.

"Was it IVF?" I ask Mrs. Green, flipping through her chart.

"Lord, no," Mrs. Green says. "More like an unfortunate accident."

"We already have two children," Mr. Green pipes in. "Both of them are in college. This was... a big surprise."

Mrs. Green looks embarrassed. "I thought I was going through menopause. My cycles were so irregular, I thought there was no point in bothering with birth control. It took me four months to even realize I was pregnant because I was only getting two or three periods a year."

"Not that we won't love the baby," Mr. Green says quickly. "We were planning a romantic trip to Paris this summer, but it wasn't hard to postpone that."

"For 18 years," Mrs. Green adds.

I guess I don't blame them for being shaken. I can't imagine thinking you're completely done with child-rearing and then have to start all over again with diapers and nighttime feedings.

"Are you interested in adoption, Dr. McCoy?" Mrs. Green teases me, batting her eyes.

"I'll get back to you on that," I say.

Mrs. Green is five centimeters dilated, so I admit her and put her on the list to get an epidural. Within the day, I'm pretty sure that the Greens will be middle-aged parents.

———

Thankfully, the beginning of my call runs rather smoothly. Triage is quiet and there are no emergencies. I don't even have to call our attending, Dr. DeAngelis. Maybe if I can deliver a quiet call to her, she'll forgive me for what I did in the ER.

At around four in the afternoon, Mrs. Green successfully delivers an eight pound two ounce baby boy. It goes very smoothly, with Dr. DeAngelis just standing in the corner of the room, nodding her head. Mrs. Green has only a few minor second degree lacerations from the delivery.

"You can handle sewing her up, right?" Dr. DeAngelis says to me.

"Of course," I say. She still seems to trust me again, thank God.

Mrs. Green is still numb from her epidural, so I get to work sewing her up. She has pretty standard tearing, but anything more than a first-degree tear needs to be sewn up. It's something I've done probably hundreds of times and is not a big deal.

I'm passing the needle through her perineum when I suddenly feel a sharp pain in my right thumb. I wince and yank my hand away. Christ, did I stick myself? That would really be a rookie mistake.

I look at my glove. It looks intact. I probably just imagined it.

I glance up and see Mr. and Mrs. Green cooing over the little baby boy that they didn't want. I quietly change needles and continue sewing.

When I get out of the room about ten minutes later, I peel off my rubber gloves. Now it's unmistakable. I see the large puncture mark on my thumb, which is still oozing blood. Crap. I can't believe I stuck myself.

This isn't a big deal though. I mean, I just stuck myself with a suture needle. And it's not like Mrs. Green is riddled with disease. I'd really rather not have to report this to Dr. DeAngelis.

"What happened to your hand?"

I look up and start. Eric is standing in front of me, his eyebrows raised. I feel my cheeks flush. "Nothing."

His green eyes flicker down to my thumb. "You stuck yourself."

Even though I realize it's a bit childish, I hide my hand behind my back.

"It's none of your business."

Eric laughs. "Are you embarrassed?"

"No," I mumble.

"I stuck myself a few times." He shrugs. "It's not a big deal, especially up here. It's not like your patients are high risk. Here, I know the protocol like the back of my hand."

Eric takes me by my non-bloody hand and pulls me in the direction of the nearest sink. He hasn't touched me since my conversation with Hillary, and I have to admit that I miss it. His callused palm feels pleasantly warm against my hand. He doesn't make any comments about how freezing my own hand must be.

"Now scrub your hand really well," he instructs me.

Eric watches me as I soap up and wash my hands thoroughly, scrubbing up to nearly my elbows. When I finish, I grab a paper towel. I look down at my thumb, which is still bleeding slightly.

"Give it here," Eric says, holding his hand out to me.

"Yeah, right."

"Come on," he says. "Don't be a baby."

Reluctantly, I allow him to take my hand. My fingers are now pleasantly cool from being washed, and his hands are very warm. He places gentle pressure against my thumb, milking blood out through my wound.

"Expressing blood gets rid of any contaminants," he explains.

"I see," I murmur.

"And now," he says, "I have to suck out the poisons with my mouth."

I stare at him.

"Kidding," he says with a crooked smile.

Confession: I was sort of hoping he wasn't kidding.

"You've got to report the needlestick," he says. "And you need to talk to the patient, see if she'll submit to blood testing."

"Great." That should be humiliating. And I'm sure Dr. DeAngelis will be thrilled with me.

Eric's hands are still holding mine. His green eyes are studying my face and I feel my breath catch in my throat.

"We would've had a great time at our dinner tonight," he says.

"I guess it wasn't meant to be," I murmur.

"You would have loved the restaurant," he says. "Best Moroccan food in the city."

It's obvious that Eric's hands on mine are no longer therapeutic. He's not massaging toxins out anymore. He's just massaging. And it feels kind of amazing.

But I can't afford to fall in love with this guy.

"You ever take Mary there?" I ask him.

Eric yanks his hands away from mine like my flesh was suddenly burning hot. (Obviously they're not. My circulation still sucks.) He shakes his head at me.

"So that's the way it's going to be, huh, Emily?"

I shrug.

Eric sighs and turns away from me. He makes it a few yards, before he turns around.

"The reason I didn't tell you," he says, "is because I was sick of being the poor schmuck who fell apart when his wife died."

I don't say anything, so he turns around and walks away. Though what I really want to say is that if he doesn't want to be that guy, he should stop being that guy.

I've got to go talk to Mrs. Green about the blood testing. Obviously, I'm dreading it. As a doctor, it's incredibly hard to admit to making a mistake. She trusted me and I did something dumb. Admittedly, it was a minor mistake, but I feel like it's not the sort of thing I should be doing at this point in my training. Not that experienced surgeons don't stick themselves sometimes, but still.

When I come into Mrs. Green's room, she's cradling her new baby son and her husband is taking a million photos with his camera phone. Considering how miserable they seemed about their imminent delivery earlier today, they certainly seem to be doting parents. I guess the adoption plans have been abandoned.

"Hello again," I say.

"Hi, Dr. McCoy," Mrs. Green says. She seems tired but cheerful. "Am I being moved to the postpartum unit now?"

"Very soon," I promise. "There's actually something else I need to talk to you about."

Mrs. Green frowns, concerned. "What is it, Doctor?"

"So while I was sewing up your lacerations," I begin, the heat rising in my cheeks, "I actually stuck myself with the needle."

"Oh my," Mrs. Green says, her eyes widening. "And that's especially scary, considering I'm HIV-positive."

I feel my stomach sink. "You are?"

Holy shit. I had no idea that Mrs. Green was HIV-positive. I even glanced at her chart for any mention of communicable diseases and there was nothing. If that's the case, her baby should receive some sort of prophylaxis for—

"Just kidding," Mrs. Green laughs.

Mr. Green grins at me. "You should've seen your face, Dr. McCoy."

Ha ha. Hilarious.

"I don't have any diseases," Mrs. Green says. "But you're welcome to do any blood tests you want if it would make you feel better."

"Thank you," I say. I guess this went as well as it possibly could have.

"By the way, Dr. McCoy," Mr. Green says. "Did you know you have the same name as the doctor on 'Star Trek?'"

"Yes," I say, smiling tightly. "One or two people have mentioned to me."

That joke will truly follow me for the rest of my life.

Chapter 39

The rest of the Saturday call is relatively quiet, but I still feel exhausted when Monday morning rolls around. I'm going to be spending the entire shift with Holly, which is usually a great treat, but today I'm not looking forward to it. I know she's still really pissed off at me for not supporting her when Jill was throwing her hissy fit. Holly holds grudges longer than the Mafia.

Sure enough, Holly is very blatantly not speaking to me on Monday morning. In fact, the only person who seems to be in good spirits is Ted, who is giving sign out.

"Let me tell you about Jill and Ted's Excellent Adventure last night," he says.

An exhausted Jill glares at Ted. "I swear to God, if you make that joke one more time, I will kill you with my bare hands."

Jill and Ted head out after sign out, and Eric goes upstairs to see the postpartum patients. Holly and I are left alone in The Pit. She's sitting in a chair with her feet up, playing with her cell phone.

I want to tell Holly that I'm sorry, but somehow I can't get the words out. Maybe it's because I'm not entirely sorry. I meant some of what I said and she knows it. Holly won't fall for a half-assed apology. I've got to use my *whole* ass for this one.

"Doctors," Pam, the nurse on Triage, shows up at the door of The Pit looking breathless. Pam is one of our best and most experienced nurses, so if she looks freaked out, I know I should be freaked out.

"What's wrong?" I ask. I brace myself.

"We have an emergent transfer from home coming in," Pam explains. She winces as she says it.

Oh no. I hate those.

"What's the story?" I ask.

"Baby was breech," Pam says. "The head got stuck during an attempted home delivery, apparently."

I suck in a breath. When a baby is being delivered breech, the head getting stuck is a huge obstetric emergency, because the umbilical cord is compressed while the head is in the pelvis and the baby is deprived of oxygen. It's scary in a hospital setting, and in a home setting, it's fatal most of the time. I'm scared that by the time the patient gets to us, it will be far too late.

This isn't a delivery. It's a rescue mission.

I glance over at Holly, who knows this and looks very white.

"Let me take this one," I say.

She nods but doesn't say thank you.

A few minutes later, Dr. Shepherd has arrived on the floor in anticipation of the arrival of this patient. Dr. Shepherd is a huge crusader against homebirth. I think she's seen a few homebirths that have gone very badly and that's soured her permanently. It doesn't matter if the woman has given birth to a dozen times before, if the birth is uncomplicated, or if they live in the backyard of the hospital. If a patient even hints at the idea of giving birth at home, Dr. Shepherd launches into a 15-minute speech that ends with her nearly yelling at the patient. I don't think she can help herself.

Dr. Shepherd's speeches always end the same way: "Even if you live five minutes away, that's not close enough. Can *you* hold your breath for five minutes?"

She doesn't say it now, but she looks very tense. The fine lines around her eyes and between her pale eyebrows have deepened. She says to Pam: "Do we know who the midwife was?"

Pam shakes her head. "Wasn't one we're familiar with. Not one of the nurse midwives, I'm pretty sure."

My understanding is that nurse midwives are more experienced, have hospital privileges, and are a reasonable alternative to an obstetrician. So-called "professional" midwives have less standardized training, and can't deliver in hospitals, which Dr. Shepherd seems to feel makes them more hesitant to transfer the patient to a hospital. Basically, it makes a dangerous situation all the more dangerous.

Personally, I feel anyone who tries to deliver a breech baby at home has got to be out of her mind.

While we're waiting for the patient to arrive, doctors start accumulating on the floor. First the NICU team arrives, followed by anesthesia. We're all just standing there in a huddle, poised to save this one tiny baby. I can see some of the residents in scrubs are bouncing from foot to foot anxiously.

The patient is rushed in a minute later with a gaggle of nurses and EMTs surrounding her stretcher. One of the EMTs quickly passes on the vital information. The patient is Julie O'Neill, age 26, second pregnancy, second delivery. She's been laboring over a day at home and finally the baby's body started to emerge feet first. Unfortunately, the head did not follow. Also unfortunate is the fact that the midwife who was delivering her is nowhere to be found.

That last fact is not a huge surprise though. If I were responsible for unnecessarily jeopardizing the life of a newborn, I'd disappear too.

Mrs. O'Neill is conscious, but barely. I think she's running solely on adrenaline right now. She looks pale and frightened, and the sheets underneath her are drenched in blood. The group of doctors descends on her immediately, but Dr. Shepherd tells the EMTs to wheel her directly to the OR before anything is done, just in case there's a chance we can save the baby through surgery.

"What's going to happen?" Mrs. O'Neill whispers to me, as I jog along with her gurney. "Is the baby going to be okay?"

I can't answer that question honestly, so I just say, "We'll do our best."

Mrs. O'Neill rolls her head up to look at the ceiling. She's very pretty in a youthful and natural sort of way—she has wide brown eyes and freckles dotting her slightly upturned nose. She looks like a very trusting type of person.

"I didn't know he was still breech," she murmurs. "The midwife said that he turned."

Once we're inside the OR, Dr. Shepherd doesn't waste a minute before yanking back the sheets covering Mrs. O'Neill's lower half. Before I can stop myself, I gasp. Dr. Shepherd shoots me a look, but I can't help myself. Aside from what looks like about two liters of blood on the sheet, I see the body of Mrs. O'Neill's baby hanging out of her.

I can see nearly the entirety of the tiny body. It's a perfectly formed newborn boy. The arms and legs have ten fingers and ten toes, tiny little sausages budding off from tiny hands and feet. His abdomen bulges slightly the way all newborns do and I can see the outline of his rib cage. His chest doesn't move.

Also, he's blue. So blue that I know before we even check that we won't find the heartbeat. The baby is dead. He's probably been dead for a while, judging by how stiff the tiny body looks.

Despite the sheer number of people in here, the room goes completely silent. Everyone realizes that the baby has died and there's nothing we can do about it. But at the same time, nobody wants to give up. We still can try our best to defy nature and bring this newborn back from the dead.

Dr. Shepherd pulls out the piper forceps. These forceps are designed to rescue an entrapped head. Dr. Shepherd positions herself between Mrs. O'Neill's legs and glances over at me.

"You have to hold the baby steady," she tells me.

I grasp the tiny body with my gloved hands. It's cold to touch. Dr. Shepherd inserts the forceps into the birth canal and applies pressure, but the head is really stuck. It's clear that she needs to cut an episiotomy, but I guess she's hesitant to do it considering that nothing will save the baby at this point, so why slice up the mom?

After several minutes, Dr. Shepherd lets out a sigh. "I have to cut an episiotomy," she says, resignation in her voice.

She works quickly, but there's no real urgency anymore and everyone knows it. After making the incision, the baby's head slides free. The umbilical cord is wrapped twice around his neck. We pass the baby over to the NICU team, who quickly surrounds him, making a valiant effort at resuscitation.

"How did he look?" Mrs. O'Neill manages.

Dr. Shepherd opens her mouth, but no words come out. She doesn't want to tell Mrs. O'Neill and neither do I. But somebody has to.

————

The task falls on the attending from the NICU team. He delivers the news to Mrs. O'Neill, who looks shocked and bursts into hysterical wails. In the back of my head, I assumed she must have already known. But she had no idea.

After the staff clears out of the room, Mrs. O'Neill asks to hold her baby. This is a common request in the cases of stillbirth, and I've always found it very difficult to watch. Many women even want photographs taken of them with their deceased newborn. There's a company that comes in and does it for them. I suppose it serves a purpose, although it honestly really creeps me out.

"Let's go talk to the husband," Dr. Shepherd says after we exit the OR.

Crap. I was hoping she would do it herself.

We head to the waiting area where a dark-haired man in his early thirties is pacing across the room. It's almost mesmerizing to watch him, the way he marches those eight feet, spins on his heel, and then marches back the same eight feet. I'm guessing this is Mr. O'Neill. When we show up, he stops pacing abruptly and stares at us.

"Mr. O'Neill?" Dr. Shepherd asks gently.

He nods and gestures at the only other person in the waiting area, a woman in her 40s with frizzy black hair wrapped in a kerchief and large bags under her eyes.

"This is Hannah," he says. "She's our midwife."

So the midwife isn't on the next bus headed out of town. Dumb move.

Dr. Shepherd glares at Hannah with such venom that I'm scared I may have to hold her back. On her part, Hannah appears completely unperturbed. Does she have any idea what she's responsible for? Doesn't she care?

After an uncomfortable moment of silence, Dr. Shepherd clears her throat.

"Mr. O'Neill," she says. "I'm very, very sorry, but we were unable to save your son. Your wife is saying goodbye to him right now and you are welcome to join her."

It's incredibly painful to watch the way Mr. O'Neill's face crumples. Men don't cry much, but I see it sometimes. On the day that a man's son is born or dies, he has a license to cry. I look away.

"How could that happen?" Mr. O'Neill demands to know. His voice breaks on every word.

"The baby was deprived of oxygen for a long time," Dr. Shepherd explains calmly. "The umbilical cord was compressed during the attempted delivery."

"Those sorts of things can happen sometimes," Hannah speaks up. Like she's some sort of voice of knowledge. Ha. "There isn't much that can be done about it."

"Not at home, no," Dr. Shepherd says. She glares at Hannah for a second before turning her attention back to the father. "A breech baby that size should have been delivered by C-section."

Mr. O'Neill looks down at his hands, which are trembling badly.

"What am I going to tell my other son?" he whispers.

"I'm sorry," Dr. Shepherd says again.

We all stand there in silence for what seems like an eternity. I try not to imagine the conversation that Mr. O'Neill is going to have with his other son. In these situations, it's best to try to think of something else. Anything else. I attempt to guess what the cafeteria might serve for lunch, even though odds are very good I won't have time to get lunch today. Again.

Finally, Mr. O'Neill turns to look at Hannah. His sadness seems to be evolving into anger. When he speaks, his voice dripping with accusation.

"You *said* the baby had turned. You *said* he was head down."

Hannah's face is completely expressionless. Shouldn't she be crying? Apologizing? Something? I mean, the newborn baby of a woman she supposedly cared for is dead. If I were her, I would be on the ground weeping. And begging for forgiveness.

"We *thought* he was head down," Hannah says. "It's hard to be 100% sure."

"Not at home, no," Dr. Shepherd says again.

Mr. O'Neill is just staring down at his feet. I'm not sure if he's going to cry or scream or what. I can't even begin to imagine what the guy must be feeling right now. Instinctively, I take a step back.

Hannah stands up and puts one of her long white hands on Mr. O'Neill's back. He bristles slightly at her touch, but she does not move.

"Kevin," she says. "Some babies just aren't meant to live."

Hannah can't see it, but I do. This is clearly the worst possible thing she could have said. Mr. O'Neill's eyes fill with quiet rage and I take another step back. His right hand balls into a white fist, flies through the air, and lands squarely in the center of Hannah's face with a resounding crack.

Hannah screams and clutches her nose with both hands. Bright red blood streams down her chin, dripping down onto her loose-fitting brown dress. I think he broke her nose.

"My son was meant to live," he hisses at her.

Dr. Shepherd and I exchange looks, wondering if we need to call security. The thought of calling a guard to haul off this grief-stricken man on the worst day of his life seems too awful to contemplate. But then Mr. O'Neill raises his hands in the air and takes a step back.

"I'm sorry," he says, not sounding the slightest bit sorry. "Can you... can you please take me to see my wife and son now?"

"Yes," Dr. Shepherd says before Hannah can protest. She puts a hand on Mr. O'Neill's shoulder and guides him in the right direction. "Go ahead inside and the nurses will show you where she is."

Hannah is still gripping her face, her eyes squeezed shut in pain, whimpering. Dr. Shepherd turns her gaze on the midwife.

"I wouldn't press charges if I were you," Dr. Shepherd says to her.

Hannah opens her brown eyes and just stares at Dr. Shepherd.

"I did nothing wrong," she says.

Dr. Shepherd snorts. "Go home," she says. "Go find a lawyer who can defend you against manslaughter charges."

Dr. Shepherd starts to leave, but Hannah calls out to her: "Wait. Please. It's hard to breathe." To prove her case, she gives a strangled sounding breath.

Actually, she doesn't sound too good.

At first I think that Dr. Shepherd isn't going to stop and I'll be left to deal with this situation by myself. But I guess she isn't quite that cold.

"Emily, go ask Dr. Kessler if he can attend to this woman," she says. She turns on her heels to leave the waiting room, and I hear her final words, just loud enough for me to make out: "Take your time. I'm sure she can hold her breath for quite a while."

Chapter 40

Eric reports that Hannah does in fact have a broken nose. Actually, what he says is, "Hey, that guy broke that bitch's nose!" He says it right in front of a bunch of nurses who saw Mrs. O'Neill get wheeled in, and they burst into spontaneous applause.

Because it would be unethical not to, Eric brings Hannah down to the ER. In the meantime, I try to find Holly, to let her know that one of her patients is likely headed for a C-section.

Holly isn't in The Pit or in Triage. I check a few of the patient rooms before I decide I should probably just page her. Unfortunately, she doesn't return her page right away. Or after five minutes and then after ten minutes.

And that's when I start to get worried.

I head down to Triage and start quizzing the nurses about the last time they saw Dr. Park. She hasn't been spotted for at least an hour.

A lot can happen in an hour.

I'm on the verge of panic by the time I go to the call room. Hopefully, she just decided to lie down for a bit and lost track of time. Even though that would be incredibly unlike Holly.

I try the door to the call room, and it's locked. That's a good sign, meaning I found her. I knock on the door. "Holly?"

I hear Holly's voice, thin and weak: "Go away."

This is less promising.

"Holly, we need you." I hesitate. "Are you okay?"

"Wonderful," is the response the other side of the door.

"Holly," I say as calmly as I can. "Can you please let me in?"

Silence.

Crap. I wonder if there's a key to the call room around somewhere. I know Jill has one.

Before I have a chance to weigh my options, I hear a click as the door unlocks. It swings open a few centimeters and I push it open the rest of the way. Just in time to see Holly collapsing to the floor, clutching her belly.

Oh no.

"Holly," I say, falling to the floor beside her. I reach out and almost touch her shoulder, but then think better of it. "You need to be admitted. Right now."

"I'm okay," Holly insists, breathing through what looks to be a pretty intense contraction.

It doesn't matter what Holly wants. I stand up and grab for the phone to dial the number for the front desk at Baby City, and tell them to send a stretcher to the call room stat. Then I page Dr. Reynolds, Holly's OB/GYN.

"You're going to be okay," I say to Holly. Then I add, "The baby is going to be fine."

Holly, still on the floor clutching her belly, looks up at me. Her eyes are filled with tears, but at the same time, I can see another emotion there besides fear and sadness. Venom.

"What do you care?" Holly practically spits at me.

"I care," I try to tell her, but by this point, the stretcher has arrived. And anyway, Holly would never believe me.

Chapter 41

About a week before my intern year started, I was forced to take an advanced life support class. It mostly consisted of watching endless videos, where people collapsed in a multitude of different situations: on a beach, in a restaurant, and even one at what appeared to be a teenage sleepover.

At some point, I stopped paying attention and just started daydreaming. You can only watch so many manikins be saved by well-trained bystanders.

I can't remember what I was thinking about when I heard the loud snoring coming from my right-hand side. I glanced over, and saw a cute, chubby Asian girl with her head drooped forward, her mouth hanging open, and a little bit of drool threatening to spill from her lips. I nudged her hard and she jerked her head up. She looked around, completely baffled by her surroundings.

"You fell asleep," I whispered to her. I decided not to tell her she'd been snoring. And drooling.

The girl looked around, and finally nodded. "Shit," she commented.

"It could have been either one of us," I said sympathetically.

She grinned at me. "You keep me awake and I'll keep you awake?"

I nodded. It was the start of two fun days of jokes with Holly about super sexy manikins and how we had become completely adept at saving the life of anyone made of plastic. It was the start of Saturday nights out, margaritas, and about 500 million text messages, joking or whining about our respective lives. It's weird because as a kid, you always have tons of friends. But as you get older, and realize who you are and what you like, you have fewer friends and those friendships are more meaningful. I'm not sure if I've ever had a friend that I connected with as much as I did with Holly.

When I show up for work the morning after Holly goes into labor, I am informed by a nurse guarding the door to her room that I'm not allowed inside.

"I know she's a private patient," I tell the nurse. "I'm her friend. Her *best* friend."

"Family only," the nurse growls in my face.

I've already got a letter in my file, so I decide not to push it further. At least I know that Holly probably hasn't had the baby yet, but I want to see her. Mostly because I really want to make things right again.

I walk back to The Pit, dejected. Eric is inside, sitting on a chair, lazily fiddling with his phone. He looks up at me, and his eyes are so green and sexy, I almost forgot how bad I'm feeling. Almost.

"Holly hates me," I say, plopping into a chair next to him. "Dr. DeAngelis hates me. You hate me. Everyone hates me."

Eric shoves his phone into his shirt pocket.

"Well," he says thoughtfully, "Your parents probably don't hate you. Right?"

I frown at him. "No."

"There you go." Eric folds his arms across his chest. "*Everyone* doesn't hate you."

I just stare at him.

A smile touches Eric's lips. "I don't hate you either."

"Well, that's a comfort," I mutter.

I stand up again and head over to Triage. I have to stay busy so I can stop thinking about Holly. She needs to keep from having her baby for at least 48 hours so that she can get the full dose of steroids in order to help her baby's lungs mature. But even if she gets it, 30 weeks and change is way too early for the baby to be born. I hope they can keep it in there at least another two or three weeks.

After delivering the baby of the 49-year-old woman, it's a big contrast to see a chart waiting for me in Triage, stating the age of the mother to be 16. If 49 is the oldest patient I've delivered, 16 will be one of the youngest.

Her name is Veronica Gibson. I hate to stereotype, but I'm immediately picturing some girl with huge boobs, too much makeup, and a slutty skirt. I mean, what kind of 16-year-old gets herself knocked up anyway? I hate to tell you what I used to do on Saturday nights when I was 16. My most exciting evening revolved around watching Saturday Night Live.

When I open the door to the examining room, I get a surprise. Veronica Gibson is a sweet-faced girl, with round cheeks and about ten extra pounds of baby fat. Bright blue eyes hide behind slightly oversized glasses. Her somewhat frizzy brown hair is pulled back into a long braid going down her back.

She actually sort of reminds me of me at that age. Well, except for the huge, round belly.

"Miss Gibson?" I say as I walk into the room. "I'm Dr. McCoy."

"Ronnie," she corrects me as her round cheeks turn red.

A woman in her 40s, presumably Ronnie's mother, is standing next to the examining table, looking about as exhausted and enthusiastic as the mother of a 16-year-old pregnant girl could possibly look. She puts her hand on her daughter's shoulder protectively.

"Ronnie is having contractions every five minutes," she says. "We timed it."

The monitor strapped to Ronnie's belly confirms her story. Actually, the contractions are now every four minutes.

"And how do the contractions feel?" I ask Ronnie.

"Awful," she says. "Like a jillion times worse than period cramps."

It's really hard to wrap my head around the fact that this cute, young girl is actually pregnant. Every time I look down at her belly, I feel surprised.

I do a cervical exam and Ronnie is four centimeters dilated. It looks like she's going to have this baby pretty soon. Hopefully, she'll deliver vaginally. With very young patients, I hate the idea of exposing them to a C-section when they have so many years left for childbearing. Unfortunately, Dr. Buckman is the attending on call tonight.

"I think you're a keeper, Ronnie," I tell her. "I hope you packed your bags."

Ronnie nods. "Mom, can you call the Littmans and tell them that the baby is coming?"

She sees the expression on my face and adds, "The Littmans are the family that's adopting the baby."

Okay, that makes sense. If I somehow got pregnant at 16, I wouldn't want to raise the baby either. Frankly, I think it's surprising she went through the pregnancy at all, considering the other options available. It must be hard to be a pregnant high school student, especially for a nice, middle-to-upper class girl.

"That's great," I say as Mrs. Gibson leaves the room to make the call. "Are they nice?"

"*Really* nice," Ronnie says. "They live in Long Island and they have this ginormous house with a lawn, and they've been trying to have a baby for like the last ten years. They have the nursery for the baby already made up. They painted the walls pink." She smiles. "The baby is a girl, in case you didn't know."

"It sounds like she'll have a really happy home," I say.

Ronnie nods. "I wanted to keep her at first, but that was dumb. The Littmans will let me see her. They're even going to name her in honor of me."

"Veronica?"

Ronnie shakes her head. "Violet. Which I actually like better than Veronica."

"I like it too," I say. "But I also like Veronica."

Ronnie just smiles shyly at that.

I reach out and pat Ronnie on the shoulder. I want this delivery to go well for her. I want her to have the baby, hand her over to a new loving family, and then go back to her friends and her school. There's no reason it shouldn't work out that way.

———

With Dr. Buckman on call today, there is the usual barrage of C-section patients. They come in, one on top of another, Eric and I trading off first assist.

"Do babies ever come out of the vaginas anymore?" Eric asks me at one point. I'd been wondering the same thing.

As I'm walking out of my hundredth C-section of the day, I see there's a commotion on the floor. A few NICU residents in scrubs are rushing to one of the rooms. One of them shoves past me so roughly that I have to grab the wall to keep from falling. There must be some big emergency going on.

Holly…

I see Eric standing at the nursing station, just watching from afar. I grab him by the shoulder.

"What's going on?" I ask him.

He shakes his head. "I… I think Holly's having the baby."

The door to her room has been left ajar and I could just walk in if I wanted. But I shouldn't. If she doesn't want me there, I have to respect that. But it's really damn frustrating to be an OB/GYN, staring at the hospital room of your best friend in labor, and know that you can't go in.

Eric and I just stand there for what feels like an hour but is probably more like ten minutes, watching the door to Holly's room. I just want to hear a baby crying. A newborn testing out her new healthy lungs by bawling her little heart out.

Please, baby, cry…

But I don't hear that. All I hear are scattered words and phrases, most of which I can't make out because I'm afraid to get any closer. At one point, I make out the word "intubate." That's definitely not the word I want to hear. That's pretty much the *last* word I want to hear.

And then I see a group of people in scrubs emerging from the room. They're moving quickly, which I try to take as a good sign. If anyone had died, there would be no need for speed. Then I see the little plastic-edged cart holding Holly newborn baby, and my optimism fades when I see that the baby is intubated and receiving oxygen. She isn't moving or crying or doing anything that a healthy baby ought to be doing.

Eric puts his hand on my shoulder. I'd almost forgotten he was standing there until he did it.

"They'll save her," he says. "Hell, they save 24 weekers."

"They shouldn't have to," I say. I don't say the other words I'm thinking: *They wouldn't have to if not for me and Jill bullying Holly.*

I swallow hard. I've seen so many terrible things here on Baby City, I've gotten really good at suppressing my emotions, and like I said, I'm not much of a crier. I never,

ever cry. Anyway, if you cry, you look weak and nobody respects you.

I'm not going to cry.

I'm not.

"Dr. McCoy?"

I take a deep breath and turn around to face the nurse standing behind me, Paula. I force a smile. "Yes?"

"Veronica Gibson is ready to push," she says.

At least this will take my mind off of Holly.

Chapter 42

Ronnie is a superstar when it comes to pushing. She's only 16, but she's a natural. I want to bring her in as an example to all the older women who give these tiny pathetic little pushes and we have to wait around all day for the baby to come out. Ronnie is pushing so well that after about 15 minutes, I tell the nurse to page Dr. Buckman to come in for the delivery.

Dr. Buckman shows up about ten minutes later, but he's not wearing scrubs. He's dressed in a nice suit and tie and smells vaguely of cologne. Did he think he was being paged to attend a dinner party? I can only assume he must have.

When they are on call, attendings are required to stay in the hospital. Even though the residents take care of most of the vaginal births on our own, we are just residents. If something goes wrong, there needs to be an attending around. Fast.

That said, if nobody is currently in labor, occasionally attendings will take off for an hour or two. Mostly just Dr. Buckman, actually. If nobody is close to giving birth, presumably nothing can go wrong so quickly that you can't make it back to the hospital in time.

Although if it were me, I wouldn't take that chance.

"Don't you look nice, Dr. Buckman," Paula comments. She's either flirting with him or being sarcastic. I can't tell.

Dr. Buckman tugs at his tie.

"I've got tickets to a Broadway show at six," he says. He glances down at his watch. "Should be plenty of time. You said she's close, Emily?"

"Real close," I say.

Dr. Buckman nods. "I hope so."

Or else what? You'll miss opening curtain? Or will you be cutting Miss Gibson open if she doesn't deliver in a timely fashion?

Okay, that was mean. I'm sure Dr. Buckman wouldn't rush to do a C-section on 16-year-old.

When we get back into the room, Ronnie is already crowning. I put my hand on her thigh.

"You're doing great," I tell her.

She beams at me. She doesn't even look tired. Maybe 16 is the best age to have a baby.

Two more pushes and we've successfully delivered a healthy baby girl. Unlike Holly's baby, this one is pink and squealing and perfect. We cut the umbilical cord, and hand the baby over to Ronnie. Ronnie gazes down at the newborn, beaming into her little face. She seems really happy. I guess it's sort of bittersweet though, because she won't be keeping the little girl.

"Okay, great job," Dr. Buckman says, clearly relieved that he's going to make his show. Good thing his priorities are straight. "Emily, are you all right to take it from here?"

I'm about to deliver the placenta, so I tell him, "Yeah, I'm fine."

Generally, the delivery of the placenta is incredibly anti-climactic. I do my usual maneuver of applying pressure to remove the placenta, expecting it to slide free. But strangely enough, it doesn't budge. I massage the uterus manually, but still no luck.

"Can you give her some Pitocin?" I ask the nurse.

With stubborn placentas, Pitocin stimulates contractions. It usually works pretty quickly, but this time it doesn't seem to help.

"Shit," I mumble under my breath. Then I say louder, "Can you get Dr. Buckman back to the room?"

Luckily, Paula manages to catch him before he leaves the floor. He returns the room, not looking very pleased. I quickly explain about the placenta, feeling only mildly embarrassed. This just isn't my day.

Unfortunately, Dr. Buckman doesn't have much better luck. This is a vindication, but also sort of scary. We've got the Pitocin running, I'm massaging her uterus manually, and the placenta is still fixed. "Accreta," I hear Dr. Buckman mumble.

Placenta accreta is an obstetric complication in which the placenta becomes deeply attached to the uterine wall. It's hard to detect prior to delivery, so it's not surprising that it wasn't recognized until now. But it's scary, because it puts Ronnie at higher risk of hemorrhage once we remove it.

"Is everything okay?" Ronnie's mother asks.

Dr. Buckman looks up at the clock on the wall and sighs loudly, which I think is extremely tacky.

"Everything is fine," he says.

Dr. Buckman squares his shoulders as he looks down at Ronnie's vagina, with the umbilical cord still hanging out. He wraps his fist around the cord, gives a mighty tug, and all of a sudden, the placenta pops free.

Paula claps Dr. Buckman on his shoulder. "Nice job, Doctor," she says to him.

I look down at the placenta that the nurse has taken, and I frown. I've seen a lot of placentas and this one doesn't look right to me. It's the wrong shape.

"Is that all of it?" I ask.

"Of course," Dr. Buckman says as he rips off his gown.

I'm not quite so sure, but I guess it's bad form to second guess my attending. I don't want Dr. Buckman to hold a grudge against me forever because I insisted on examining the placenta. I'll just keep a close eye on

Ronnie while she's still in Baby City. I'm sure she'll be fine.

———

It's about half an hour later when I'm sitting in Triage and Paula comes running over, looking somewhat breathless.

"Dr. McCoy," she says. "I just checked Gibson and there's a lot of blood on her sheets."

My heart speeds up. "How much would you say?"

Paula bites her lip. "I'd guess about two liters."

Crap. I knew that placenta wasn't whole.

Paula, as if reading my thoughts, says, "He didn't get out the whole placenta, did he?"

"I…" I can't say anything negative about Dr. Buckman. Even though I'm thinking it so hard that I'm certain she must somehow hear it. "Let me go see the patient."

I drop the chart I had been holding and run over to Baby City. When I get to Ronnie's room, the baby and Ronnie's mother are both gone. Ronnie is all alone and she looks incredibly pale.

"I don't feel good, Dr. McCoy," she tells me.

I look down at her arm and can see that she's got an IV in place. That's good, at least.

"Type and cross two units," I tell Paula. "And type and screen another two. And please put in another IV."

Paula starts to run off, but before she can go, I add, "And page Dr. Buckman!"

He's just going to have to miss his show. Too goddamn bad.

I put the pulse oximeter on Ronnie's finger. Her heart is running fast, but that's no surprise. The cuffs on her arm inflates automatically to take her blood pressure, and I see that those numbers are starting to dip as well.

"Am I going to be okay?" Ronnie asks me. She gives me this tiny, nervous smile that just about breaks my heart. This is why I could never do pediatrics.

"Absolutely," I say. "By tomorrow, you'll be as good as new."

I hope.

Paula took away the old bloodied sheets, but when I lift up the new ones, I see that they're soaked with fresh blood, bright red and still warm. At this point, my heart is beating just as fast as Ronnie's. I'm vaguely aware that she's asking a question, but I can hardly hear it.

"What?" I say.

"Do you think I'll be able to go back to school in September?" she asks.

"Absolutely," I tell her, looking back at the door. Where is Paula? And where the hell is Dr. Buckman?

Ronnie is just about as white as a sheet on her bed. She looks like she's about to pass out. I can't let that happen.

"What's your favorite subject in school?" I ask her. I know I'm just stalling for time, but I have to believe that Dr. Buckman will be here any second.

"Science," she says. "I kind of want to be a doctor."

"That's awesome," I say. I stare at the door, willing it to open and for help to arrive.

"But not an OB/GYN," she adds.

That makes me smile. "Why not?"

"You guys work too hard," Ronnie says with the tiniest of smiles.

I get my wish and the door opens. But it's only Paula. "The blood is on its way up," she tells me.

"And Dr. Buckman?"

Paula shakes her head and lowers her voice a notch. "I tried twice. Not answering his pager."

Shit, shit, shit.

I instruct Paula to stay with Ronnie, and I race out of the room. If I can't have my attending here, there is definitely another person that I'd like to have around when my patient is crashing. And I find that person sitting in The Pit.

"Eric," I say breathlessly. "I need you."

"I knew you'd come to your senses," he jokes. Then he sees the look on my face and sobers up. "What's wrong?"

I quickly fill him in on the details, including the placenta accreta, the hemorrhage, and the fact that Dr. Buckman is not answering his pager.

"Christ," Eric says. "It sounds like she needs surgery. At least a D&C."

"I can't do that without Dr. Buckman here," I say.

He shakes his head. "Why the hell isn't he answering his pager?"

Maybe he's waiting until the intermission. Who the hell knows?

We page Dr. Buckman one more time and Dr. Shepherd too, then head to Ronnie's room together. By this point, the blood has arrived and is flowing into her vein. The sheets underneath Ronnie are completely saturated though. If we don't stop the bleeding, this new blood is just going to go right through her.

"Hey, Ronnie," Eric says, squeezing her hand as he speaks to her. "My name is Dr. Kessler. How are you doing?"

Ronnie just shakes her head, too weak to respond.

"Dr. Kessler works in the emergency room," I tell her. "That's the kind of doctor you want to be. Trust me."

Ronnie doesn't even smile this time.

An alarm goes off. Ronnie's heart rate is too high, and her blood pressure is too low. I look at her face, and see that she's barely clinging to consciousness.

"I don't feel comfortable managing this here," Eric murmurs to me. "Especially without an attending around. I think we need to transfer her to the ICU right now."

"Yeah," I agree.

Eric shakes his head. "Where the hell is Dr. Buckman anyway?"

"There was a show he was trying to go to," I say weakly.

"A *show*?" I see Eric's hands ball into fists. "He's not calling back because he's watching a show? That's inexcusable!"

I glance over Ronnie, who is lethargic but not unconscious.

"Keep your voice down," I murmur.

Eric looks like he has more to say, but he's interrupted by a nurse bursting into the room. "Dr. McCoy," she says. "Dr. Shepherd is on the phone."

Oh, thank God.

I leave Eric in the room, and race to pick up the phone. I almost faint with relief at the sound of Dr. Shepherd's voice.

"One of my patients is hemorrhaging," I say. I quickly fill her in on the details of Ronnie's case. "She's lost at least five liters of blood. I can't reach Dr. Buckman. I've been paging him for half an hour."

"Are you transfusing her?" Dr. Shepherd asks.

"Yes," I say.

"I could be there in 15 minutes," Dr. Shepherd says. "Get her set up for a D&C."

"Right." I feel my shoulders relax ever so slightly. Now that Dr. Shepherd is on the case, I'm not nearly as scared.

"Also," Dr. Shepherd says. "I hope you're using your discretion in not mentioning to the patient that the attending isn't answering his pager. That would be incredibly inappropriate."

I frown. "Of course," I say softly.

"Thank you, Emily," she says.

I glance at the room, where Eric is tending to Ronnie. It may already be too late.

———

Dr. Shepherd and I complete a D&C on Ronnie Gibson. Jill and Ted are arriving as I leave the procedure, and there's part of me that desperately wants to stay and make sure that Ronnie is all right, that the bleeding stops. But Jill assures me that she'll take good care of the patient.

"Go home and get some sleep," Jill says to me. "Otherwise you'll be useless tomorrow."

When I leave Baby City, Dr. Buckman is still MIA.

The events of the last couple of hours have drained all the energy out of me, but I can't make myself go home quite yet. Instead, I take the elevator to the third floor. The third floor is where the NICU is located.

It occurs to me as I walk to the NICU that I don't even know the name of Holly's baby. She had been talking about naming her Emma, after yours truly. But I have a feeling that plan got scrapped.

A nurse named Gail, with short gray hair and horn-rimmed glasses, is guarding the NICU tonight. With my scrubs and my ID badge, if I had walked by her purposefully enough, there's a chance she might not have stopped me. But I hesitate for just a beat and that's enough.

"Can I help you, Dr. McCoy?" she asks me, reading my name off my ID badge.

I feel sweat breaking out on my palms. "I... I was hoping to see Baby Park."

"Are you with the NICU team?" she asks.

She knows very well that I'm not. It says on my ID badge that I'm with obstetrics and gynecology.

"No," I admit. "It's the daughter of a friend."

"I'm afraid I can't let you in then," Gail says.

I sigh. I deserve this, I know it. But it still hurts. "How is she doing?" I ask.

Gail hesitates. She's not supposed to tell me, but I guess she takes pity on me. "Stable," she says.

Stable.

Could be worse.

Chapter 43

When I come into work the next morning, Jill grabs me before I can get into The Pit. She looks exhausted. She has the appearance of the resident who didn't get even a minute of sleep last night.

"Emily," she says. Her voice is low and serious. My stomach bunches up into a knot and I'm suddenly certain that she is going to tell me that Holly's baby died last night. I don't want to hear that news. I get a sudden urge to stick my fingers in my ears start singing.

"What's wrong?" I ask.

Jill takes a breath. "We had to do a hysterectomy on Gibson last night."

The relief of Holly's baby being all right lasts for about five seconds before the news hits me. I clasp my hand over my mouth. "Oh my God…"

"The bleeding never stopped." Jill shakes her head. "We tried everything. Then it looked like she might be going into DIC."

Disseminated intravascular coagulation (DIC) is a potentially fatal condition in which the clotting cascade gets set off all throughout the body. Clots form everywhere and organs can start failing. And as all the clotting factors and platelets are used up, the patient can start hemorrhaging. When you get to that point, the prognosis is not good. If there's a choice between hysterectomy and death, there's only one choice.

"Is she okay now?" I ask.

"Seems to be," Jill says. "As of this morning, her labs looked good. Her hematocrit is stable. No signs of DIC. So I think she'll be fine."

"Except that she's 16 and we just took out her uterus."

"Yeah," Jill says. "Except for that."

I shake my head. What do you say to something like this? "Does Eric know?"

"He knows," Jill confirms. "He was having a hissy fit about it when he first came in. I didn't tell him… he must've looked it up in the computer or something. Or maybe gone up to the ICU. He thinks Dr. Buckman screwed up big time."

Well, he's right. But it's not a great idea to go around saying that to everyone.

"We need to round on her today," Jill says, "and I'd like you to be the one to do it. Don't let Eric near her. Seriously."

"Of course," I say.

Easier said than done.

———

Baby City is busy today, which is good, because it takes my mind off everything awful going on right now. I check in the computer and I notice some new labs that have been drawn on Holly's baby, which I take as a sign that the baby is still alive. More than anything, I want to go down and see the baby and talk to Holly. But even if I had time for that, Holly would never talk to me at this point.

Just before noon, I managed to make it to the ICU to see Ronnie Gibson. From her chart, it looks like she's doing very well postoperatively. The bleeding has completely stopped (obviously, since she has no uterus left to bleed) and all her vital signs are stable. She'll probably be able to be discharged to the postpartum unit later today.

When I reach Ronnie's room, I see that her mother is sitting beside her, holding her hand. Ronnie is very pale still, and something about her slightly damp hair and her scared expression makes her look so much younger than 16 years.

"Hi," Ronnie says to me in a tiny, high-pitched voice.

"Hello, Dr. McCoy," Mrs. Gibson says. She does not sound friendly. Not that I can blame her.

"It looks like you're doing really well," I tell the Gibsons. "There are no more signs of bleeding. I just want to take a look at your incision."

Ronnie dutifully lifts her gown so that I can see the row of staples hastily applied across her abdomen. I remember when my biggest worry was that she might have a C-section.

"It looks great," I say, mustering up a big dose of enthusiasm.

Neither Ronnie nor her mother smile.

"And I hear the baby is doing great as well," I say. "The Littmans must be very happy."

Ronnie and her mother exchange looks. Ronnie looks down at her hands. Her mother says in a sharp voice, "Well, go ahead. Tell her."

I look at Ronnie, who is toying with the sheet on top of her. She bites her lip then looks up at me.

"I'm keeping the baby," she says. "I decided."

Mrs. Gibson throws her hands up in the air, like she cannot believe anyone could do something so stupid.

"I was going to give her up, I really was," Ronnie says. As the words tumble out, her voice takes on a whiny edge that makes her sound even younger. "But now I know that she's the only baby I'm going to have and I want her. She's *mine*. I shouldn't have to give her up. It's not fair. The Littmans could have another baby from another girl, but this is the only baby I'll ever have."

"You're 16," her mother snaps. "You can't raise a baby. You have no job, and you have no money. You have to finish your education."

"I don't care about any of that anymore," Ronnie says, sticking her chin up in the air. "This is my only baby. I want to take her home and raise her."

Mrs. Gibson flashes me a look.

"Maybe you can talk some sense into her, Dr. McCoy," she says. Then she gets up and storms out of the room, like she can't bear another second of it.

For a minute after Mrs. Gibson leaves, it's very quiet in the room. There are things I could tell her to talk her out of it, like that her chances of becoming a doctor after becoming a mother at 16 are pretty small. That she's not mature enough, that babies are more work than she could ever imagine, that she'll likely spent her life in poverty if she doesn't complete her education. That she's giving up her youth to raise this baby.

Except the truth is, if I were Ronnie Gibson, I think I would do the same thing.

It's Ronnie who finally breaks the silence.

"The condom didn't break," she says.

"What?" I say.

Ronnie smiles wryly. "I told my mother that the condom broke. But it didn't. There was no condom. Jake didn't have one and we decided to take the chance."

"Oh," I say.

"I know that sounds really irresponsible," Ronnie says. "I thought after this all happened, I would just go back to school and be a normal kid again. It would be like this mistake never happened. But... I can't do that anymore."

"I don't blame you," I say. I'm glad that Mrs. Gibson isn't in the room right now. She'd probably strangle me with her bare hands.

"I know it's going to be hard," Ronnie says. "I know I'm going to be broke and finishing my education is going to be really difficult, but I still want to do it." She pauses. "I know I'll never regret keeping her. I'll only regret giving her up."

"You're really brave," I tell her.

Ronnie giggles little bit. "Actually, I'm really scared."

"That's part of being brave," I say. "Being scared, but going ahead and doing what you need to do anyway."

"Thanks, Dr. McCoy," Ronnie says. She grins at me. "Maybe I'll be an OB/GYN after all."

I smile back at her.

Then she adds, "But probably not."

———

As I'm leaving Ronnie's room, I nearly run smack into Mrs. Gibson, who is carrying a cup filled with apple juice. I was more focused on Ronnie when we were in the room so I didn't realize how incredibly tired Mrs. Gibson appears. She has dark circles under both eyes, and her hair is coming loose from a hasty ponytail.

"Dr. McCoy," she says.

I nod in greeting. I know she's upset and rightfully so, but I've got too much to do to get sucked into a conversation consisting of me getting yelled at.

"Hang on," she says, putting her hand on my forearm.

So much for a quick getaway. I plaster a smile on my face. "Yes?"

"I just want to apologize for being snippy in there," Mrs. Gibson says. She forces a smile of her own. "It's just... it's been a stressful day."

"Very understandable," I say.

"I support Ronnie wanting to keep the baby," she says with a sigh. "I just don't want her to ruin her life. We don't have the money to support this baby and for her to go to college. I'm just worried that this is going to destroy all her dreams."

"Yeah," I mumble, not wanting to say outright that I agree.

"But the important thing," she goes on, "is that my daughter is alive. And that's thanks to you, Dr. McCoy. And of course, to Dr. Shepherd and Dr. Buckman too."

My stomach turns when she praises Dr. Buckman. He doesn't deserve that. It's because of him that Ronnie is in this situation. Yeah, maybe she would've wound up with the same outcome either way. But if he had taken her into the OR when he recognized the placenta accreta, maybe she would've had a fighting chance. Maybe if he had made sure that the placenta was whole before he took off, she would have kept her uterus.

Honestly, I believe the whole thing is his fault. And it's very hard to live with that knowledge.

I think of Jill and the way she always does what's best for her patients, even if it means she's going to get into trouble and jeopardize her career. I always thought she was a fool, but now suddenly I sort of understand. I close my eyes and take a deep breath.

"Mrs. Gibson," I say. "Can we talk for minute? In private?"

———

Dr. Shepherd arrives at signout that day looking scarier than the Grim Reaper.

If she looked angry when she was dealing with the Holly situation before, she looks completely enraged now. Even though her mouth is shut, I can tell from the way her jaw sits that her teeth are clenched tightly together. She glowers at the five of us.

"Caroline," Dr. Shepherd says.

Caroline looks up, completely terrified. "Yes?" she squeaks.

"Go home now," Dr. Shepherd orders her.

Caroline's eyes widen. "But I—"

"Now," Dr. Shepherd repeats, in a voice that leaves little room for argument. "I need to have a talk with the residents alone."

Caroline looks relieved, then quickly grabs her books and scrambles out of the room. Lucky girl.

Dr. Shepherd shuts the door behind Caroline. She eyes the four of us, a sneer spreading across her lips.

"Get up," she orders us.

Ted, Jill, and I stand up. Ted jumps up so quickly that his chair falls over behind him, then he assumes a military pose. Eric lags in his seat an extra moment, then reluctantly gets up as well.

"I just had a talk with Veronica Gibson's mother," Dr. Shepherd says. "They're planning to bring a lawsuit against us."

My stomach flips. That's not entirely unexpected though, considering what happened.

"Unfortunately," Dr. Shepherd says, "Mrs. Gibson is extremely upset about the fact that Dr. Buckman did not immediately take her daughter to surgery when he identified the placenta accreta, and then he disappeared for an extended length of time." She pauses for what seems like an hour. "Apparently, one of the residents told her about this and encouraged her to sue."

My knees almost give out under me. Oh my God. She told. She *told*.

"She wouldn't give me the name of the resident," Dr. Shepherd continues, the anger growing in her voice. "But I know it must be one of you four." She pauses. "Would anybody care to come forward?"

I look over at Eric, who is standing up straight, staring ahead, not looking at Dr. Shepherd but almost looking past her. Jill, to my right, is shaking her head like she can't believe this is happening. Nobody is looking at me. They haven't guessed the truth, even though it seems like it ought to be painfully obvious considering I was the one taking care of Veronica Gibson.

"Nobody?" Dr. Shepherd prompts us.

Jill whips her head around to stare in Eric's direction. Her eyes narrow and she glares at him. She must think it's him. But he just keeps staring straight ahead.

"Fine," Dr. Shepherd snaps. "If nobody is honest enough to come forward, then all of you will suffer the consequences of one person's actions."

"But that's not fair!" Ted cries out. "I never even met that patient!"

"Shut *up*, Ted," Jill hisses under her breath.

Ted starts to whimper, but he keeps his mouth shut. I taste bile in my throat, wondering what punishment the four of us will have to endure. Dr. Shepherd is not well known for her lenience.

I can't let this happen. I have to come forward. I don't know what Dr. Shepherd will do to me, but I can't let everyone take the blame for something that I did. I have to tell her the truth and live with the consequences. Even though the consequences might mean the end of my career.

I open my mouth to speak, but before I can get a word out, Eric cuts me off.

"I did it," he speaks up, no longer staring past Dr. Shepherd, but instead staring right at her. His green eyes are full of defiance. "I was the one who talked to Mrs. Gibson."

What?

"No kidding," Jill mutters.

Dr. Shepherd descends on him like a starved lion. Her blue eyes are flashing, and her white teeth are bared. It's actually slightly terrifying. As guilty as I feel that he's taking the blame for what I did, I'm desperately relieved that her anger is aimed at him and not me.

"What you did was completely unacceptable, young man," she hisses at him.

"You mean telling the truth?" Eric retorts.

"You criticized your colleague," she says. "You jeopardized the entire department and the entire hospital."

"No," Eric says. "*Dr. Buckman* jeopardized the entire department and the entire hospital when he didn't do his job properly."

"If you don't realize what you did was wrong," Dr. Shepherd says, "then you're not fit to be a doctor."

In her heels, she's exactly his height, and now only inches away from his face. He must be able to feel her hot breath on his face, but he doesn't flinch.

"I could say that about other people as well," he says.

Dr. Shepherd narrows her eyes at him. "You are dismissed, Dr. Kessler."

He raises his eyebrows at her. "Excuse me?"

"You are suspended from residency until further notice," she says, allowing the tiniest smiles to touch her lips.

For the first time, Eric looks slightly shaken. "You don't have the authority to do that."

"I believe I do," she says.

At that point, Eric would be wise to shut up. But I can tell he's not going to.

"Really nice," he says. "Kicked out for doing the right thing."

With those words, he pushes past Dr. Shepherd, flings open the door to The Pit, and storms out, slamming the door behind him. The three of us remaining residents jump at the noise, but Dr. Shepherd doesn't even flinch.

"I knew it had to be him," she says. That satisfied smile is still on her lips. "My residents would never do anything like that."

As soon as Dr. Shepherd clip-clops out of the room on her heels, Jill turns to me and grabs me by the shoulder.

"Holy shit," she says.

"Yeah," I breathe.

"What was he *thinking*?" Jill says, shaking her head. "I mean, you just don't *do* something like that. You don't rat out an attending. Ever."

"I guess he felt like it was the right thing to do," I say.

St. Eric always does the right thing, no matter what the cost. I guess this time the right thing was taking the fall for someone else.

"Maybe so, but..." Jill shakes her head again. "I actually feel sorry for him. Dr. Shepherd is going to do everything she can to get him kicked out. Lucky for him he's not an OB/GYN resident."

"You think she'll be able to do it?"

Jill shrugs. "Dr. Shepherd is a big cheese. And she's used to getting her way."

I can't let that happen. If it comes down to it, I'll have to confess.

Chapter 44

As soon as sign out officially ends, I start searching the neighborhood surrounding the hospital. I dig deep into the crevices of my memory, making right turns, then doubling back to make a left. I spot garbage bins that looked familiar and soak my right foot in a puddle up to my ankle. I must walk for at least half an hour before I get my pay off:

The sign that says "Burger." With the R partially scratched off.

I walk inside and the heat hits me like a punch in the face. I see Eric sitting at the counter, a half-eaten burger in front of him, along with two bottles of beer, one half-empty and the other completely drained. He lifts his green eyes when I enter, but he doesn't say anything.

I plop down onto the stool next to him. The gorilla grunts at me until I order a beer and a burger. I nudge Eric's shoulder and he nods at me.

I sit there awkwardly for another minute while he chews on his burger. He slides his beer over to me and I take a sip. It's warm.

"Are you okay?" I ask.

"I'm fantastic," he says tonelessly. "I never have to deliver another goddamn baby ever again."

"I'm sure Dr. Shepherd is just angry right now," I say. "I don't think you're going to get kicked out of residency."

Eric laughs. "You really think I'm worried about that, Emily? When you see your wife die in front of you, that's kind of a get out of jail free card for the rest of residency. At worst, they'll send me in for a few more counseling sessions with the shrink." Eric shrugs. "No big deal. He and I are great buddies by now."

Basically, he saying that whoever did it is off the hook. Which means nobody needs to know it was me, including Eric.

The gorilla places my own beer and burger down in front of me. The burger tastes good, but not quite as good as I remembered it.

Eric, noticing the expression on my face, says, "It's always best first time you have it."

"It's still really good," I say.

"Yeah," Eric says. "It is."

We both chew in silence for a few more minutes. Finally, I say, all casual, "So why did you tell on Dr. Buckman?"

Eric puts down his burger. His green eyes meet mine and he frowns. The whites of his eyes are slightly bloodshot, but he's still really sexy.

"Come on, Emily," he says. "You know I didn't do it."

I force a smile, but it comes out crooked. "What do you mean?"

Eric cocks his head slightly. "I know that it was you. I know that you talked to Mrs. Gibson."

My heart almost stops. "That's ridiculous," I sputter.

Eric looks me straight in the eyes. "I *heard* you."

I just stare at him.

"I heard the whole conversation," he says. "You were in the filing room that has the copy machine. Maybe you thought you closed the door, but it was cracked open. I heard every word."

I don't know if it's the heat in the restaurant or the things that he's telling me, but I really feel like I'm going to faint.

"Can we go outside?" I ask.

Eric nods. He throws a few bills on the counter, then gently grabs my arm and leads me out of the restaurant to the street. As I walk beside him, my own words echo in my ears: *Mrs. Gibson, I need to talk to you. It's about what happened last night. I think you need to know...*

Eric leads me to the steps of a nearby brownstone and makes me sit down. He peers at my face.

"Are you all right?" he asks.

"Yes," I manage.

He sits down next to me, an inch or two closer than he really should.

"I also know about the Nair crack you made to Marissa Block," he says.

I look up at him sharply. "How...?"

He grins at me. "I went in to check on her right after you went in there, and she gave me an earful."

"If you tell Jill..."

Eric laughs. "Yeah, I know exactly what will happen if I tell Jill. Firsthand."

I lower my eyes. "Sorry. I just didn't like it that everyone was laughing at Marissa. I thought I was helping her. But she kind of took it the wrong way."

"If you were a man, you would've known better."

I pick at a loose thread on my blue scrubs. "Maybe."

"I'm sorry I gave you guys a hard time when you were making jokes about Marissa," he says. "I know we're all under a lot of stress, and you were just blowing off steam. I mean, it's not like I'm any saint myself."

Yeah, we can't all be like his dead wife.

Eric's scooches a little bit closer to me, bridging the already small gap between our bodies.

"The truth is," he says quietly. "I didn't have the guts to tell Ronnie myself about how Dr. Buckman screwed up. You're really brave. Really stupid and really brave."

"Probably more stupid than brave," I say.

"Possibly," Eric agrees. "But I still think you did the right thing."

I lift my eyes to meet his. "Almost as good as St. Mary, huh?"

Like always, my comment about Mary manages to shut him up. I didn't mean to do it this time. Eric just saved me. I should be grateful to him.

It's just frustrating that I can never ever live up to his ex-wife.

"Here's the thing," Eric says, his eyes lowered to stare straight down at his sneakers. "Mary and I were getting separated."

What?

"What?" I say.

He heaves a sigh. "Nobody knew. But it was a long time coming."

I can't even believe what I'm hearing.

"I thought you two were the perfect couple," I say. "Hillary said that you did everything together."

Eric snorts. "Amazingly, Hillary is not the world's expert on my marriage." He sighs again. "Emily, do you know what it's like to be married to St. Mary? It sucks."

I just shake my head.

"At first, I thought she was completely amazing," he muses. "And she *is* amazing. She's the most selfless person I've ever met. She wanted to help everyone who was less fortunate. It was, like, her life's work. I admired the hell out of her. It also didn't hurt that she's... well, she was gorgeous, okay? I thought I was the luckiest guy in the world to be marrying her."

"So what happened?"

"On our honeymoon," he says, running a hand through his hair, "we went to Zimbabwe to dig a well for the townspeople. That was how I spent my *honeymoon*. Breaking my back, digging a well." He shakes his head. "I mean, would it really have been so sinful for us to go to the Bahamas or something? Would that really have been so wrong? But no, not if there was a well that had to be dug."

He goes on, getting a bit angry now. "And every time she had a day off, she had to go volunteer at the free clinic. What's so wrong with spending her time off with me once in a while? We had so little of it, just a few days a month. Why couldn't we just go see a movie or spend the day in bed?" He clenches his hands into fists. "And I know the world is overpopulated, but would it really have been so awful to have a child of our own? Just one?"

He's breathing hard now, getting really furious at the memory of it.

"The last straw was when my dad died," he says. "I was really close with my dad and it wrecked me when he died. But Mary had some missionary-type trip she was supposed to go on, so even though I needed her, she went on the trip anyway. She wasn't even there for me during the goddamn funeral."

He squeezes his eyes shut for a minute. "I know they needed her. But *I* needed her. And I was her husband."

I reach out and take his hand. He gives me a squeeze.

"Did you tell her how you felt?" I ask him.

He snorts. "I was done telling her how I felt. When she came home again, I wouldn't even speak to her. I couldn't even *look* at her. I just knew I didn't want to be married to her anymore. Finally, I told her I wanted to move out."

"What did she say?" I breathe.

"She cried," he says. I see his eyes are getting wet and he clears his throat. "She asked if there was anything she could do. But she didn't mean it. We had conversations like this before, where I begged her to cut back on the charity, and she did. But it was always temporary. I mean, that's what she loved. That's what she was born to do, and I sort of felt like I was being selfish by getting in the way."

He wipes his face with the back of his hand. "The marathon was the next day. I told her that I wouldn't run, but she said that I had to because we had collected money. For some charity. I can't remember what. You'd think I'd remember."

Actually, I can see why he wouldn't.

"I was the one who got her into running," he says. "I always loved to run. When I was pissed off at Mary, I'd always go out and take a run and it would make me feel better. She liked the idea of running because we could use it to raise money. So she trained for the marathon. At first she trained with me, but then after I got pissed off at her, she did it alone."

His eyes get this far off look. "I was about half a mile ahead of her because I didn't want to be near her. I heard somebody collapsed, so I went back to see if I could help. When I saw it was her, I just…"

I give his hand a squeeze, and he looks at me in surprise, as if he had forgotten I was there.

"I just keep going over it in my mind," he murmurs. "I keep thinking that maybe if I had been next to her, I could've saved her. I could've given her CPR faster, maybe I could've gotten to her while she still had a shockable rhythm. Maybe she'd still be alive right now."

"Probably not," I say gently.

"But I don't *know*," he says. "That's the thing. Even though I didn't want to be married to her anymore, Mary was a great person. And I feel like… like I *killed* her."

I can tell that he's trying really hard not to cry. I feel bad for dredging up all these memories, but at the same time, I think maybe it's good for him to talk about it.

"I felt like I had to compensate for causing her death," he goes on. "I went on the trip to Bolivia like she was supposed to. I picked up all her shifts in the free clinic, no matter how exhausted I was. I just wanted to make things right again." He sighs. "But it didn't help. Nothing made me feel any better. I even gave up running marathons, even though it was one of my most favorite things to do."

Eric's words are scaring me a little bit. Basically, he's telling me that it's hopeless. That he can't be happy ever again. That he gave up things that he used to enjoy. Don't they say that's the sign of major depression? He doesn't seem depressed, but he's proven that he's very good at hiding things.

"What happened today," he says, "I mean, saving you from Dr. Shepherd… that's not the kind of thing Mary would have done. She believed everyone should be accountable for their actions. It's the kind of thing that *I* would've done. And I think it was a good thing. It made me feel like *me* again." His eyes un-cloud as he looks up at me. "Maybe I can be a good person without having to live Mary's life."

I smile at him. "I thought you said you didn't like saving women. You said it was a turnoff."

Eric smiles back. "There's nothing that's more of a turn on than getting to come to the rescue of a woman who's as strong as you are, Emily."

He looks at me for a long time, and for a moment I think he's going to kiss me. I desperately want him to kiss me. But he doesn't. Instead, he pulls away from me and fiddles with his left hand. Before I have a chance to ask him what he's doing, he grabs my hand and slips something small and cold inside my palm.

I open up my fist and looked down at Eric's wedding ring.

"Time to move on," he says.

I frown at him. "What am I supposed to do with this?"

He shrugs. "I don't know, give it to charity? Throw it in the dumpster for all I care."

He stands up and brushes off the legs of his scrub pants. I get the sense he wants to be alone, so I don't get up. I close my fingers around the ring. I haven't quite decided what I'm going to do with it.

"I'm going to head home," he says. He pauses. "I know things are weird right now, but... don't lose my number, okay?"

"I can't," I say. "It's programmed into my phone."

"Well," he says, "then don't lose your phone."

"Even if I did," I say, "all my information is in the Apple iCloud, so I would be able to get all my phone numbers and information from that."

Eric squints at me. "I'm trying to say something romantic here. You're sort of ruining it."

"Oh," I say. "Sorry."

I'm a doctor, not a poet, dammit.

But Eric just grins at me so maybe I haven't ruined it after all. He gives me this cute little wave, then he walks away.

Chapter 45

A week later

All babies are cute.

That is a fact. There's no such thing as a disgusting baby. I've seen babies with six fingers or horrible double cleft palates, and they were still just completely adorable. When I rotated through the NICU as a medical student, I saw a baby with something called "prune belly" where the baby's abdominal muscles were missing and his belly was this bloated mess of unrestrained abdominal organs. And even that baby was really adorable.

So it's no surprise that Holly's baby is really cute.

I stop at the NICU near the end of my shift. All I want is to catch a glimpse of the baby and make sure she looks all right. I know they won't let me inside and they definitely won't let me see her chart, but I'm sure I could tell from across the room how she's doing.

I make it as far as the entrance of the NICU when I see Holly sitting beside one of the many incubators, gazing at the baby inside. I almost do an about-face, but then she sees me. Our eyes meet, and she nods at me that it's all right for me to come in.

The general public is not allowed in the NICU because we're covered in germs, but I get away with it because I'm in scrubs and all. I walk past rows of adorable but sick newborns, ranging in size from tiny to miniscule, and finally come to a stop in front of Baby Park.

The baby isn't the smallest in the NICU, but she's very, very small. She has soft, downy black hair covering her scalp, and her tiny eyes are squeezed shut. Her little curved legs are pressed together, one of them bandaged from a recent blood draw. One hand has an IV in it, but the other is squeezed into a tiny fist. The baby is intubated, and I see her chest rising and falling with each breath. Two leads on her chest monitor her heart rate.

"She's beautiful," I say.

"Thank you," Holly says tonelessly.

Holly turns away from me and looks down at her daughter. She gently strokes the side of the baby's cheek through a hole in the incubator.

"What's her name?" I ask.

"We haven't decided yet," Holly says.

The two of us to stand there for a minute, watching the baby breathe. I think this is the most beautiful baby I have ever seen in my life. And that's saying a lot, because I see a lot of babies.

Holly is the one who breaks the silence.

"I don't forgive you," she says.

She doesn't know. She doesn't realize that I was the one who went to Dr. Shepherd and told her that Jill was refusing to change the schedule. I told her that Holly needed time off, and she wasn't going to take it if she didn't get forced. I told Dr. Shepherd that she had to do something right away, that I was scared for Holly's baby. Nobody knows about that except me and Dr. Shepherd.

And of course, I let Eric take the blame for it. But even he didn't figure that one out.

It doesn't matter though. When Holly needed me to stand up to Jill for her, I didn't do it. And that's all she'll ever remember.

"Maybe someday," I say to Holly.

She's quiet for a minute. "Maybe," she says.

We watch the baby breathe together until it's time for me to leave for signout.

———

I'm running two minutes late for signout in Baby City, so of course Caroline picks this moment to stop me in the hall in Triage. She ought to be in signout herself. Jill says she's been doing better on the rotation, and even getting through C-sections without fainting, but it's not enough that she can afford to slack off.

"Emily!" she says. Still with the exclamation points. Oh well. You can teach a person medicine, but you can't teach them not to be enthusiastic. Maybe that's a good thing.

"What is it?" I ask.

"Today is my last day!" Caroline says.

"Oh," I say. I clear my throat. "Well, um, good job this month, and… we'll miss you."

Caroline beams. "I'll miss you too."

Geez. Let's not get too sappy here.

"I just want you know," Caroline says, squeezing her hands together, "this rotation has been a really amazing experience for me. And… I've been thinking about specializing in OB/GYN."

I stare at her. "Really?"

Caroline nods eagerly. Her blue eyes are shining. "It's just so intense. I don't think anything else could compare after experiencing this."

"You still have a lot left in the year," I point out. "Maybe you'll find something else you like."

"I don't know," Caroline says. "I don't think I could be happy doing anything else."

That's what they say about OB/GYN. Don't do it unless you couldn't be happy doing anything else. Of course, that's what they say about medicine too. Apparently, I've chosen the most challenging specialty within the most challenging career. No wonder I'm so tired.

"I just want you know," Caroline goes on, "that working with you has been a really amazing experience. You're totally the one who inspired me to be an OB/GYN." Her eyes fill up with tears. "I want to be just like you."

Aw, shucks.

And now she's crying and hugging me. Even though I know she has a long road ahead of her, I actually think she might be really good at this job. She seems to love it and she really seems to care. So I let her hug me, even though she's getting tears and snot all over my scrub top.

I knew I was going to make her cry, dammit.

Epilogue

Four years later

There's nothing worse than a patient who thinks she knows everything.

That, in my opinion, is the most difficult sort of patient, even worse than the crazies. And you can tell that the patient giving birth in this room is one of those incredibly difficult patients by the stressed expression on the face of the labor nurse as the time to push draws closer, despite the fact that the labor is completely uncomplicated. Pam is one of our most experienced nurses, but right now, she's got the deepest worry lines I've ever seen between her eyebrows.

"We've got to reposition," Pam is saying. "The baby's heart rate—"

"—is fine," I say.

Pam folds her arms across her chest and glowers at me.

"Dr. McCoy," Pam says, "I don't think you are in any position right now to make that decision."

I have a speech in my head that I probably shouldn't give. About how she's the nurse and I'm the doctor, so really, she has to listen to me, no matter which side of the bed I'm on. Luckily, I get saved from saying anything irretrievably stupid by Dr. Holly Park bursting into the room, in a typical Holly-style entrance.

Holly's straight black hair is clipped into what I think of as a typical mommy haircut—short and practical, and her brown eyes are bright. She's wearing blue scrubs, which conceal the bulge of the first trimester of her second pregnancy. She narrows her eyes at me.

"Making trouble, are we?" she asks, clucking her tongue.

"Of course not," I say innocently.

Holly snorts. "Okay, let's see if you're ready to push yet."

A lot of people have asked me how I could allow my best friend to deliver my baby. Isn't it weird to have her doing a pelvic exam on me? Yes. A little. But the truth is, we both do so many of them that it's about as routine as brushing our teeth. Actually, more so since I don't brush my teeth nearly as often as I check cervixes. But what it all came down to is I wanted somebody I could trust. If I can't deliver my own baby, she's the next best thing.

So yes, Holly is my best friend again.

It didn't happen overnight. When she returned to work after taking an extended leave, things were awkward for long time. Then one day, I was eating lunch alone in the cafeteria and Holly plopped down across from me with a chicken pesto sandwich and started talking to me like nothing had ever happened. Now we're both attending physicians at Cadence Hospital, and back to our monthly margarita nights, except obviously we're both getting Coca-Cola now.

Of course, it helps that Holly's daughter Lauren is healthy and thriving.

Holly's brows furrow in concentration as she feels my cervix. I can't feel her fingers at all, because I got an epidural hours ago. I've ordered epidurals for lots of women in the past, and now that I've had one myself, I think these things are the greatest miracle ever invented. I went from feeling like I was having the worst menstruation cramps of all time to a state of blissful numbness. If they had a bottle of epidural on the market, I would definitely keep one in my medicine cabinet.

"You're ready to push," Holly declares. "The head is *right there*. The baby's in a great position."

I scrunch up the sheets with my fingers. "I can't yet. He's not here."

I look at the door to the room pointedly. How can I start pushing when my husband is still absent?

Holly sighs. "Well, where is he?"

"Just getting me something," I say. I add, "He said he would be right back. He'll be really fast—he was running."

"He's *always* running," Holly says, rolling her eyes.

I'm about to start panicking, when the door cracks open, and I see those now familiar green eyes and matching green scrubs. He raises his eyebrows at me. "Can I come in?"

"*Please*," Holly says. "And tell us what was so important that you had to abandon your wife while she was transitioning into active labor."

Eric Kessler, my husband of two years, steps into the room and triumphantly holds up a bottle of vanilla Coke Zero. My spirit lifts. "You found it!" I exclaim.

Holly's eyes widen. "You can't have that now!" she protests, shaking her head.

"It's for after," I say. "I just got an unbelievable craving. I can't explain it." I smile at Eric. "Was it hard to find?"

"Practically impossible," he says. He places the bottle down on the table by my bedside as a drop of condensation drips down the wrapping. I nearly start salivating. God, I wish I could have it now. "I went to the cafeteria, looked in every vending machine... I was about to start circling the block, but then you'll never guess who I ran into."

"Who?" I ask.

"Your star resident, Caroline," he says. "I told her what I needed, and she got me the bottle in two minutes. What's up with that? Does she have a stash in her locker?"

Believe it or not, he wasn't being facetious when he called Caroline our star resident. The enthusiasm that made her annoying as a medical student got translated into being an incredibly hard-working resident. She's one of our favorites. Plus she has an eerie ability to locate bottles of vanilla Coke Zero.

"Are we ready to push now?" Holly asks. "Are there any other snacks or beverages we need to obtain first?"

"I'm good to go," I say.

I don't think Holly notices the tremor of nervousness in my voice, but Eric does. He reaches out and takes my hand in his. He winks at me as he gives my fingers a squeeze.

Eric and I have been together for about four years now. I never lost his number, but for a long time, I was nervous about calling him. I must have picked up my phone a hundred times with my finger over the call button, but I was never able to go through with it. And then one day, while I was staring at his number, my phone started ringing and his name appeared on the screen.

Eric is great. I mean, really great. Maybe Mary never appreciated him, but I do. He's not perfect, but he's perfect for me, or something cheesy like that.

For a long time, I wasn't sure what to do with Eric's old wedding ring. I thought about selling it and giving the proceeds to some sort of charity, like he suggested. But when I went to a store to get the ring appraised, it turned out that Eric and Mary cheaped out on their rings. I still could've donated the money to charity, but it wasn't very much. Instead, I used the money to treat us both to a nice dinner out, and also to sign him up for his first marathon since Mary's death.

He was reluctant at first, but as soon as I talked him into it, I could tell it was right thing to do. He's been running ever since. It's made him really happy, almost as happy as the baby I'm about to expel from my vagina is going to make him.

I never told him how I paid for that first marathon.

Eric grabs on to one of my legs and Pam holds the other. Holly positions herself where the baby is supposed to come out. The epidural has been running down, so I feel my next contraction coming, and I know to push, even before Holly says, "Push for me!"

I ride the waves of the contraction, pushing the best I can as Pam counts to ten. The pain eases up, and I look over at Holly.

"How was that?" I ask.

Holly shakes her head. "Come on, Emily. You can give a better push than that."

I try again, and then a third time, but don't have much better luck. Without even asking, I can tell from everyone's faces that I'm doing terribly. The baby is the right size, he's in a good position, but I'm not making any progress because I'm not pushing the right way. I'm one of those first-time mothers who can't get the hang of pushing, the ones I always looked down on. And now we're all going to be in here for the next 20 hours because I don't know how to push.

Oh God, I'm so embarrassed.

Eric squeezes my hand again as he keeps his other hand on my leg.

"Emily," he says. "Listen to me."

I wipe the sweat from my forehead. "Okay."

"I need you to push," he says, "like you're having the biggest bowel movement of your life."

They're the most inspiring words I've ever heard in my life.

The next contraction arrives. This time, I focus on Eric's words and give it all I've got. I'm not going to give any more little girly pushes. No way. I'm getting this baby out of me. I look over at Eric, and I can tell from his face that I did good.

"Great job, Emily!" Holly exclaims. "I need you to keep pushing just like that. Just like that. Come on, push! Push! Push!"

Push!

Acknowledgements

Kelley Stoddard would like to thank...

I would like to thank, first and foremost, my husband, Kevin, for supporting me through working the toughest job that you will ever love, and loving me even when working that job gets the better of me. I would like to thank my children, Victoria and Ryan, not only for teaching me how to be a better and more compassionate physician, but also for being the lights of my life. My favorite job is being your mother. I would also like to thank my parents, for being my cheerleaders, for teaching me perseverance, and for showing me the importance of setting goals and achieving them. Finally, I want to thank the patients, the nurses, and the physicians with whom I've had the pleasure of working throughout the years for all that you have taught (and will continue to teach) me as I continue on this journey. I'm so lucky and blessed to have known each and every one of you.

Freida McFadden would like to thank...

Thank you so much to my family—my husband, for supporting me throughout my medical training, and my children, for having the good sense not to be born until I finished my internship. I want to thank my mother, who would read anything I wrote even if the entire book were fingerpainted in ketchup. I would like to thank my wonderful beta readers Jessica Schuster and Dr. Orthochick, who have been kind enough to read and comment on all my books with only minimal eyerolling. I have to give a shout out to my editor Jenica Schultz, for her excellent work as usual. And I would like to thank the residents on my OB/GYN clerkship, who inspired me with your tireless efforts to safety herald tiny babies into the world while ensuring there was also time to make absolutely certain that we medical students knew that everything we were doing was completely and utterly wrong.

We would both like to thank...

We would like to thank Dr. Amy Tuteur of The Skeptical OB, for both her guidance on a difficult scene in the book, and for being a strong Internet presence in support of safe birth. We would also like to thank Dr. Katherine Chretien of Mothers in Medicine, who is responsible for bringing us together, so without her there would be no book at all.

Made in United States
Orlando, FL
26 January 2024

42946944R00233